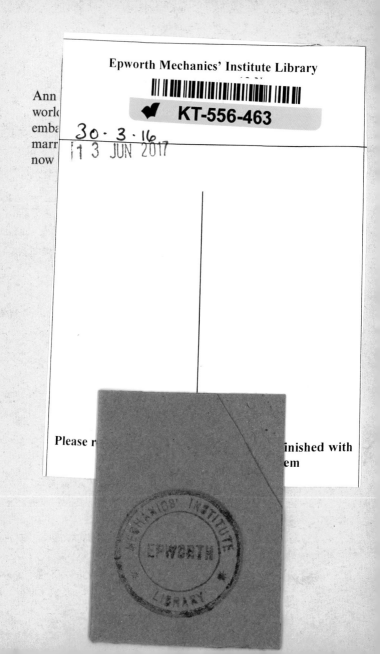
Ann
worl
emba
marr
now

Please r   inished with
                                              em

Risking It All

Ann Granger

First published in 2001
by HEADLINE BOOK PUBLISHING

First published in paperback in 2002
by HEADLINE BOOK PUBLISHING

8

ISBN 978-0-7472-6801-7

Printed and bound in Great Britain by
Clays Ltd, St Ives plc

HEADLINE BOOK PUBLISHING
A division of Hodder Headline
338 Euston Road
LONDON NW1 3BH

www.headline.co.uk
www.hodderheadline.com

To Christopher, a source of stories and on hand when something goes amiss with the computer . . .

Chapter One

'What's more,' I said to Ganesh, 'there's my independence to consider.'

Ganesh replied, rather rudely I thought, 'What independence? You're broke, you're homeless, you're dossing here in Uncle Hari's garage. You keep all you own in a plastic binbag and the only family you've got is that perishing dog.'

At this point, Bonnie barked. Ganesh looked at her and she flattened her ears and uttered a throaty whine.

'Dogs are worried by eye contact,' I told him. 'They see it as a challenge.'

'Oh? Well, in my experience, you don't turn your back on them.'

Ganesh doesn't get on well with dogs. I suspect he's afraid of them. He may have a phobia like some people do with cats. Whatever it is, dogs know it and they give Ganesh a terrible time, even little dogs like Bonnie.

I explained to him that he was being illogical. None of the things he'd listed meant I wasn't independent. If anything, they meant I was.

'You're the one who's not got any independence,' I argued. 'You're tied to your family. You either work for your dad or you work for your Uncle Hari, which wouldn't matter if it was work you enjoyed. But you don't. You hate it.'

'That's different,' said Ganesh sniffily.

We were sitting on a couple of upturned crates in Hari's garage at the rear of the newsagent's he runs. Ganesh and I had seen in the New Millennium on Blackfriars Bridge with a horde of others, watching the fireworks and popping champagne corks. I couldn't help thinking at the time, as I raised my plastic tumbler of bubbly to the New Year, that the majority of people there had a home to go to when it was all over. It was something they probably took for granted. I never have, nothing permanent, nothing I could think of as my home, at least not since I was sixteen.

Correction: recently I'd enjoyed the rare comfort of a basement flat, just for a brief but wonderful while. But I didn't slip into the mistake of letting my guard down, thinking at last I was 'home'. I've learned not to do that, not to let myself become dependent on anything. Dependent means vulnerable. Perhaps that was what I was trying to explain to Ganesh.

As to that flat, I'd always known it couldn't last, and sure enough it didn't, proving I'd been right not to count on it. Shortly before Christmas, Fate in the form of burst pipes took a hand and I'd been flooded out. My then landlady, Daphne, invited me to spend Christmas with her so I wasn't forced to turn to the nearest seasonal charity shelter. But no sooner was Boxing Day over than things began to plummet downhill with a vengeance.

Daphne, urged on I'm sure by her unspeakable nephews, Bertie and Charlie, announced she was putting the house up for sale with immediate effect. She was planning to live in a cottage in Cornwall and it just so happened that nephews B and C knew of one with vacant possession as of the instant.

What's more, an old chum had invited her to accompany her on a millennium cruise which involved drinking a glass of champagne at midnight on some remote atoll. Despite the short notice (owing to someone else dropping out), she felt she couldn't turn it down.

So Daphne jetted out to join the party, leaving it to nephews B and C to arrange to send nearly all her furniture to the saleroom, except what she wanted for the cottage, which would be put in store until her return. We spent the last day in each other's company going round sticking Post-It notes to everything she wanted to keep. If I felt there was indecent haste in all this, it was hardly for me to say so. But it was a lowering occasion. Even Daphne murmured it was like valuing the estate for probate.

One thing she had insisted on was that I be allowed to stay on in the empty shell of the house until it was sold. But there was never a chance of that. The minute she was out of the country, the horrible Bertie and Charlie began making my life a misery. On the excuse of packing up the house and 'keeping an eye on things', they virtually moved in themselves.

'After all,' said Bertie nastily, 'we can hardly leave security in your hands.'

'I can look after the house,' I argued. 'I'm quite capable, you know.'

'You,' said Bertie, 'will fill the place with people like yourself. That's what people like you do. You'll turn it into a squat. Your friends will take up the floorboards for fuel, be overdosing on every banned substance known to man, writing obscene limericks on the walls and urinating in the garden.'

'I will not move anyone in!' I yelled at him. 'And what do you know about squatters, anyway? What makes you think

3

they all behave like that? Any squat I've lived in has had house rules and everyone's stuck to them. Either that, or they were out. I bet I know more about keeping undesirables, as you'd call them, at bay than you do.'

'I am a solicitor,' Bertie said smugly, 'so I do know a great deal about these things. Besides, how can we ask the estate agent to show prospective buyers round with you and that disgusting little dog camped in the kitchen? Aunt Daphne was out of her mind allowing you to stay over Christmas. Now I see you are interpreting her well-meant gesture as a virtual invitation to squat indefinitely. It was not so intended and my brother and I mean to see you don't get away with it. You have no kind of contract to stay in this part of the house. You've paid no rent since you lost the basement flat. Out you go.'

'Thanks,' I snarled. 'And a Happy New Millennium to you, too. By the way, why did that antique cabinet with the marquetry panels go off in a separate van to the rest? Why didn't it go in the lorry to the saleroom with the other things?'

'None of your business,' he snapped. 'However, Aunt Daphne told my brother and myself we could each have an item of our choice for sentimental reasons. I chose the dear little cabinet. It belonged to my grandmother and I well remember it from when I was a boy.'

'Wow! Pass the sickbag!' I invited. 'Spare me dear old Grandma, at least. I bet sentiment's got a whopping big price tag on it by now.'

Bertie leaned towards me, his piggy eyes sparkling with malice. This was a man who really hated me. 'In the words of the vernacular,' he hissed, 'get lost.'

So I did. I knew I couldn't win this one. He had a point

about the estate agent. I suppose it wouldn't have looked good to a possible buyer to see me there. I put together the few belongings I had left and took myself and Bonnie to Hari's newsagent's to tell Ganesh of my eviction.

'This will never do,' said Hari, listening to my tale with growing dismay. Then he brightened. 'I have an idea. You can stay in my garage until the council houses you.'

This was a big relief. It was also the moment to tell him there wasn't a hope in hell of the council offering me, single, childless and not even born in the borough, a home. I have what they like to call 'low priority'. It's an official way of saying 'bottom of the barrel'.

But Hari had worries enough. Why add to his concerns? I thanked him and moved in towards the end of January. After this, 2000 could only get better. I hoped.

I had to share my new accommodation with piles of boxes. The air whiffed of petrol and engine oil, though it was ages since Hari had kept any kind of motor vehicle in there. Transport was symbolised by a rusty old bike with flat tyres and no saddle. When the garage doors were shut you had to keep the light on because there weren't any windows. But at least there was electricity. There was also a small door in the rear of the place leading into the back yard of the shop, so I could come and go that way. The main doors were kept locked for security. I'd got a folding bed and a sleeping bag and a Calor Gas heater. I used the shop toilet and wash basin, and if I wanted a bath, I could go up to the flat over the shop where Hari and Ganesh lived and take one there. Some evenings I ate with them. So, to be fair, everything was by no means as bad as it sounds.

Hari was happy enough with the arrangement because he

thought it was temporary. I was happy because it was free. Ganesh was grumpy and miserable because he felt it was infra dig.

'Sleeping in a doorway is worse,' I'd pointed out at the beginning of our conversation.

'No one's asking you to sleep in a damn doorway. You can sleep on Hari's sofa,' Ganesh had retorted.

'That wasn't what Hari offered.'

'Because he thought you were only going to be here a few days. You've been here over a month.'

'I told him I'll contribute to the electricity bill.'

'Sod the electricity bill.' Ganesh was getting worked up. 'I know, if you'll let me, I can talk Hari round to taking you on as a lodger in the flat.'

'No way! Are you crazy? Your family would hit the roof. They'd all be there before you could say knife, every uncle, aunt and cousin. You know what they think about me.'

'They like you.'

'Only if I keep at arm's length. They think I'm a bad influence on you.'

At this Ganesh lost it seriously, something which rarely happens, but when it does, you have to watch out. His long hair fell over his face, he waved his arms around, and words bubbled out of him in a seething stream like lava from a volcano. Even Bonnie was impressed and retreated to her little bed by the wall.

I'd realised I had to close off the argument pretty quick or Ganesh would short-circuit. So when I could get a word in, I'd said the bit about my independence and Ganesh stomped off angrily back to the shop. I went down the road to the Chinese takeaway and bought special fried rice and took it back and ate it in solitary splendour. I didn't want to go up to the flat and start arguing all over again. I particularly wanted to keep Hari out of it. Like I said, Hari worries. He worries on a heroic scale. He's a nice, kindly, hard-working man and the most stressed person I know. Most businessmen worry about profits and overheads and things. Hari worries about everything, like his health (and mine or yours if he knows you), the state of the nation and the millennium bug, which then, early in the year, he was still sure was lurking somewhere ready to gum up the works. Hari mistrusts computers. He particularly mistrusts the Internet because he is convinced it will ruin newsagents like himself.

'They don't buy magazines. They don't watch videos. They sit in front of that damn box playing with mice.'

He reads all the newspapers in the shops and worries about each and every item. 'See here? Some poor child has turned orange because of something she drank. I sell cold drinks. Suppose someone drinks something he bought here and he turns orange or pink or whatever it is and sues me?'

'It's not going to happen, Hari,' we tell him. 'It's about as likely as space debris falling through the roof.'

'Hah! You think this can't happen? One piece fell on a cow in America and killed it stone dead. You think it can't fall on me or you?'

I think he actually likes worrying. It's a sort of hobby.

Anyway, the whole row with Ganesh had taken place the evening before events really began happening. Perhaps it was an omen heralding some sort of bug like the millennium one but only targeted at me and designed to mess up my life (again). Perhaps my stars were out of true, and if an astrologer had drawn me a personal map the planets would've been zig-zagging around like dodgem cars.

When Bonnie and I had finished the fried rice, I settled down in my sleeping bag and slept very badly. I don't like being at odds with Ganesh, who is the best friend I've ever had or am ever likely to have. He's always there, and although we have the occasional bust-up (as then), when things quieten down we pick up where we left off. When I first knew him he was helping his parents out in their greengrocer's shop in Rotherhithe and I was squatting in a condemned house. In the end, developers knocked down both the squat and the little parade of shops which included the greengrocery. Mr and Mrs Patel moved out to High Wycombe because a cousin was already in business there, and anyway, people in the commuter belt have more money and buy expensive upmarket items like avocados and lemon grass. In Rotherhithe they sold an awful lot of spuds, onions and the smallest, cheapest bananas and oranges. 'Lousy profit margins,' explained Ganesh to me gloomily.

There wasn't room for him in High Wycombe so he'd gone up to Camden to help his uncle in the newsagent's. I did ask whether he'd ever contemplated working for someone not a family member but he got tetchy and said I didn't understand. Saying I didn't understand was Gan's way of closing off any argument he was losing.

In our Rotherhithe days his family had always been nice to me and I'd helped out sometimes at weekends in the shop, rather as I'd been doing for Hari up here in Camden. (This family business is creeping, like ivy.) The trouble is, I don't have one, a family, I mean. I think that's what worries the older Patels most. It's something they just can't understand. I'm young, single, female and batting round on my own. It both shocks and worries them. Someone, they feel, should be looking after me. Only they don't want it to be Ganesh. They doubtless have their own plans for him, although so far they've been keeping them up their sleeves. This does tend to make him jittery and he's happy to be out of their way.

The next morning, when I woke up, still tired and fed up, I realised I was going to have to do something to patch up the quarrel, straight away. If it meant going up to the shop waving a white flag, so be it. I decided to go about a quarter to eleven. Hari and Gan usually take a coffee break then, after the early-morning paper rush. But being Saturday, the rush would be on all morning and they'd be grateful to have someone make the coffee and stand in for them in turns while the released one drank his reviver.

I went in the back way, from my garage home, through the cluttered yard and in the back door which leads to the storeroom. The storeroom is a treasure house which looks as if a whirlwind has hit it. Boxed sweets of all kinds are wedged higgledy-piggledy on the dusty shelves. Cans of soft drink are stacked in wobbly towers. In between all these are boxes of oddments like ballpoint pens and sellotape rolls, last year's diaries (don't ask me why; perhaps Hari hopes that somehow the date will come round again . . .) and unsold Christmas wrapping paper which Hari is definitely planning on selling next season. It looks chaotic, but believe me, Hari knows the number and location of every bar of peppermint cream or disposable cigarette lighter. I wove my way between it all and emerged into the shop.

I'd caught a brief lull between customers. Hari and Ganesh were huddled in the corner by the till, apparently arguing about something, and I was nearly upon them before either of them became aware of it. Hari saw me first. He made an urgent flapping movement of his hand to shut Ganesh up and hailed me.

'Fran, my dear!'

Ganesh gave me a shifty look. Right, I thought, they've been arguing about me. Gan has been moaning about my being in the garage when I could be a lodger in the flat. Hari is starting to worry how long I'm going to be in the garage and is even more worried that if he brings me indoors the family will be on his neck. I got annoyed because I felt I was being discussed as if I was a stray cat they might adopt or not.

As it turned out, I was both right and wrong. They had been talking about me, but not about the suitability or otherwise of my accommodation.

Ganesh mumbled, 'I'll put the kettle on.'

'No, I'll make the coffee,' I said. 'And then we can all three of us sit down and sort it out in a civilised way.'

'Sort out what?' He scowled at me.

'My being in the garage, isn't this all about that? You don't have to worry about me. I'll find somewhere else.'

A customer came in and Hari turned to him with the deeply suspicious look on his face he reserves for customers he hasn't seen before. He's only marginally less mistrustful of the ones he knows. Gan followed me into the washroom, where I was filling the kettle from the tap. Okay, I know it doesn't sound very hygienic, but since Gan had the whole washroom completely renovated, while Hari was away in India just before Christmas, it's all very clean and nice in there. There's even a plastic air-freshener dispenser so you get overpowered by Woodland Fern as you step in.

'We weren't talking about that, as it happens,' said Gan in that way he has when he's still cross with me; sort of critical and reproachful together. It means he's about to tell me something, for my own good, I don't want to hear.

I plugged the kettle into the wall socket and said, 'Oh, right?'

'Yes, right!' He paused, then asked in a different voice, sounding a bit embarrassed, 'Look, Fran, you're not in any kind of trouble, are you?'

'What, me?' The kettle hissed gently as it came to the boil. I put the mugs ready on the little shelf there for that purpose and spooned Nescafé into them.

'Be serious, Fran. There's been a bloke here asking about you.'

That shook me up. I stood with the teaspoon in one hand and the coffee jar in the other and stared at him. 'Who?'

'No one I've ever seen before.'

'DSS checking on me?' That seemed the obvious answer. 'Perhaps they think I'm drawing the dole and still working here.'

'You can have your job back when business picks up,' said Ganesh, diverted. Then he said, 'No, it wasn't them. Anyone can recognise them straight away.'

'Not the cops?' I was beginning to get just a tad nervous.

'Not the regular sort. Here, he left his card.' Ganesh fished a battered piece of white card from his jeans back pocket and held it out to me though I hadn't a free hand to take it. The kettle boiled.

'Hold on a minute,' I said. I made the coffee, put down the spoon and took the card.

'This is a wind-up,' I said when I'd scanned it.

'He's got business cards printed, how can it be? He must be who he says he is.'

'Gan,' I said patiently, 'no one, but no one, has the name Clarence Duke.'

'Why not?' Ganesh was genuinely puzzled.

'Because he was the bloke who drowned in a cask of malmsey. The Duke of Clarence, I mean. I know my Shakespeare. *Richard the Third*.'

My ambition, yet to be fulfilled, is to be an actor. I know I didn't actually complete the dramatic arts course I went on after being expelled from school, but that, as they say, was for reasons beyond my control.

'What's malmsey?' asked Ganesh.

I said I thought it was a sort of sweet wine. Gan said he'd never seen that one in Oddbins. I asked if he'd ever looked. Anyway, it was something they drank in the Middle Ages. Gan said he thought that was mead.

'And he must have been pretty well tanked up if he fell in and drowned.'

'The story has it, he was pushed.'

'Not another one of your murders,' groaned Ganesh.

We were getting off the point here but I didn't want us falling out again. I didn't even argue that the murder investigations I'd got caught up in were not, in any sense, 'my' murders. What am I? Lizzie Borden?

'This Duke,' I said, tapping the white card. 'If he's a private detective as it says here, he may be using an alias.'

'He uses a Mazda 323,' said Ganesh, being difficult. 'A jade-coloured one. And he wants to find you, Fran.'

'Ha, ha. What for? Hey, perhaps I'm heiress to a fortune and don't know it.'

'More likely they want you for a witness. Private eyes do a lot of work for solicitors these days, digging out missing witnesses and so on. Have you been on the scene of any trouble lately? I mean, since the last lot.'

I studied the card.

INVESTIGATIONS OF ALL KINDS UNDERTAKEN.
WE ARE KNOWN FOR TACT AND RELIABILITY.

Who were 'we'? I was willing to bet that Clarence Duke, if that really was his moniker, was a one-man band. His card looked the sort you print out yourself at one of those machines. Perhaps I ought to print some for myself. I'm by way of being a private detective. Oh, not a proper one, no office or anything like that. That means National Insurance contributions and tax returns, things which haven't figured very large in my life so far.

I've had a lot of other jobs, all sorts, while working towards getting my Equity card. Whatever I do, it never seems to last more than a few weeks, so that's why I thought I'd be an enquiry agent. That and the fact that I've had a little experience in these matters. (What I call 'experience' Ganesh tends to call 'trouble'.) Anyway, I'm prepared to take on enquiries ('run into trouble', in Ganspeak) for people who can't go through the usual channels. Now, Clarence of the business card, he was one step up from me. He'd got stationery and probably an office in his front room and perhaps his wife or girlfriend manning the phone. That last was guesswork but I'd bet on it. One thing I was sure of, I didn't want to meet him. I said so.

'What did you tell him, Gan? And what exactly did he ask, anyway?'

'He understood we'd employed you in the past. Did we have a current address for you? I said you hadn't worked here since the Christmas rush . . .'

'Rush?' I interrupted. 'In this shop?'

'Hey, we do all right. Could be better but we do all right. I told Duke I had no address for you, and the way I see it, I wasn't lying. I couldn't have told him you were camped out in Hari's garage, could I? Even if I had been prepared to tell him anything, which I wasn't.'

'Was he satisfied?'

Ganesh looked uneasy. 'I think so.'

I took Hari his cooling coffee. 'Ganesh has told me about the private detective,' I said.

'A very strange fellow,' said Hari disapprovingly.

'What did he look like?' It suddenly occurred to me that I might have run across Clarence Duke, under some other unlikely name, at another period in my eventful life.

Ganesh wandered up and he and Hari exchanged looks. 'Short,' said Hari, taking first turn.

'Moustache,' added Ganesh. 'Bit straggly.'

'Jeans and a leather jacket,' said Hari, brightening. 'Yes, yes, I remember.'

'Bad teeth,' said Gan. 'Needed to see a dentist.'

'Why do I get a private eye who looks like a health warning?' I asked. 'Why don't I get the ones who look like Jonathan Creek?'

'This is real life,' said Gan.

'They must be out there somewhere, the dishy ones.'

'Probably, but they're not interested in you, Fran.'

That's what friends are for. To destroy your fragile self-esteem. I thanked them both for not telling Clarence Duke where to find me, and resolved to avoid anyone short with a moth-eaten moustache and galloping halitosis.

As it happened, Hari wanted to leave the shop for a couple of hours that afternoon and asked if I could put in some temporary time. We agreed I should be paid cash, just to avoid awkwardness – should Clarence Duke be working for the DSS after all.

The afternoon was quiet and they didn't really need me. Ganesh and I chatted about this and that, carefully not mentioning the morning's visitor. We sold the odd Mars bar and packet of ciggies. Just after four, when Hari returned, I collected Bonnie from the storeroom where she'd been snoozing while I worked, and left the shop by the front entrance. Bonnie needed a walk.

I set off briskly, but I hadn't gone far, only to the next corner, when a small, moustached figure stepped out of a doorway and confronted me.

'Francesca Varady?'

'Shove off,' I advised, my heart sinking. This had to be the guy who'd been round earlier.

He ignored the brush-off. He was used to it in his line of work. 'Clarence Duke,' he introduced himself. 'Private detective. My card!' He produced another home-made effort with a flourish.

I again advised him to take himself off asap, this time rather less politely.

'Don't be alarmed,' he urged.

'I'm not alarmed,' I told him. 'I just don't want to talk to you. My mother warned me about strange men.'

A funny look came over his face. 'Your mother?'

I was immediately sorry I'd said it. Since she'd walked out when I was seven, I'd never seen or heard from my mother again. A day doesn't pass that I don't miss Dad and Grandma Varady, who brought me up. But my mother I've never missed. Kids are resilient. Once I'd realised she wasn't coming back, I'd cut her out of the scheme of things. I didn't need her, and obviously she'd had no need of me.

'I'd like to talk to you on a matter of business,' said Clarence Duke, attempting an honest expression and failing dismally. 'Can we go and have a cup of tea somewhere?'

'No,' I said. 'I have to walk my dog.'

He eyed Bonnie. 'Then perhaps I could walk with you and we could have a little chat?'

He was a creep. On the other hand, I'm incurably curious. 'All right,' I said. 'But you do the talking. All I'll do is listen until I get bored. I don't guarantee any replies.'

'Fair enough,' said Clarence. 'I don't think you'll be bored.'

He smiled. He did have bad teeth.

Chapter Two

We strolled along the path by the canal. After we passed under the bridge, I let Bonnie off the lead. She pottered happily ahead of us investigating interesting whiffs, of which there are plenty just below Camden Lock. The canal was on our left. The road on the other side of us was invisible high up behind a bank of dusty shrubs and a brick wall. There weren't too many other people around. I like it down there by the canal, even though not all the memories it has for me are nice. Someone I knew died down there in that debris-strewn grey-green water lapping at the concrete rim. In my imagination, which is always active, I could picture his body, kept afloat by his old ex-army greatcoat, face down, arms outspread. But like I say, that's my imagination. I never saw him dead. I just heard about it later.

Thinking about that, I almost forgot Clarence Duke and had to pull myself together, realising he was talking to me. I wondered where he'd left his car. Parking places in Camden are like palm trees in the desert. They're rare and they draw travellers to them from all directions. Being a motorist hadn't stopped him donning running shoes. At any other time I'd have laughed. They were so clearly insurance. Few people are happy when they find they're being trailed by a private investigator. I wondered how many quick getaways Duke had managed – and how many times he'd got caught and duffed up. He was of puny build. He ought to put in some time at the gym.

'You don't mind,' he was saying, 'if I just check with you I've got the right Fran Varady?'

'I've never come across another one,' I said sourly. 'And I'm not answering questions, remember?'

'If you're not the right girl,' he pointed out, 'then I'm wasting my time and yours and I'll be off. So we might as well be sure.'

'You are wasting your time, anyway. As far as I can see, you're definitely wasting mine.'

He gave me a thin smile. He'd had difficult interviewees before. He cut out the chit-chat and got to his questions. 'Could you tell me your father's name?'

A prickle of alarm ran up my spine. Sure, I could tell him my dad's name. But how would Clarence know I'd given him the correct one? Only if he knew something about Dad. As much to find out what, as to oblige him, I told him my father had been called Stephen.

'Only,' I said, 'he was christened Istvan. They were Hungarians.'

'Yes,' he said in a way which told me he already knew this. Who the heck was this guy? 'How about your mother's name?'

My mother again. I'd spent fourteen years doing my best to forget her, and here was Clarence making me think of her. He had no right to do that. No one had that right.

'She was called Eva,' I said. 'But she skipped out, so don't ask me anything about her, all right?' I drew a deep breath.

'Look, I don't know who you are. A scrap of card means nothing. Anyone can print them off and stick any daft name on them.'

I'd offended him, not by doubting whether he was legit, but by attaching the adjective 'daft' to his name.

'I can't help my name!' he said sharply. 'I was called after my grandfather. Clarence is no ruddy name to have, I can tell you. I had a hell of a time at school.'

Fair enough, I couldn't help my name either. But I felt I'd evened things up between us a little. He was wanting to know about my family. He'd been obliged to tell me something about his. Being such a little fellow, if he'd been bullied at school as he said, he'd have been unable to do much about it.

For a moment, I even stopped disliking him. Not that I'd got good reason for taking against him, other than the fact that he was bothering me. But dislike's an instinct and connected to distrust. I didn't trust Clarence Duke. But I did sympathise with his having been the target of bullies when he'd been a kid. Children are ingenious and implacable tormentors of other children. They form gangs like stray dogs and hunt like them, seeking the weak, the isolated.

My first year at the private girls' school Dad sent me to was wretched. I was the outsider and every other girl in my year knew it. They circled me from the first, predatory, waiting. I couldn't tell anyone. The picked-on child never can. When you're young, failure to be accepted is a thing of shame to be borne in silence. I couldn't tell a teacher; that would be telling tales and dishonourable. I couldn't tell Dad and Grandma. They were congratulating themselves that the sacrifices they were making were worthwhile. They were giving me a good start in life. To have confessed that I was miserable would have distressed and disappointed them. Worse, it would have shocked them and destroyed the image they'd created of the school being full of nice young ladies who didn't behave like street urchins. They wanted so much to believe I was happy there. I couldn't take that delusion away from them, especially as I knew that Dad was desperately trying to make it up to me that my mother wasn't there. Poor Dad. He thought he'd solved my problem for me. Instead of that, he'd made it worse. Dad always had good ideas. I don't remember any of them working out.

'Tough,' I said to Duke. 'I mean it. Like, bad luck.'

He chuckled to himself, the last reaction I'd expected. 'That's until I found out how to deal with it.'

This I wanted to hear. Sooner or later the victim generally susses out a form of defence, though sometimes there are real tragedies when a kid doesn't. In my case, a talent for acting got me off the hook, to an extent. I could imitate any teacher with a marked manner or voice. I disarmed my persecutors by making them laugh.

The staff members concerned soon guessed what was going on. It must have been then they put me on that staff-room unofficial blacklist. Perhaps they'd been waiting for a chance to put me on it from the first. They, too, knew I was different. My family had neither money nor class. I had a foreign name, no mother, a father who was a loser and a grandmother who was loudly and flamboyantly barmy.

I avenged myself on the entire staff by behaving badly. I saw them as fair game. I thought of myself as some kind of resistance heroine fighting an occupying power. They saw me as a subversive revolutionary who didn't know and would never learn what was acceptable behaviour, but had a sure-fire instinct for what wasn't. A rotten apple in their snooty little barrel. From then on, until my eventual inevitable expulsion, life was one long running battle. They brought up the big battalions. I sniped from behind cover and sabotaged their lines of communication.

I got a reputation and in turn that got my original persecutors off my back. Lest you think they admired my fine disregard for authority, my dash and derring-do, let me correct that. My school-fellows scented danger to themselves, that they'd be damned by any kind of association. So they left me alone to rampage among the school rules at will. They were sharper than I was. I was too dumb to realise I was doing harm to no one but myself. The school won the last battle, as it was inevitable they would. I was not, wrote the headmistress to Dad, taking advantage of what the school had to offer. They all felt that was such a pity. I was bright but unruly. I seldom if ever handed in homework on time. When it did arrive, it gave the impression of having been scribbled out on the bus that morning on the way to school. (She was right.) It hardly seemed fair to let me continue to be a subversive element when I wasn't even benefiting from the education on offer. I was out. Poor Dad. Poor Grandma. I'd like to add, poor me. But seeing as I'd brought it all on myself, I've never been able to indulge in self-pity. Just as well.

So it was with real curiosity that I asked Duke, 'How?'

He wiped the smug look from his weasel features and gave me a funny sideways glance, as if judging how I'd take what he was going to say. 'Everyone's got secrets. Even school bullies. In fact, especially school bullies. So you find out what the secret is and you let them know you know it. Then they leave you alone.'

I could see how he'd ended up a private detective. His investigations had started early, sneaking around finding out the sordid little sins and embarrassments that schoolkids hide behind bluster and aggression. He could finger this one for shoplifting. That one's mother was on the game and had been up before the magistrates again. Another one lived in unbelievable squalor with drunken parents. The RSPCA had been round to rescue the dog, but the child had been left to social services and they'd done sod all. Clarence had put himself in the position of being able to start a whispering campaign, and even the most violent playground thug is powerless against that. I understood it. But I didn't like it.

'Something tells me you fancy you know a secret about me,' I told him. 'And I'd like to hear what it is. For a start, I'd like to know who hired you. I'm entitled to be told, I think.'

'Eva did,' he said simply. 'Eva Varady, your mother.'

I stopped dead and whirled to face him. He looked alarmed, as well he might. I guess my expression told him this wasn't welcome news. We were about the same height and I think I'm pretty fit. It's not only men who can dish out the aggro. He backed off a little and then hopped back some more when I yelled in his face:

'That's a lie! She didn't. She couldn't have. It's not true. She's gone. She's dead!'

He put his head on one side in that bird-like way of his and dealt me another of his strange looks. 'Who told you she was dead?'

I was silenced. No one had told me. I suppose, as a child, I'd decided in my own mind that she must be. She had never come back for me. Death was the only acceptable explanation.

Later, I'd assumed that I must be as dead for her as she was for me, even if we were both living. The idea of my mother as a flesh-and-blood creature intervening in my life had become too incredible even to be imagined. I still couldn't imagine it. This had to be some kind of trick. Who was pulling it and why or what he or she hoped to gain, I couldn't even guess. But that was it, it must be. I seized the explanation, demanding, 'Who put you up to this? What's your game? If you think I can't deal with a slimy little runt like you, you're badly mistaken. I don't like people trying to put one over on me and I always do something about it.'

But even as the words left my mouth, I knew in a small cold corner of my heart that it was going to turn out to be just as he'd said. *She'd* sent him. Any other explanation was grasping at straws. She'd walked out and now, on this cold, overcast February morning by the canal, she'd walked back in again in the person of this sad little bloke. How could she do this to me? And why?

Clarence Duke was looking hard done by. 'You asked me,' he snivelled. 'So I told you. That's what you wanted to know. It's always the bloody same. People say they want the truth and when they hear it they go off the deep end and start yelling. No one put me up to it, except Eva herself. It's my job. I do things for people. Things they can't do themselves. She wanted to find you so I found you for her. It's a job to me, right? You needn't make it sound so personal. What's it to me whether you're happy about it or not?'

Fair enough, I had no right to take it out on him. He was a hired snoop, a messenger boy, just as he said. He did jobs for people who couldn't do them themselves, just as I'd been flattering myself I did in my investigating career. I didn't like the idea of looking on Clarence as a colleague, and I dare say he wouldn't have fancied me as one. But I owed him basic respect as one professional to another (almost). Besides, he had no reason to lie to me. I ought to be glad he hadn't, because that certainly wouldn't have helped. But I didn't want to know any more. No more questions, and above all, no more painful answers.

We were still standing on the towpath. 'This is as far as we go,' I said eventually. I was trembling. I couldn't help it. I had to force myself to speak calmly, but inside the pressure had built up as if I was going to explode.

'Give me one more minute, Fran—' He held up his hands placatingly.

'No!' I shouted at him. 'You've done your job, just like you said. Now clear out of it and leave me alone!'

Bonnie, hearing me raise my voice, had already come running back, ears pricked enquiringly, looking around with anxious brown eyes to see where the trouble was. She decided it was Clarence, barked at him and made a dive for his running shoes.

'Call the dog off!' he whined, jumping around to keep out of the way of Bonnie's teeth. 'I don't like dogs. They always bite me.'

'They've got sense. Scram before *I* bite you,' I told him.

I turned my back on him, whistled up Bonnie, and started off walking as fast as I could. I could hear him pattering behind me. He was a persistent little sleazeball.

Without turning, I told him, 'If you don't clear off, I'll shove you in the canal and tread on your fingers if you try to climb out. Even if you can swim, there's enough toxins in there to give you the runs for a month.'

'She said you'd be upset,' he said.

'Upset?' I whirled round again and he jumped back quickly out of my reach. The news hadn't just upset me. I was devastated by it. Everything I'd built up over fourteen years, every little brick in a wall protecting me from the fact that my mother had abandoned me, walked out and left me and never sent so much as a birthday card afterwards, all came tumbling down. I had no point of reference any more. I wasn't the Fran Varady I'd thought I was, without any family since Dad and Grandma Varady died. I was a new, strange Fran who had a mother. She was alive, she was near at hand, she spoke to me through this skinny little bloke with his tatty business cards. Why? Did she want something from me? Because I had nothing I could give her. Nor had she anything I wanted.

'I am more than upset, Clarence,' I managed to say evenly, but he could surely hear the anger in my voice, and, probably, the pain. 'I'm hopping mad. Don't push your luck. Go back and tell her you found me. You've done your job.'

'She wants to see you, Fran.' His tone was cajoling.

'Well, I don't want to see her. You tell her that. She's had fourteen years to come and see me. She could've come to see me when I had bronchitis at eight, or chickenpox at twelve, or was in the school play, or after Dad and Grandma died and the landlord threw me out in the street at sixteen . . .'

I knew I was losing my cool. I managed to get it back. 'Tell her,' I said, 'that the times she could've come to see me have been and gone and now she's missed that particular bus.'

'She's dying, Fran,' he said, looking at me with watery little grey eyes.

'That,' I told him, 'is despicable. If you're going to lie, think of something else.'

'It's the truth, I swear. She's in a hospice. She's got leukaemia.'

'On the level?' I heard myself ask.

'On the level,' he said. 'So, what do I tell her? Will you go?'

'Will you go?' asked Ganesh.

I'd told him all about Clarence and the thunderbolt he'd delivered. Not straight away. I'd gone home after leaving Duke down by the canal, and sat for ages on a crate in my garage home, just thinking, or trying to. My thoughts spun round crazily. Eventually I became aware someone was speaking to me. My eyes focused and I saw Gan, balanced on his heels in front of me, his face, framed by long black hair, filled with concern.

'What's up?' he was asking. 'Come on, Fran, what's wrong?' He reached out and put a hand on my arm.

So I told him. I pretty well tell Ganesh everything and he's usually got good advice which I don't always take. But I was in need of advice now like never before.

'You need to think it over,' he said. 'Sleep on it. Come up to the flat and eat with us tonight. You should have some company.'

They shut up the shop at eight, and when I got up to the flat at just before nine, Hari was frying onions in the kitchen and watching a video of some Bollywood epic on the little TV in there at the same time.

'How are you feeling now?' Ganesh asked.

'Still churned up. I don't want to see her, Gan. I know it sounds mean, when she's so ill, but what can I say to her?'

'Perhaps she's got things she wants to say to you?' he suggested.

'I don't want to hear them. What can she do? Apologise? You can't abandon a child and then, years later, say you're sorry.'

'Why not?' asked Ganesh. 'What else can she say? Everyone regrets things they've done. If you can't put them right, all you can do is tell the person you've hurt you wish you hadn't done it. Why *did* she do it, do you know?'

'No,' I said. 'Since I grew up I've tried considering her and Dad as a marriage and I can see it wasn't perfect. He was a nice, loving, happy man, even if not what you'd call a good provider. He always had lots of ideas, they just never seemed to work out. But he loved her and so did—' The next word stuck in my throat.

Ganesh finished the sentence by saying, 'And so did you.'

'Yes. Little kids love their mums. But she didn't love us, either of us, did she? She particularly didn't give a hoot about me or she'd have taken me along with her.'

'Depended where she was going,' said Ganesh.

'Or with whom!' I snapped back, sick of hearing him fight her corner.

'Was there another bloke involved?'

I told him I didn't know and then nodded towards the kitchen. 'Don't tell Hari. He'll worry.'

Ganesh grinned briefly. 'How did you guess?'

I sank down in the corner of the battered old sofa, arms folded tightly across my chest, knees pressed together, not quite resorting to the foetal position, but coming pretty close. I was frightened, floundering about, knowing what I had to do, wishing with all my heart I could get out of going to see her, but aware that I was being pushed inexorably towards it. Ganesh sat at the other end, leaning forward with his arms

27

resting on his thighs, hands loosely clasped, watching me with concern in his eyes. For all his able playing of devil's advocate, he didn't know what to do either.

After we'd eaten, Hari disappeared to do some balancing of the books in his untidy little office. Gan and I washed the dishes, then slumped in front of the TV, watching – or pretending to watch – a late-night political discussion.

Gan said nothing because he knew I wasn't in the mood for more talk. There was only one subject, and we'd said all we could on that. To try and talk about anything else would've been ridiculous. Eventually he dozed off, with his arms folded, his legs stretched out and his head propped on a faded red velvet cushion. He gets up all week at an unearthly hour to take in the newspapers.

I was left with my thoughts. It was easy for Gan to take the moderate view. I also considered it a tad hypocritical. I wondered whether anyone in his family would've forgiven an erring wife. But then he wasn't talking about his lot, was he? He was talking about me. Close as I am to Gan in so many ways, there's always this divide between us, something we can't bridge. I feel it more than Gan. We get along so well but we have often surprised ourselves with our different viewpoints.

Equally, it was easy for someone like Clarence to deliver his message as he was paid to do. I didn't know how he'd found me. I hadn't asked, not wanting to know anything more. But despite the seediness of his appearance, he must be a good detective. He'd done his part and was waiting now for my response to take back to his client, my mother. I had a last try at persuading myself he had been lying, after all, about her being in a hospice. But I knew he hadn't been. The worst news was always true. To refuse to go and see her seemed cruel. But what did she want? To make amends before she died? Despite all Ganesh had said and, all right, despite all I told you, how do you make amends for the bewilderment and despair of a seven-year-old child?

I struggled to find mitigating circumstances, some excuse for her behaviour towards me. She had known I'd be well looked after by Dad and Grandma. It wasn't as if she'd dumped me on social services. But I remembered how crushed Dad had been by her defection. I could see him in my mind's eye, sitting at the table with his head in his hands. He got over it outwardly, as one does, as I did. But the hurt never left our hearts. We never spoke of it to one another, but we knew. It was as though we shared a secret.

Sometimes Grandma would refer to her, generally when defending me after I'd done something wrong. 'What can you expect of a motherless child? What kind of woman walks out on her own flesh and blood? Ah, poor little one . . .' All this as she sat on her chair, patting me on the head and weaving from side to side as if she was about to keen over the dead. She'd then seize my head, nearly pulling it off, and kiss me soundly.

After this, I'd be force-fed with goulash and sticky cakes by way of compensation. Grandma worked on the theory that calories solved any problem.

I hadn't got much in life, as Ganesh was fond of pointing out, but I had considered myself adjusted to my circumstances. I knew who and where I was, what life was likely to offer me and what it wasn't. I had found a kind of equilibrium inside myself, despite everything. I was being asked to risk that. To risk everything. For what? To go and see a woman who had so effectively screwed up three lives?

Hari reappeared and sat down to read his newspaper. Ganesh stirred and woke up.

'Terrible things are happening,' said Hari from behind his newspaper.

'Yes, they are,' I said.

'What are the police doing, that's what I ask!'

'Generally,' I said churlishly, 'they're making life difficult for people whose lives are already difficult.'

'Here is a poor woman,' said the invisible Hari, 'has lost her only daughter.'

Gan and I both looked at the newspaper and Hari's fingers gripping it to either side.

'What woman?' asked Ganesh truculently.

'A nice respectable lady, a doctor's widow.'

Gan and I heaved a joint sigh of relief. On reflection, it was hardly likely to have been my mother, advertising in the paper for news of me. But she might've done. She'd hired Clarence Duke. She didn't have much time. She could've put in an ad. *Anyone knowing the whereabouts . . .*

'See, here is a photograph of her daughter.' Hari rattled the paper at us as if that would enable us to see the picture, which we couldn't. He carried on. 'Such a good girl, a nurse. Now she's missing. She went off shift one evening and she didn't get home. No sign of her. Her flatmate reported her missing the next day, but did the police do anything? No, they did not, not for three days. Now her mother, at her wits' end, is making a big fuss. Quite right, too.'

Hari emerged from behind the paper to stare morosely at the talking head on the TV screen. 'And the politicians, too? What are they doing? Nothing. What a terrible thing to lose your child like that. What would that poor woman not give to get her back again?'

It seemed as if God or someone was sending me a message, making up my vacillating mind for me.

I whispered to Gan, 'If I go, will you come with me?'

'Sure,' said Gan.

Like I said, he's a true friend.

'You ought to make it soon,' he said hesitantly.

'Yes, I realise that.'

'Tomorrow's Sunday,' he went on in a low voice. Hari's a trifle hard of hearing. 'It'll have to be in the afternoon.' In the morning the shop was open for the Sunday-paper trade until twelve. 'So, what are you going to do, phone this bloke Duke? You can use ours.' He nodded towards the phone.

'I'll do it in the morning,' I said.

'Better do it now.'

'Hari will hear.'

'Use the one in the shop.'

Hari appeared from behind his newspaper. 'What is all this?'

Gan said loudly, 'We were saying, if they haven't found this nurse's body, she might turn up. People do go missing and then walk in the door years later.' He glanced at me and whispered, 'Sorry, Fran.'

'It's OK,' I told him. 'People certainly do go missing and they do turn up. I just hope the doctor's widow's daughter doesn't take fourteen years to walk back into her life.'

Chapter Three

I did phone that night, from the shop, on my way out. I got through to an answering machine and Clarence's voice telling me to leave my number and he'd get back. If I did that, when he got back, the odds were Hari would pick up the receiver. I put it down without leaving a message.

This in itself was enough to prevent me spending a good night. General conditions in the garage made doubly sure. I'd left the Calor Gas heater on low and could hear it hissing gently at me in the darkness, but even so, the temperature struggled to rise above freezing. The wind poked icy fingers through the cracks between wall and roof. They prodded at me maliciously if I showed signs of dropping off. The smell of oil and fuel from the ghost of the motor vehicle once kept here seemed stronger. There were scattering noises in the corners which I kept telling myself could not be mice, because Bonnie would've taken care of them. She was snoring happily at my feet. Halfway through the night it began to rain, and the noise on the corrugated roof was horrendous. I couldn't live here much longer. I'd have to try the housing department again. I'd already put word out on the street that I was looking for a squat to share. Response so far had been zilch. It was discouraging in more than one way. Sharing a squat is a skill.

You learn it, and if you don't use it, you get rusty. I feared I'd become used to being on my own, even in the few months I'd had the flat. Heaven help me, even in my present less-than-perfect circumstances, the thought of sharing again worried me.

Around three in the morning, just as I had finally fallen asleep, Bonnie growled and I awoke. I sat up with that sense of panic you get if you've not been sleeping well and something disturbs you. Bonnie was making a low, resonant, primitive sound. I'd got to know Bonnie's growls. There was the one when we played tug-of-war with an old rag which was her make-believe-I'm-fierce growl. There was the tentative one when she wasn't sure about something. Then there was the danger one, like now. I sat up and put out my hand to communicate with her. She was standing by my folding bed and I could feel the hackles raised on her neck.

Running footsteps sounded in the access road outside the garages. They ran past my unit, then seemed to hesitate before turning and running back again. I could guess what was happening. This little roadway is a dead end, leading only to the garages. Someone was being chased, and had turned into the poorly lit entry only to find he couldn't get any further and was obliged to run back. He could've been running from anything or anyone, a mugger or something quite different. Why he ran didn't matter. He ran.

If you live on the streets you see people running and you don't ask why. You just get out of the way. You never see the pursuers. If they pass you within spitting distance, you don't see them. Life on the streets requires a kind of blindness and deafness which can be switched on and off. It isn't only street-dwellers who develop this. People who work at night – refuse collectors, street-washers and gully-emptiers, night-shift workers, tarts – they concentrate on what they're doing, where they're going, make sure no one is coming after them, and get the hell out of it if trouble blows up. Perhaps this runner had simply been in the wrong place at the wrong moment and realised it. He ran.

He may have left it a fraction too late. I thought I heard voices in the distance, shouting. A car screeched nearby, an engine throbbed, was revved up, and the vehicle made off at speed.

After that I lay there, dozing fitfully, to the sound of London waking up and starting a new day, echoing through the locked main doors. Newspaper delivery vans began to arrive. That meant Ganesh would be up and about. I crawled out of the sack and got dressed, which didn't take long as I slept in most of my clothes for warmth. I pulled on my jacket, laced up my boots and, with Bonnie at heel, left through the back door and tramped across the yard towards the bright light of the shop.

'You're early,' said Ganesh, yawning.

I mumbled at him and went to make coffee in the washroom. Bonnie was out in the yard, pottering around. Ganesh had the radio on. I gave him a hand assembling the Sunday supplements into the relevant papers. They seem to get fatter and fatter. You wouldn't think people had time to read them all. But if you forget to put, say, the motoring supplement in the *Sunday Telegraph*, the buyer is back within thirty minutes angrily demanding to know why he doesn't have the complete set. So then you have to pinch one from another made-up copy because there's never a spare. If he's short, it probably means you've put two motoring supplements in someone else's set. Get my drift? But when you've taken one from another set, that set is incomplete and the whole thing is linked into a sequence of robbing Peter to pay Paul.

So it was a normal day and yet wasn't normal. It was a day like no other. It was the day I was going to make contact with a woman who'd walked out of my life fourteen years before and whom I'd been confident I'd never see again.

I breakfasted upstairs with Hari and Gan, and when they'd gone down to the shop, rang Clarence Duke.

'You're early,' he said, sounding a bit miffed. It was just after eight. 'It's Sunday.' That meant I'd got him from his bed for sure.

I told him I'd been up a couple of hours. There's a particular feeling of virtue which comes from telling someone you've been busy while they've been dead to the world.

'What's more,' I said, 'I rang last night and you'd left your answering machine on. It wasn't convenient to leave a message. It wasn't my phone.'

'I've got a private life, you know,' he said.

'I thought I had one until you turned up,' I retorted.

I heard him make a noise which sounded like a yawn. 'Does this mean you're going to see Eva?' he asked.

'I'm thinking about it,' I told him, unwilling to commit myself aloud, despite the fact that my mind was made up and Ganesh, even as we spoke, was arranging to borrow his mate Dilip's car.

He said, 'Right, glad you're going.'

That annoyed me. It wasn't what I'd said. But it was what I'd meant and he'd realised it. He gave me the address and phone number of the hospice. He sounded offhand, which surprised me a little. But perhaps he had another case to follow up and, now he'd concluded this one satisfactorily, he'd lost interest. Or, more likely, he was going back to bed.

As I hung up it occurred to me that he referred to my mother, his client, in a very familiar way. Never Mrs Varady or whatever name she used these days. Always Eva. But it was too late to ask him about that. There were a lot of questions I probably should have asked him and hadn't. There's nothing like going into a strange and frightening situation absolutely stone-cold ignorant.

The hospice was at Egham. I hadn't expected it to be out of London. But possibly there is a scrap of consolation in passing your last days in nice leafy Surrey, rather than among the bricks and traffic of a big city.

'It's going to take us half the afternoon to get there and find it,' I said to Ganesh.

He told me not to worry; even in Dilip's car we'd do it easily. I decided not to phone ahead first. Simply, I was afraid they'd put my mother on the line and I wasn't ready for that. I wasn't ready for any kind of meeting, but I'm never at my best on the phone, anyway.

We rattled through Egham in Dilip's beat-up elderly Datsun, rather lowering the tone of the place. They're very upmarket in Egham.

I didn't know what to expect of a hospice; something like a hospital, perhaps. But it wasn't like that at all. It was a large brick house halfway up a hill outside the town, set in a big garden with lots of trees between it and the road. We clanked and bounced down the drive and parked where a noticeboard said *Visitors*.

There didn't seem to be too many visitors at the moment

despite it being Sunday. It was just as well, I thought, as we climbed out. Gan wore a saggy waxed jacket which looked as though it might have been worn for heaving bales of newspapers around since dawn. I had on black leggings, my new zip-sided boots and a bright yellow puffa jacket I'd bought at Oxfam. It was warm but unflattering. I looked like a Winnie-the-Pooh who'd hit hard times. I'd also experimented with dyeing my hair a purplish red, having got fed up with its normal mid-brown. At least my last close-trimmed haircut had started to grow out and I had a bit more hair these days to dye. Ganesh had kindly said it didn't look bad. 'Better than it did, anyway,' he'd added.

We had left Bonnie behind in the storeroom at the shop. Though Ganesh is definitely anti-dog, Hari rather approves of Bonnie. He thinks she's a good watchdog. She certainly barks. But she's only small, a Jack Russell type. I don't think villains of any sort would find her too much of an obstacle, especially as she tends to identify with anyone wearing smelly old jeans and to distrust the better dressed and well-heeled. She and I both.

We stood before the main entrance and stared at the glass doors leading into a spacious lobby, the only sign this wasn't a regular private house.

'There'll be an office of some sort inside,' Gan said. 'We should go there first and tell them who we are.'

'Do you think we'll need identification? I haven't got any.'

Gan had his driving licence, but that didn't verify my identity. All I had was Duke's business card and I'd have to use that to back up my story if need be. We rang the bell.

After a wait, a middle-aged woman in a grey cardigan and matching pleated skirt appeared on the other side of the glass.

'It's open!' she mouthed at us. To demonstrate it, she pulled the door towards her.

We sidled in, apologising.

'No matter!' she said cheerfully. 'I'm Sister Helen.'

Viewed closer at hand, she could've been anything between forty and sixty. Her skin was extremely clean-looking, shiny, pink and white like a milkmaid in a nursery-rhyme book. She wore no make-up. 'Sister' might mean she was a nurse but I was more inclined to believe she was a nun. They don't wear long black habits these days but I'm tuned in to nuns, as you might say, being a long-lapsed Catholic.

There was a strong scent of flowers in the hospice. Large vases of them stood all around. But they couldn't disguise a lingering odour hard to pinpoint but which came from sick bodies.

I took a deep breath. 'I'm Fran – Francesca Varady. I believe you've got my mother here.' I should've asked Duke what name she was using. I'd feel a fool if Sister Helen didn't recognise Varady. Fortunately, she did.

'Eva,' she returned in the same cheerful manner. 'I'll take you along to her, this way.'

She beckoned with a hand as scrubbed clean as her face, nails neatly trimmed, turning to lead the way as she did so. Ganesh looked nervously round the flower-filled hall and whispered, 'Shall I stay here?'

'No, I need you with me!' I grabbed his hand and towed him along in the wake of Sister Helen.

'I'm glad you've come,' she said chattily over her shoulder. 'Did Mr Duke find you?'

'Yes,' I said tersely.

So she knew all about Clarence. I wondered if she'd

suggested my mother hire a private eye. We passed a dayroom on the way with people sitting around in it, some watching TV, one or two reading. One woman was knitting, a long strip of work like a scarf, all different colours. She was surrounded by scraps of wool and her fingers moved methodically, creating something which had a beginning but no end other than hers. She'd go on adding to it until that moment came when she laid down the knitting needles for ever. I guessed it occupied her mind. The atmosphere was peaceful, by no means depressing.

Our guide opened a door. 'In here. Eva? Are you awake, dear? Here's a visitor for you.'

She stood aside. I could do nothing else but walk in, but once I'd got over the threshold, I froze. My legs wouldn't take me any further. On the way to the hospice, I'd conjured up all sorts of ways to deal with this moment, but as it was, my mind was a complete blank. Ganesh, behind me, bumped into me. I felt him give me a little push in the middle of my back. His breath tickled my ear as he whispered, 'Go on!'

I couldn't. I stayed rooted to the spot just inside the door, staring across the room to the woman who was propped up in the bed by the window. She turned her head and our eyes met. I opened my mouth, hoping something would come out.

I heard my voice, distant, floating out on the air. It said, 'Hello. I'm Fran.'

She said, 'I'm glad you've come, Fran.'

Everyone was glad I was here, Clarence, Sister Helen, my mother. I had never felt so lost in my life.

Then Sister Helen closed the door and left us, me, Gan and the woman in the bed, together.

Ganesh was shuffling about behind me. I introduced him

hastily. That bit, at least, was easy.

He said, 'Good afternoon, Mrs Varady. I just came to keep Fran company.'

'It's nice to meet you,' she said, and held out a thin white hand. Ganesh walked over to the bed and took it. He held her hand for a moment then said gently, 'I'll wait outside.' He glanced at me. 'I'll be around, Fran.' And he was gone.

I edged over to the bed and sat down in a wicker chair, not because I was relaxed, but because my legs were wobbly. I didn't know what to say and I didn't want to stare. She seemed quite calm and was studying me with large pale-blue eyes.

My memory of her was of a small, attractive woman with thick dark-blonde hair. She'd hardly any hair at all now, just wisps combed neatly back. In contrast to her thin hands, her face was round, cheeks full, and the skin beneath her eyes was puffed. I wouldn't have known her. Only her voice struck a chord in my memory. Not exactly recognition, but something familiar which hit me mid-chest and made me feel almost physically sick. I hoped I wasn't shaking. I felt as though I was. Every nerve in my body quivered.

'Your friend is nice,' she said. She was handling this much better than I was. It seemed unfair. She was ill. I was fit.

'Yes, he is,' I muttered, adding, 'but he's only a friend, nothing heavier, in case you were wondering. It works better that way.' I knew I sounded awkward. People don't understand about me and Ganesh and it's not easy to explain.

But she smiled and nodded before disconcerting me by saying, 'You're as I thought you might be, Fran. You're pretty.'

I was taken aback. 'In this outfit?' I indicated my clothes.

'They don't matter,' she said. She looked away, her eyes seeming to focus on nothing in the room, perhaps on something in her imagination. 'I used to like clothes,' she said. 'Always sewing and altering, do you remember? What a silly thing to fuss about.'

I'd forgotten, but in a flash of memory I saw her now, seated at a treadle sewing machine which had belonged to Grandma. It was a wonderful contraption, that sewing machine. When not in use, it looked like a table with a fretwork metal footplate fixed between its side supports. When needed, the machine itself was lifted out of a recess within the table and sat on top. That was the image I saw, Mum bent over the wheel, which hummed round, powered by her foot on the plate, the length of material moving steadily under the hammering of the needle.

When I was small, I liked to play with that treadle machine when it wasn't in use. I rocked its footplate back and forth with a satisfying clank and gave my toys rides on it. I pulled open the little wooden drawers in the table, stuffed with coloured silk thread, buttons and lengths of something called bias binding which stretched if you pulled it. (Though that was strictly forbidden, as it rendered it useless.)

Grandma had bought that machine in a junk shop soon after her arrival in England in the fifties. She'd used it to set up a little dressmaking business. At one time, she'd got quite a reputation for wedding dresses. She still got the odd request for a wedding dress when I was a kid. I have memories of yards of white satin pinned on a headless, armless canvas torso on a single polished wooden leg. I acted out little plays in which I had the title role and that dressmaker's dummy was my leading man. There were other materials connected with weddings. Silk which rustled, shot taffeta which changed its colour as you moved it. That was generally for the bridesmaids' dresses. My favourite was mauve. I longed to be a bridesmaid so I could swank in shot taffeta, but no one ever asked me. Needless to say, no one asked me to marry them, either, so I didn't get to reign over all in ballooning skirts over stiffened gauze petticoats. I imagined Grandma's brides floating down the aisle looking like the Good Witch in *The Wizard of Oz*, the one who travels by bubble and floats in to help out Judy Garland.

I'm still unlikely to walk down the aisle. But if I did, it wouldn't be in a white dress, and not only because now I'm older, I'm less keen on ballooning skirts and tinselly glitter. I wouldn't wear a wedding gown of any design for the simple reason that Grandma isn't here now to make it for me. I wouldn't want one made by anyone else.

One thing was for sure. I could never have learned to sew for myself. Grandma tried to teach me to use the treadle, but every time I started rocking the footplate, the whole tabletop machinery ran backwards, sending the material towards instead of away from me. Don't ask me why. Perhaps it was trying to tell me something about my future.

Now, with all these memories flooding back for the first time in years, I wanted to cry. I felt that desperate. But I couldn't cry. I needed to say something but could only think to ask her how she was feeling. Even that seemed an impertinence. She was dying.

'Not too bad today,' she said, and added, 'it must have been a shock when Rennie Duke found you and told you about me.'

'Yes, it was a bit.' The image of Clarence Duke came to me and I asked, 'How did you choose him? Did he advertise?'

'Oh no, that is, he does advertise sometimes. But I know

him of old. I worked for him for a while. That's why I chose him, I knew he was good.' She smiled. 'And he wouldn't charge for his services, for old times' sake.'

'That's nice of him,' I said lamely. It seemed un-Clarence-like, the image of loyal friend not squaring with the seedy little character I'd met.

'I expect you didn't like him much.' She had a way of going to the heart of things. Perhaps approaching death gave you insight. 'Don't be put off by Rennie. He isn't all bad. As a PI he's very good.' She shifted a little in the bed and I wondered if she was, despite appearances, in pain.

'I hoped you'd come,' she said. 'I wanted to see you again – and I've got something to tell you.'

'I don't want explanations,' I said quickly. 'They're not necessary.'

'Oh, explanations?' Her large blue eyes looked amused. 'There aren't any I could give you, not for why I went. Nothing you'd understand. I could tell you I'm sorry, and it'd be true. But it wouldn't help, would it? Even if you believed me, and just now, you probably don't. I hope you will one day. It was a terrible thing I did to you in walking out when you were so young. But sometimes you have to make hard choices in life, and whatever you choose, you have to live with it afterwards.' She waved a hand to stop any reply I might want to make.

As it was, I couldn't have replied at once, which was as well. I'd probably have blurted out that yes, we'd all had to live with her decision. But then I felt ashamed because what she was saying, that she would be wasting her time apologising, was what I'd said to Ganesh. Only I'd said it in anger, and she said it in a simple way which somehow made things seem logical. But then she said something which put them out of sync again.

'I wanted to see you, Fran. It's nice to know you don't hate me so much you wouldn't come. There's something very important I need to tell you. Something that happened after I left Stephen. I need your help, Fran.'

'Is it something I really need to know?' I asked, my voice sticking in my throat. I felt a spurt of resentment. Was this why I was here? Why hadn't she asked, how are you, Fran? What are you doing? Where are you living? As to the last, it was better she didn't learn I was dossing in Hari's garage. But she could've asked.

'Yes, you should know it, and you're the only person I can tell about it. When I have, you'll see why. Whether you'll understand is another matter.'

She folded her thin hands on the coverlet. She wore no rings. I wondered if she'd left her wedding ring behind when she'd walked out, all those years ago. Her nails were clipped short as tidily as Sister Helen's were.

'I didn't leave your father for another man,' she said. 'In case you all thought I did. But after a while, I did meet someone else. We weren't together very long, only a few months. Then he left.'

So she, too, had been dumped. It was hard not to feel a glimmer of satisfaction. I'm not proud of all the feelings I had then, just telling you what they were.

'There was a further complication,' she was saying. 'I was pregnant.'

'This man's child?' I said. 'I mean, you weren't, when you left home?'

'No, not Stephen's child.' She paused, picking at the top

45

sheet with her fingers. 'I didn't try to contact the father of the baby. I knew he wouldn't want to know anything about it, and besides, I'd no wish to have him back in my life. I had the baby in St Margaret's maternity hospital, a little girl. I called her Miranda.'

Just like that. This time yesterday I'd had no family. Now I was acquiring relatives faster than I could take it in.

I asked hoarsely, 'Where is she? Where's – my sister? How old is she?'

'She's twelve now, just coming to her thirteenth birthday,' my mother said. 'As to where she is, I don't know. Let me tell it in order, Fran, or it will get confusing. In the same ward, at the same time I was there, was a young woman called Flora Wilde. She was a nice young girl with a nice husband who visited and brought flowers, sat by the bed and held her hand. I envied them so much because I had no one to visit me. They'd moved down to London only recently from the North. She'd had a little girl too, the same day Miranda was born. But Flora and Jerry Wilde weren't blessed with a healthy baby as I was. Their little girl was very frail. Flora had been told she'd be unlikely to have another. It was a miracle she'd had that one. She had a condition which resulted in spontaneous miscarriage and had lost two or three babies in the early weeks. She'd spent most of her pregnancy lying in bed, frightened to move. When I took Miranda home, she and Jerry had to leave their little mite in the hospital. I thought about them a lot.'

My mother's formerly colourless face had become flushed. I realised all this was stressful for her. I asked her if she wanted anything, should I call Sister Helen?

'No,' she said quickly. 'I've got to tell you it all, now, today. Tomorrow I might have a bad day and not be able . . .

I know this must all sound sudden and rushed, but I haven't got time to do it any other way.'

'It's all right,' I soothed.

She relaxed and picked up her story in a dogged, rehearsed way. She'd been practising this in her head, ready for when I came.

'I found it very hard to manage with the new baby. I only had part-time work and had to pay a neighbour to mind Miranda. It left me almost nothing. One day, I was walking home from work past the hospital. I walked everywhere. I couldn't afford the bus. There, just coming out of the hospital gates, were Flora and Jerry Wilde. They were both in a terrible state, and when they saw me, Flora set up a great howl. Jerry came hurrying over. He told me their baby had died. They had been warned of the possibility, but for a while she'd done so well that they'd allowed themselves to hope, even to be optimistic. Then, suddenly, everything had fallen apart. I felt desperately sorry for them. It seemed all wrong. Here was I with a healthy baby I couldn't afford to care for properly, and there they were, comfortably off, longing for a child, Flora unable to have another . . .'

My mother stopped.

My heart in my boots, I said dully, 'I can guess what you're going to tell me.'

I supposed she'd had no choice but to give up the baby for adoption.

'It seemed right at the time,' she said defensively. 'It seemed meant. They had registered the birth of their little girl, refusing to believe she'd never come home, so there was a proper birth certificate for a Nicola Wilde. They had no family or close friends in London and they'd had no time to notify anyone further away of the tragedy. No one knew their child had died, and if the poor little soul was cremated quietly in a private ceremony, there was no reason anyone should – not if they brought home an infant of the right age and sex. I explained my circumstances to them and asked if they would like to take Miranda. I knew she'd have the best possible home and loving parents and no one need ever know. She'd just take on the identity of the dead child. Instead of Miranda Varady, she became Nicola Wilde.'

Now just wait a minute! This wasn't exactly what I was expecting. A private, totally unofficial arrangement? A baby just handed over to people who, after all, were as good as strangers? People who'd take away her identity and give her a false one? This was what she'd done? No wonder she couldn't tell anyone, only me.

'It was crazy,' I exclaimed. 'Why didn't you go through the proper channels? They could've adopted her legally.'

'I wasn't sure of that!' She was growing animated and it wasn't doing her any good. Her breathing had become laboured. 'You know what happens when social services get a foot through your door! They'd have taken Miranda into care, fostered her out with someone I knew nothing about, and there'd have been no guarantee the Wildes would've been allowed to adopt her. This way, no one knew. I had to make a decision on the spot. I hadn't got time to think it over. Once the Wildes had told anyone at all that their baby had died, it would be too late. It was then or never.'

'But didn't anyone ask you where your baby, my sister, was?'

'I was on my own, who cared about me?' She rolled her head from side to side on the pillow. Then, with an air almost of triumph, added, 'I moved, several times, to different areas. You know how it is. I wasn't a council tenant. I rented private rooms. No one cares, Fran.'

Yes, I knew how it was. London is full of single women on the move. A fair number of them have a baby or even a couple of little kids. If the support services were infallible, there'd be fewer tragedies, fewer horrendous court cases, fewer battered or dead babies. Instead, the courts, the social services, the charities and all the others struggling to deal with those who fall through gaps in the system are stretched to breaking point, groaning under the load.

So little children die despite being on an 'at risk' register. Elderly people die cold and hungry for all the winter heating payments and the day centres. Mentally ill patients released into 'care in the community' get no care at all, stop taking their medication and descend into spirals of violence directed against themselves or others. Runaway kids sleep on street corners and are picked up for prostitution. I'd seen it myself. In my early days on my own, I'd been approached by kindly men or women offering me a 'job and a roof, good money'. I'd always ducked out and run for it. Such people don't like being refused.

My mother had been one more woman with a baby. Local council departments are delighted to cross someone off their list if they get a phone call saying that person is moving elsewhere to be someone else's problem. Delighted to have someone who doesn't keep asking for things. Too busy struggling to cope with those demanding help to have time to worry about those who don't.

If you want to lose yourself, London must be one of the easiest cities to do it in.

My mother with her baby had simply faded from view. No one knew. No one had asked. No one.

'Included in the people who don't know,' I said aloud, 'is Miranda – or Nicola, as she is now. What if she finds out?'

'How could she? And they can hardly ever tell her. There's a proper birth certificate for Nicola Wilde. There's no reason why she should ever find out.' My mother struck her thin hand on the bed.

Of course, a birth certificate. All you need in life. Heck, this is a country where you can go to earth and turn up as someone else. We have a culture which makes it easy. No one's required to carry identification, except to enter specific buildings. It's not illegal to use an invented name unless you use it in a criminal deception. (There'd be an awful lot of authors and actors in gaol if it was.) You want to be someone else? You find out the name of someone deceased, who'd be about your age if alive, in a given locality, and you write off for a birth certificate. With a birth certificate, you *can* be someone else. My sister had become someone else. The Wildes, obviously in deep shock and, psychologically speaking, in denial at the loss of their baby, had made it so. If later they'd realised the wrongness of what they'd done, it was by then too late.

'Take it easy,' I soothed. I poured my mother a glass of water. She sipped at it while I tried to work out what was coming next. I had a fair idea.

'You're going to ask me to find her, find Nicola, aren't you?' I said.

'I can give you the Wildes' last address.' She looked at me pleadingly. 'Don't refuse, Fran. I wrote it out ready, just in case you came and I – I wasn't able to give it to you.' She was scrabbling beneath the pillow and pulled out a crumpled envelope which she shoved into my hand.

My fingers closed on it automatically. It was warm with her body warmth. A warmth soon to be extinguished. But this wasn't the time to let emotion stop me saying the obvious. 'Look,' I argued, 'you said there was no need for Nicola Wilde ever to find out she's really Miranda Varady. But if – and it's pretty unlikely – I were to find her, well, that would let the cat out of the bag, wouldn't it? Me jumping up saying, "Hi! I'm your sister, Fran!"'

'But I don't want you to do that!' She clutched at my hand and the envelope got crumpled up even more. 'All I want is for you to find out where she is and try to get a look at her. Hang round and wait till she comes home from school, something like that. Then come and tell me what she looks like. You see, I don't know, or I didn't until today, know what either of you looked like now. I knew that the image I've carried in my head's been out of date. You were a little girl. Miranda just a tiny baby. The only thing that's seemed important to me these last weeks has been knowing what you both looked like now. That's why I asked Rennie Duke to find you, that and to try and make some sort of peace with you. Now here you are, I've seen you. As to making peace, I hope we can do that. I'm grateful to you for coming. I can understand how hard it's been for you to decide to do it. Mir— Nicola is another sort of problem. I can't ask her to come here. I can't see her myself. I want you to be my eyes, Fran. Also, I want the Wildes to know that I'm not going to be around much longer, so if they have still been worrying that I might change my mind one day and claim Miranda back, well, I'm not going to, am I? All I need is for you to make my farewells for me. There's no need to go into details.'

'But if I start asking questions about these people's whereabouts, someone's bound to get suspicious. I mean, what excuse can I give?' Surely she could see how awkward it would all be.

'When you find the Wildes,' she repeated obstinately, ignoring my objection, 'just tell them I haven't got long. I don't want to go without telling them how grateful I am for all they did for me. Tell them, Eva wanted to send her love. That's all. Miranda needn't be brought into it. They'll understand.'

No, they wouldn't. They'd be petrified. Even if I didn't mention Miranda – Nicola – they'd guess what all this was about. A secret they'd been burying for nearly thirteen years and which they'd believed was known only to three people, themselves and my mother, was known to a fourth – me. I hated it. I hated every part of it. I hated the deception being forced on me and long practised on someone who was my half-sister. I hated the deception my mother and the Wildes had been practising on themselves for the past thirteen years. Of course, it had seemed easy at the time. My mother tells the neighbour who's been caring for Miranda that the baby's gone into care. Miles away, a young couple with a baby move into a house somewhere, perhaps on a new housing estate. No one questions them. They can produce the necessary birth certificate which will get the child into school, get her a passport, get her any legal document she needs. Relatives living a long distance away, who knew the Wildes' baby was poorly and in intensive care, are told that the baby is now well enough to go home. Do they question that? Of course not. They'd be overjoyed.

But they were all wrong about no one ever finding out. It was there in the maternity hospital records, if anyone cared to check. Mrs Flora Wilde gave birth to a baby which died a couple of months later without ever leaving the hospital. But then, who was going to check? I was. I was checking on them. This was the part I hated most of all.

I replied as gently as I could because it was obvious how much she was counting on me and the extent to which she had persuaded herself it would be as simple as she'd explained it. 'Suppose I don't find her?'

'But you will,' she said simply. 'I've got a sort of sixth sense about it, Fran.'

Great. A thought struck me. 'Why didn't you ask Clarence – Rennie Duke to find her? He found me.'

She looked a little embarrassed, avoiding my eye. 'It's not the sort of information I'd put in Rennie's hands. Not even a bit of it, not even if I left out the child and just told him I wanted to contact the Wildes. He's – too thorough. Can't we just leave it at that? He's been a good friend to me, he found you. But that was a different matter. It didn't involve other people. Rennie, well, he might be tempted.'

I understood well enough. I remembered him telling me of his childhood playground blackmail schemes. Because that was what I was prepared to believe they'd eventually become. Originally he'd only wanted to bargain with bullies to be left alone. I accepted that. But I'd seen his face, heard his voice, when he told me about it. A puny little kid, the butt of practical jokes and rough usage, had suddenly found a road to power and he'd learned how to use it. How many other kids had he checked up on, found out some little secret about, and then demanded payment in kind for his silence? No, my mother couldn't tell him about Miranda-Nicola. She couldn't even give him a hint which might put him on the trail. To Rennie it would have suggested money in the bank.

'I understand,' I said.

'You mustn't tell anyone else, Fran!' She sounded desperate. 'I told you because you're my daughter. Miranda is your sister. Blood protects blood, Fran. I haven't even told Sister Helen. Swear you won't tell anyone.'

'There's Ganesh,' I said. 'I might need his help.'

'No, no one!'

She had pushed herself off her pillows and looked so distressed I had to take five minutes calming her. There was still one question I had to ask, even if it upset her again.

'When all this happened, were you working for or did you know Clarence Duke? Because if so, he must—'

She was shaking her head vigorously. 'No – I met Rennie Duke later. He knows nothing of my having a daughter – other than you. He thinks you're my only child.'

I bit my lip but let it go. She'd worked for Duke. She knew him better than I did. On the other hand, two things she'd told me about him made me anxious. One was that she didn't entirely trust him, any more than I would. The other was that he was a good private detective. Add to that the fact that I knew he liked ferreting out people's secrets. I knew I couldn't discount Rennie, as she called him, much as she was assuring me I could.

There was a discreet tap at the door. Sister Helen put her head through the gap. 'Everything fine?' I realised she was giving me a hint that my visit had lasted long enough.

'I'm just going,' I said. I pushed the envelope into my pocket.

'Eva takes a nap around now, don't you, dear?' she said to my mother.

My mother smiled at her and then turned her head on her pillow to look at me. She did look exhausted. 'Don't forget, Fran.'

'I won't,' I said, thereby committing myself. I added, 'I never hated you.' It was true. I could hate what she'd done, but not her. I'd obliterated her memory and thought of her as dead, but that wasn't because of hatred. It's betrayed love which has to be forced into some secret place and locked up because it never loses the power to hurt. 'I'll come again,' I said.

'Yes,' she said. 'I'd like you to come. We didn't get much time to talk about you. Come back and tell me all about yourself.'

I thought Sister Helen had a curious look in her eyes as I passed her on my way out. It wouldn't do to underestimate her, either.

Chapter Four

Gan had been waiting for me outside the hospice, sitting in the car and studying *MicroMart* magazine. As I got in, he folded it and asked simply, 'Everything OK?'

I said, 'Yes.' That was it. We drove back to London in near total silence. However, as we neared the end of our trip I told him how grateful I was for all his support that day.

'I didn't do anything,' he said, avoiding a motorcycle messenger.

'You drove me there and back. You were there. That's enough.'

'Any time,' he said.

We exchanged glances. Gan smiled and returned his attention to the traffic. Despite what I'd said to my mother about my relationship with Ganesh, it'd be plain hypocritical of me to claim we never, either of us, had thoughts of taking it further. Of course we did. But the obstacle wasn't just his family's entirely understandable objections to a liaison of any sort with me. After all, what family in its right mind would welcome me as a new member? I think what really stopped us, stopped me certainly, was fear of tampering with a relationship which worked, only to find we'd got ourselves into a relationship which wasn't working. That sort of situation isn't reversible. You can't go back to being the way you were before. So we leave things as they are. It's safer.

Mind you, I sometimes get the impression Gan is waiting for me to sober up, settle down and turn into a model citizen. Then he and I can open up that dry-cleaning business he's always on about. I tell him it's the last line of business I'd ever go into and I can't think why he wants to. Just the thought of standing over the steam press all day is enough to turn me off completely. In fact, I don't fancy any sort of shop. Look at Hari. After working all day, he spends most of his evening balancing the books and messing round with orders and VAT returns. To me he's like a mouse on a wheel, running round and round. No wonder he worries.

I felt badly about not being able to tell Ganesh everything my mother had told me, and especially what she'd asked me to do. But perhaps it was better Gan didn't know, certainly not while he was driving the car. He'd hit the roof and rightly warn me in no uncertain terms that I was getting into something I'd probably regret.

I already regretted it, but it didn't stop me, the next morning, getting ready to tackle my task. Delay wouldn't help. Get on with it and get it over, that was best. Moreover, the quicker I was about it, the less likely it was Gan would find out. I can only fool him for so long.

Before leaving, I read through for the umpteenth time the letter my mother had pressed into my hand the previous day. It was short and selective, written in a kind of code for my eyes only. She had probably worried that circumstances might result in someone else opening it. I wondered if the person she was worried about was Sister Helen. Well, if she had jibbed at putting down in writing every detail of the story she'd told me, it was certainly wise of her. It was pretty explosive stuff, powerful enough to blow away at least three people's private lives.

I scanned the letter. She'd simply asked me to check the given address, which was in Wimbledon, and discover if 'old friends' Jerry and Flora Wilde still lived there, or where they'd gone, and to find out how they and 'their family' were.

'Tell them, Eva sends her love and not to worry,' were her closing words.

There was nothing there which anyone else reading it should suspect referred to anything other than my mother's terminal illness. Nevertheless, once I'd memorised the address, I burned the note. I had this feeling at the back of my mind all the time that I had to cover my tracks. I couldn't rid myself of the thought of Clarence Duke, or Rennie, as my mother called him. He was out there somewhere, and the more I thought about his attitude when I'd rung on Sunday morning, the more his casualness seemed suspect. My caution was already in vain, but I didn't know that then. *Beware Clarence!* I told myself.

Furtiveness was, in fact, the order of the day. I dropped Bonnie off in the storeroom and peered through the door into the shop. When I was satisfied both Hari and Ganesh were busy serving customers, I slipped into the shop, grabbed an A – Z from the shelf and scurried back into the storeroom with it. I found the street I wanted, promised Bonnie I wouldn't be long and fed her a bar of some chocolate-flavoured sweet. (I know chocolate is bad for dogs but I've not heard the substitute stuff is.) Then I sauntered nonchalantly back into the shop.

Gan was still serving a customer. I slipped the A – Z back into place and made for the door. As I passed the till, I reached across to put some coins on the counter, muttering, 'Choccy bar!' and then bolted out before anyone could ask me any questions. I could feel Gan's eyes tracking me mistrustfully. He'd have questions when I got back, all right.

Travelling a long distance by London Underground gives you plenty of time for thought, especially if any part of your journey is on the elderly rolling stock of the Northern Line. My thoughts made me feel depressed and apprehensive. I gazed resentfully at the youngster seated opposite me. A headset clamped his yarmulke to his curly hair and he was lost in the world transmitted to him by his transistor radio. He was lucky. The rest of us stared morosely at our surroundings, the tatty seats, the sweet papers and bits of free newspaper littering the floor. We rattled along at a snail's pace to Embankment, where I transferred myself to the District Line for a long, slow journey to Wimbledon. By the time I got there, I was pretty well all Tubed out. My mood hadn't been helped by having opposite me from South Kensington to East Putney a young woman with a baby in a buggy. He was a nice little kid with curly hair and blue dungarees. Every now and then the mother leaned forward to speak to him and he listened carefully. Adult and tiny child had already built a real relationship. Anyone coming along to bust it up in any way, at any time, would be taking a grave responsibility on his shoulders. I wasn't seeking to bust up the Wildes' bond with the girl who thought she was their natural daughter. I only wanted to satisfy a dying woman. But fools rush in and all the rest of it. I suspected I was being spectacularly foolish and was glad I didn't have Ganesh there to tell me so.

Much of the latter part of my journey had been overground. From West Brompton onwards there were so many trees and grass and stuff I might've been forgiven for imagining I was travelling out into the country. As we finally rumbled into Wimbledon, I glimpsed prosperous-looking Edwardian villas just before they were blotted out by the bulk of a DIY warehouse. Would the house I was going to be like that?

Wimbledon's shopping centre was a busy place but with none of the controlled lunacy of Camden High Street, with its sellers of exotica of all kinds. The shops here in SE19 were nice, steady high-street names selling nice things to people with taste. Nothing here like the pair of fluorescent rainbow-hued platform-soled sandals I'd spotted in Camden and secretly hankered after. None of the huge model boots, tanks, skulls, you name it, attached to the upper frontage of the shops. No one talking to himself. No one like me, unless you counted a solitary *Big Issue* seller who was bucking the trend but getting nowhere. Here people didn't just walk past him, they actually took time to refuse. I parted with a pound coin to support a spiritual colleague. He looked surprised.

Well, now I'd seen the place and it was time to work out what I was going to do next. I took refuge in the Prince of Wales pub for a coffee and a place where I could sit anonymously to plan my strategy. I had realised that if I was going to knock on doors I had to look reasonably respectable myself. Now that I'd seen the area, I was glad I'd taken the trouble. I wore clean jeans and a navy blazer I'd discovered rummaging through a local church jumble sale. My sweater looked new, because it was – though it had been bought at one of those shops which sell 'imperfect' goods with the labels cut out. I could ring any doorbell reasonably sure I didn't look as if I was casing the place prior to break-in.

The pub, to my great relief, presented a familiar aspect, an old London tavern with maroon anaglypta on the ceiling, apricot and maroon anaglypta walls, lots of dark wood and flickering slot machines. Some of the furniture looked as if it had been there since the place was built. It held a sprinkling of men downing elevenses pints and talking business, and a couple of elderly women having an early meal. Watching them made me hungry. I'd intended only to have a coffee but I ordered a bowl of pasta and, while I waited, tried to get my ideas straight.

When I emerged three-quarters of an hour later my ideas were no clearer and I'd had to force myself out on to the street. The temptation to hide in the warm pub for a couple of hours and then go home had been great, but I'd resisted it. I felt quite noble – and doomed.

The house proved to be a thirties-built semi, with bow windows and a bit of mock-Tudor woodwork, in a depressingly respectable street. People here painted their front doors, polished their windows and kept their cars washed. I could see why the DIY store had set up here. Any house that hadn't already been revamped was in the process. This was commuterland, and there was an air of understated prosperity about it. I could see why my mother had thought Nicola (as I had to call her) would be better off with the upwardly mobile Wildes than in a squalid bedsit with her natural mother, farmed out half the time to a neighbour who probably hadn't much cared.

Because most of the houses were older few had garages. Some residents had solved the problem by sacrificing their front gardens to hard-standing for a car. On such an asphalted area before the house I was about to call at stood a nippy little Fiat. I took that as a sign someone was home.

For a minute or two after ringing the bell I thought I might be wrong. Then, from some distant recess of the house, came the sound of an outraged infant yell. Feet clattered towards the front door. It was jerked open by a thin young woman in a short kilt, sweater, black tights and penny loafers. Her long fair hair hung dead straight in two expensively cut wings. She had a pointed nose, thin lips and frosty eyes.

'Yes?' she asked curtly.

'Sorry to disturb you,' I said. (There was another outraged yell behind us even as I spoke.) 'I'm looking for Mrs Flora Wilde.'

I'd considered whether to ask after 'Mr and Mrs' or just one of them. I'd decided it would be less suspicious if I took the latter option.

'Wrong house!' she said impatiently and began to close the door. The yelling started up more insistently than ever. She paused in closing the door to turn and shout, 'He wants his Ribena, Marie-Cécile!'

The yelling was now interspersed with the sounds of someone with a heavy foreign accent trying to placate someone else who was intent on kicking in the kitchen door. I felt sorry for the au pair, but she'd given me the chance to ask a further question.

'Perhaps they've moved,' I said. 'This is definitely the address I was given for Flora.'

The pointy-nosed one scowled at me and flicked back

her gleaming hair curtains. 'We've only been here two years. We bought from some people called Georgievich. I don't know who used to live here before that. How long ago was it?'

When I told her it was perhaps as long as twelve years, she said triumphantly, 'Well, there you are! You can't expect people to still be in the same place twelve years later, can you?' It then occurred to her that given my age, I was asking about someone who would have lived here when I was a child. I saw suspicion dawn in her eyes. 'That's an awfully long time ago.'

'Yes, it is,' I said breezily. Damn it, I didn't know how long the Wildes had lived here, or when. My mother had said it was their last address. How many had they had before this one? I should have asked her. Come to that, how many had they had after leaving here? When you've got a secret, one way of hiding it is to keep moving, as my mother had done. My flimsy strategy hatched over coffee and pasta was already revealed as less than watertight.

Since I couldn't think of a convincing explanation for my lack of precise information, and knew better than to attempt an unconvincing one, I simply ignored the implied question. 'I'm not surprised to hear she's moved. But sometimes people stay for years in one house, don't they? I thought there was just a chance they'd still be here.'

By a stroke of luck, I'd struck a chord. She had been watching me, biting at the spot where her lower lip ought to be. Now she brightened, as if she'd had an idea. 'You could try Mrs Mackenzie at number thirty-nine. She's lived here for donkey's years. She may have known these people you're looking for.'

From the kitchen regions came an almighty crash, a scream and what sounded like profuse lamentations in French.

'Got to go!' said the woman. 'Bloody hell, can't that girl do anything right?'

The door was slammed. I walked away feeling quite glad that I wasn't a harassed young mum, even with a semi-detached mock-Tudor lifestyle, my own little runabout car and an au pair. I just don't think that domesticity and I would get along. Don't get me wrong. I like kids. What I don't like, I suppose, is responsibility.

Perhaps, I thought ruefully, I take after my own mother. Perhaps, given a family to look after, I would, as she had, walk out.

I didn't like to think I had been the sort of little horror who was making Marie-Cécile's life a nightmare. But perhaps I just didn't remember far enough back. True, at kindergarten I was the one who had managed to upset the poster paints and unintentionally pulled down all the classroom decorations just before the Christmas party started. I was the one who, when builders were working at my primary school, had discovered that they'd gone to take a break leaving a pile of sand temptingly unguarded. I'd then led an infant work detail armed with anything which could be used for carrying, and diligently removed it, scoop by scoop, to an area behind the boilerhouse. There we set to work to turn it into a castle and had got up to the turrets before being discovered.

Add to that frequent spats with the neighbours, all of whom I'd managed to upset one way and another. As when I'd attempted to do a kind turn to a friendly and hungry-looking cat by opening a tin of sardines and putting it down on the floor for him. He shoved his face into it and it got stuck there, wedged on his jaws. The poor thing ran round demented, unable to see, dripping sardine oil and cannoning off the furniture. It was ages before Dad managed to catch him. Then we had to clean him up before his owner saw him. By now he distrusted our entire family and spat and scratched as we tried to remove oil from his fur and bits of sardine from his ears. All this before my disruptive progress through the private school, my eventual expulsion and the humiliation of facing Dad and Grandma which I've already told you about.

'Face it, Fran,' I told myself. 'You were ghastly.'

Mrs Mackenzie had net curtains at her bow windows. Her tiny front garden hadn't been sacrificed for a car but was paved with chequered tiles and shielded from the pavement by a clipped privet hedge. Her front door was varnished dark brown and had twin glass panels in it, long, thin and pointed like church windows. Between them was stuck a little notice. It read:

WE DO NOT BUY OR SELL AT THIS DOOR
WE SHALL EXPECT IDENTIFICATION WE CAN
VERIFY
YOU MAY BE ASKED TO WAIT WHILE WE
CONFIRM YOUR IDENTITY
YOU MAY BE ASKED TO RETURN BY
APPOINTMENT

That was a good start. I rang the bell in what I hoped sounded a confident way. From the corner of my eye I could see the net curtain, and as I expected, it was briefly twitched aside. I glimpsed a face but couldn't distinguish any particular features. The curtain fell back into place. I waited.

There was the sound of someone approaching behind the door, not a firm footstep, more a shuffle interspersed with a thud. Then there was a click and a rattle. Someone was sliding a security chain across the door before opening it, but at least she (I assumed it was Mrs Mackenzie) was opening it. The gap widened enough for me to glimpse a face again. Disconcertingly, it was at my chest level.

'Yes?' The person behind the door wasn't a child. It was a woman's voice, elderly but cool and confident. I'm not very tall. She must be unusually short, I thought.

'Mrs Mackenzie?' I found myself crouching to look her in the eye. I couldn't see much more through the crack. 'Your neighbour at twenty-six suggested I speak to you. I'm trying to trace a family called Wilde who lived here some years ago. Your neighbour thought you might remember them.'

There was a silence. 'Just give me a moment,' she said.

The door was pushed to again, but not completely. I heard faint sounds as of someone moving away, and then, surprising me, voices. Mrs Mackenzie wasn't alone. Somehow I'd imagined a widow. But she was talking to a man. Not, I thought as I strained my ears, an old man. The male voice was fairly young.

She came back. The chain rattled and fell down. The door was opened wide.

Two people stood before me, Mrs Mackenzie directly in front, and the reason for the shuffling, thudding noise was revealed. At one time, I guessed, she must have been a beauty, a tallish, slender woman. Her hair, though grey, was still thick and swept back into a knot. But now she was doubled over, fixed in a permanent stoop, and supported herself with a special stick which allowed her to rest on the horizontal handle. Her knitted skirt and tunic top hung loose on her body like wrappings threatening to come adrift. But her face was lightly made-up and her eyes, locked with mine, didn't waver. The body had crumpled with age or some progressive infirmity, but the mind within remained sharp.

Perhaps the make-up had been applied because she had a visitor this afternoon, other than myself. Just behind her, in the large square hallway, stood a young man about my age, tall and solidly built, in a rugby jersey and jeans. He had a thick mop of curling fair hair and there was a slight resemblance between him and the woman. A son? I wasn't sure.

He met my gaze over Mrs Mackenzie's shoulder and said, 'Hi.'

Mrs Mackenzie said, 'The Wildes moved away at least ten years ago.' Her eyes were studying me in a way which was neither unfriendly nor curious, either of which I'd have expected. If anything, she looked as if she was assessing me point by point. I felt I was getting marks out of ten for my speech, my blazer, my jeans, my hair, my general manner.

She said, 'The fact is, I do have an address for them but I'm not at all sure I could lay my hand on it at a moment's notice. We exchange Christmas cards, that's all. In any case, you'll understand I'd hesitate to give it to you, just like that. Perhaps if you were to tell me who you were, I could get in touch with them on your behalf, once I've run the address to earth.'

This was a tricky one and I hadn't anticipated it. She was

playing for time. If I let her contact the Wildes, I was done for. I had to get the address off her now and I didn't believe she couldn't find it. Sometimes only the truth will do. Not all the truth, in this case, but enough of it.

'My name is Francesca Varady,' I said. 'I live in Camden so I've come quite a way today. My mother, Eva, is very ill. She used to know the Wildes about twelve years or so ago.' I drew a deep breath and named the hospice at Egham. 'That's where she is, and if you'd like to phone them, you can check.' I scrabbled in my pocket and pulled out the scrap of paper on which I'd written down the hospice details given me by Clarence Duke. 'She doesn't expect them to go and see her or anything. Basically, she'd just like to know how they are and make her goodbyes.'

Mrs Mackenzie took the paper and studied it. She passed it to the young man, who read it and said, 'I'll call them if you want, Auntie Dot.'

'Would you, Ben, dear?' She looked relieved. The decision was being made for her. She turned back to me. 'Would you like to come in and wait, Miss Varady? Ben will give the hospice a ring. I'm sure you'll understand my checking?'

'Of course,' I said. Given the warning notice glued to her door, I would have expected nothing less.

I followed her into the house and she led the way, accompanying every step with a hollow thud of the stick, taking me past the telephone on a small half-moon table and Ben lounging by it waiting to make the call.

You can tell a lot from a house when you first enter, just by the smell. This one smelled of polish with a hint of lavender, of old furniture, and something else. I caught a trace of that odour of illness which I'd noticed at the hospice. Nothing like so obvious, but lurking there all the same. It's hard to define the smell of sickness. Not always, of course. When Cardinal Richelieu was dying, so I was told in a history lesson, the smell of his gangrenous limbs kept people out of the room. Visitors scuttled in and out unable to bear it. But perhaps, given Richelieu's career, people had always scuttled in and out, fearful of remaining in that dangerous and powerful presence. It probably wouldn't have bothered him. But the smell, which they could escape and he couldn't, the odour of his own body rotting, a putrefaction before death, that must have been horrible.

We'd reached a sitting room at the back of the house. As I'd expected, it was comfortably furnished and very tidy, the furniture all some years old but gleaming and dust-free. There was a fake coal fire powered by gas flickering in the grate. They had been having tea. Cups (Mrs Mackenzie was clearly not a mug person) stood on a tray, and plates with cake crumbs on them. It all looked very cosy and I wondered just how I was going to manage amid all this. I felt like the proverbial bull in the china shop.

Rescue came unexpectedly. I'd no sooner taken in all the other things than I realised the room had one curious feature. There were a lot of photographs, all over the mantelshelf, the cupboard tops, lining the shelves, even on top of the television. And all of them were of dogs. My heart rose. It couldn't have been better. They were all Jack Russells.

'I've got one of those!' I cried delightedly, pointing at the nearest JR looking perkily at camera. 'Her name is Bonnie.'

Mrs Mackenzie's stiffly courteous manner thawed instantly. She became positively gracious. 'Have you, dear?' She lowered herself awkwardly into a well-used chair with a high back and wooden arms, and indicated to me I should take a seat. 'As you can see, I've had a long association with Jack Russells. I used to breed them many years ago. I don't keep a dog now, I haven't for some while. I can't walk long distances and it would be beyond me to exercise them. They are such lively little dogs, as you know.' She'd propped the stick by her chair, and as she stopped speaking, she looked down at it, seeming for a moment almost puzzled that she had come to her present enfeebled state.

'I was given Bonnie by someone who couldn't keep her any longer,' I said. 'I'm not sure how old she is, not very, I don't think. She's very clever and a terrific house-dog.' (Even if the 'house' was a garage.)

In the background, as I spoke, I could hear Ben's voice on the phone, speaking to the hospice. Mrs Mackenzie seemed to think she had to explain his presence.

'Ben is my nephew, Ben Cornish. He's studying to be a landscape gardener.' Her voice echoed with pride. 'He wanted practice and I told him, well, he could practise all he liked on my back garden!'

She gestured towards the French windows. They opened out on to a fairly large piece of ground. It certainly looked as if someone had been working there with a vengeance. Shrubs were uprooted. Trees had been shorn of their lower branches. Debris of all kinds was stacked in a pile. It looked more like an archaeological excavation than a spot of gardening. Near the house was a raised brick construction, about knee-high, filled with earth.

'My husband,' said Mrs Mackenzie, 'was a great fish-fancier when he was alive. That was his fish-tank. After he died, I kept on with the fish for a while, but eventually they died and I didn't replace them. The pond became choked with weed. I had it emptied and cleaned then just left it. Gradually I had to leave the garden to its own devices, though once I was a very keen gardener. It got in such a state. Then Ben caught the gardening bug, as he calls it, and straightened it up. But I could see he was itching to make more of it and it is a nice position. So beautifully sunny in the afternoons.'

She smiled broadly. 'So I let him loose! He began while I was away. I went to visit my sister. Poor soul, she's not in good health. But then, neither—' She broke off and frowned, reproving herself. She was of that generation which believes it bad form to whinge. 'When I got back, Ben had swept the garden just about bare! He's got so many bright ideas and one of them was to fill the old fish-tank with earth and turn it into a raised flower bed. He's going to plant it out with spring bulbs. I'll be able to look after it just by sitting in a chair alongside it. Isn't that nice? I'm looking forward to it. He's such a clever boy.'

I guessed she had no children of her own. She'd had her Jack Russell dogs and her husband had had his fish. Now she had Ben. As she stopped speaking, the receiver out in the hall clattered back into its rest. The door opened and Ben came in.

'I spoke to someone at the hospice,' he said to his aunt. 'Mrs Eva Varady is there and she has a daughter called Francesca.' He returned my scrap of paper to me.

'You were talking to Sister Helen, I expect,' I said, as I took it. Inwardly I had misgivings about this. Sister Helen might yet prove a spanner in the works.

'That's right,' he said. 'Sister Helen it was.'

'Oh well, then,' said his aunt cheerfully, 'there will be no harm in my giving you Flora and Jerry's address.' Consternation crossed her face. 'Oh, my dear,' she said. 'Your mother is dying and I'm so sorry to have made you wait—'

'Not at all,' I said sturdily.

She pressed a concealed button on the armchair, and as I watched, fascinated, the seat began to tilt forward and rise at the same time so that she slid out, grasping her stick, and was on her feet. Now that was a nifty gadget. Still wielding the stick, she set off towards a nearby writing-desk. Ben was ahead of her and had opened it up before she got there. He took her elbow as she subsided on to a chair.

She began copying out something on to a sheet of paper. Ben left her to come and sit near me. He smiled. Either I'd passed whatever test he'd set for me in his own head, or he was softening me up for a gentle interrogation.

'You're a gardener,' I said, getting in first. 'I mean, a garden designer.'

'Hope to be,' he said. 'I'm at college at the moment. What do you do, Fran?'

'Me?' I felt embarrassed. They wouldn't understand my situation, not one bit. 'I studied drama,' I said. 'I want to be an actor. So far, I haven't had much luck.'

'Shouldn't that be actress?' he asked.

'In the profession, we don't use that term now,' I informed him. 'Though other people still do. We're all actors.'

'Tough business to be in, anyway,' he sympathised. 'So, you're resting, isn't that the expression?'

'That's it.' Too right. The most rested actor in the country.

Mrs Mackenzie had twisted on her chair and was holding out a folded piece of paper. Ben got up and went to take it.

'Here you are,' she said. 'Flora and Jerry will be sorry to hear about your mother.'

They would be sorry, but perhaps not in the way she meant it. I felt guilty because Mrs Mackenzie and Ben were such nice people, and in a way, I was conning them.

Ben brought the address to me and I took a quick look at it. The Wildes lived in Kew. Nice for the Gardens. At least they hadn't moved out of the Greater London area. It had occurred to me on my journey there that they could have gone anywhere, up to the tip of Scotland or halfway up a Welsh mountainside. Out of the country, even. (I can't pretend I hadn't secretly wished they had.) But no, they were within reach and it was too late now for me to have second thoughts. I mumbled my thanks, stuffed the paper in my pocket and got up to go.

Ben glanced at his aunt. 'I must be off as well, Auntie Dot. Can I give you a lift, Fran?'

I shook my head. 'I've got to go up north. I'll take the Tube.'

'Then I'll give you a lift to the Tube station.'

Fair enough. I guessed he wanted to check on me a little more. He looked pretty sharp. He probably knew there was something I wasn't telling.

He carried the tray into the kitchen and came back to bid farewell to his aunt. I withdrew discreetly to the hall. I could hear the murmur of their voices. I wondered if he was saying anything about me, but before I could put an ear to the door, he came out of the room.

'Right!' he said briskly.

He had one of those small four-wheel-drive vehicles. I clambered up into it and he said, 'I'm quite happy to drive you home if you want. I've got nothing else to do today.'

But that was too transparent. If he wanted to know where I lived, he wouldn't find out as easily as that. In fact, I was determined he wouldn't find out at all.

'Just the Tube station will do,' I said firmly.

He gave a sort of grin. He knew I'd rumbled him. Yes, he was smart.

As he pulled out into the road, a greenish-blue car drew out ahead of us, perhaps a hundred yards away. It dawdled along but Ben showed no urge to overtake it.

'Your aunt's very proud of you,' I said, deciding that if we were going to continue our conversation about me, I'd let him know it wasn't going to be all one-sided. People are often more keen to ask questions than answer them. They think twice if they realise they're going to have to respond in kind.

But Ben just grinned. 'I'm proud of her. She's been getting progressively more infirm for years and she's never given up. She's got wonderful spirit.'

'The sister she's just been to visit,' I said, 'would that be your mother?'

The grin was turned off, just like pressing a wall-switch. 'No,' he said abruptly. 'Aunt Dot is technically my great-aunt. She's my mother's aunt.'

I should have been able to work out something like that for myself. It wouldn't add up for Mrs Mackenzie to have a nephew of Ben's youth any other way.

'I'm sorry about your mother,' he said now.

I said, 'Yes,' which was weak but there wasn't much else I could say. I couldn't tell him how she'd walked out when I was seven.

He said, 'Varady, that's an unusual name.'

'They were Hungarians, my family,' I said. 'That is, my dad's parents brought him here in the nineteen fifties as a toddler.'

'How's your dad taking the situation with your mother?'

'He doesn't have to,' I said bleakly. 'He died quite a while ago.'

'That's tough,' he said sympathetically.

I could have told him life *is* tough. We don't all have doting great-aunts who let you play at your favourite hobby in their back gardens. That was unfair. But I'd been on my own since I was sixteen. I miss Dad and Grandma Varady and I've got them on my conscience, because they brought me up and I wish I'd repaid them better than I did. To this day I don't know how they managed to scrape together the money to send me to that private school from which I got slung out. I moved on to the dramatic arts course at a local college after that. My father and grandmother were convinced, of course, that a brilliant stage career lay before me. I thought it myself. But Dad died, then Grandma, and I was slung out again, this time by our landlord. Since then I've mostly lived in squats and my acting ambitions have been on hold. The flat I briefly rented from Daphne, on highly advantageous terms to me, was the only decent home I'd had in years. But you can see why I'd always felt it couldn't last. Nothing good ever does.

'What about your parents?' I asked. 'Are they happy you want to go in for gardening?'

'They don't mind,' he said. 'Once they got used to the idea. They're both high-flyers in the business world. At first they thought I might just be reacting to their lifestyle, like kids do. You know the kind of stuff. They think nothing of jetting halfway round the world to meet another bunch of business suits, then whizzing back to stagger off the plane and have a working breakfast with a home-grown lot. Who needs that? I don't. I've worked out what I want. I drew them up a business plan, something they could understand. I showed them where I wanted to go with the gardening. After that they were OK.'

Something told me this was the end of our conversation. Now he put his foot down and overtook the car still dawdling along ahead of us.

I don't know what made me look at the driver's window as we passed by him. Being, as I was, in the four-by-four, rather higher up, I got a good view of the interior and the driver.

'Shit!' I muttered. I hadn't meant to say it aloud. But I'd been caught unawares. The colour of the other car should have rung a bell with me, but with my mind on other things, it hadn't. No doubt about it. The car was being driven by Rennie Duke.

He was wearing a sheepskin cap, his idea of a disguise probably. But it was Rennie, I was sure of it. Perhaps if I'd seen the car myself before, and not just had Ganesh's description to go by, I might have spotted him earlier.

'What's wrong?' asked Ben quickly.

'Nothing, I just remembered something. It's okay, really.'

He wasn't convinced. I saw him look up at the mirror and take in the car now on our tail.

I was furious with Duke and sorry I couldn't ask Ben to pull up so I could jump out, storm back to the following Mazda, bash on the bonnet and give the PI a piece of my mind. The last thing I needed was his weaselly presence dogging my footsteps as I tracked down my sister. Wasn't it all difficult enough? When things are bad, we're always encouraged to believe they can only get better. Not in my experience, they don't. They can and generally do get worse. If I wanted an example of that, here it was.

Or rather, now it wasn't. Duke's car had dropped back; perhaps he feared he'd been spotted. By the time we reached the Tube station, it had long disappeared from view. Had it all just been a weird coincidence? I thanked Ben and jumped out before he could repeat his offer to drive me home or ask me any more questions.

He drove off. I stood just inside the entrance to the Tube station, concealed by a pair of chatting London Transport workers, and waited. After a few moments, a jade-green car appeared and stopped at the traffic lights. The driver, the fur hat jammed ludicrously down to his ears, was hunched forward anxiously over the wheel. He scanned the entry to the Tube station and the open area in front of it. I'd no doubt now it was Rennie Duke. I pressed back against the ticket machine. I didn't think I could be seen, or at least not well enough to be identified. The lights changed. He was in a flow of traffic now and couldn't hang about. He drove on and I heaved a sigh of relief. With luck, Rennie had lost Ben at the traffic lights. But even if he caught up with him again, he would follow Ben all the way home to wherever he lived before he rumbled I wasn't in the four-by-four.

I now knew it wasn't coincidence that had put him outside the Mackenzie house. He was following the same trail I was and I could make an educated guess as to what had put him on to it. I knew he'd visited my mother in hospital. Sister Helen knew him. Suppose, on one visit, my mother had fallen asleep, or been drowsy from drugs? And there, sticking out from under her pillow, was the corner of an envelope, the letter she'd written out for me. Someone as nosy as Rennie Duke couldn't have resisted that. A bit of water from her bedside jug dabbed along the glue line, peel it open, read the interesting contents, composed so carefully for my eyes only, but containing an address and a request. I could imagine Rennie's features twitching like a rat on the scent of food. Press it back down while it was still damp and let it dry. It'd stick again, well enough for her not to notice. Rennie was a good PI. Not a nice one, but a good one. He'd probably been waiting in the road, wondering what to do, when I waltzed up and rang her doorbell. So he'd shelved his immediate plans and decided to follow me instead. For the foreseeable future I'd be looking over my shoulder. I groaned aloud.

'Who're you dodging, love?' asked one of the LT men, amused.

I emerged from behind him. 'Just an old boyfriend,' I said.

'If he's anything like my ex-wife,' said the man, 'he'll find you in the end.'

All I needed. A Job's comforter. 'Great,' I said.

I spent the rest of the day at the housing department. There were advantages in going there late: fewer other applicants. On the other hand, first come, first served. They probably didn't have a herring box left to offer me, even if they'd wanted to.

I sat on a hard chair, staring at the scuffed and scratched paintwork around me and the door of the toilet with its notice advising anyone thinking of using it to contact security at once if they found any syringes in there. Security was a small depressed man in navy trousers and blue shirt. He kept looking at his watch. It was getting near the end of the day.

A fat woman with greasy hair was berating the official at the counter. She was accompanied by a younger version of herself, bottle-blonde and spotty, with a bulging waistline. A grimy toddler in a buggy completed the unattractive trio. He was sucking a lollipop.

'There's eight of us in the house. It's too bloody many. My daughter needs a place of her own. She's got a kid and another on the way.'

The woman at the counter took details in a weary way. It had been a long day. Mother, daughter and grandchild departed. The kid dropped his lollipop on the floor as he passed me. The security man said, 'Oi!' in an aggrieved way, but only got a dirty look from the two women. They disappeared from view. The security man and I stared at the lollipop and then at each other, as if each willing the other to pick it up. Heck, it wasn't my job. It wasn't his either. The cleaner would be coming in shortly. The lollipop stayed where it was.

The woman at the counter listened to my tale of woe. She said she'd put me down for a place in a hostel though there was no guarantee. I said I didn't want a place in a hostel. She told me, nicely, not to be choosy.

'Have you got somewhere for tonight?' she asked. She was trying to be helpful. But there wasn't anything she could do.

I told her I had somewhere for that night and she gave me a look which asked what I was doing bothering her, then. I'd forgotten the lollipop, and as I tramped out I stood on it and it stuck to my boot. I had to pull it off and drop it in the waste bin. The security man was grinning from ear to ear.

'It's nice to know I've made someone happy,' I said to him sourly.

'That's all right, love,' he said kindly.

I walked home, the sticky patch on the sole of my boot attracting loose paper, cigarette ends and dead leaves. I had to keep scraping the lot off on the edge of the kerb. It had been an eventful day. I'd got a lead on the Wildes but Rennie Duke had got a lead on me. All in all, life was getting extremely complicated.

Chapter Five

I trailed along the streets, taking my time about getting home. 'Only worry about one thing at a time!' Grandma used to say. Fine, but how do you decide which pressing worry is at the front of the queue? Should I be beating my brains out over going to see the Wildes? Or working out what Rennie Duke was up to and where he was going to appear next? Or how I was going to explain to Hari that I wouldn't be getting a council flat? In fact all these concerns were pushed into the background by thoughts of my mother, lying in the hospice, trusting me to be successful, to find Nicola and do it somehow without upsetting the Wildes or letting Nicola find out the truth. I decided to think of my sister as 'Nicola', the only name the poor kid knew she'd ever had. And then to come back and tell her all about it. To come back *in time* to tell her all about it. I couldn't muck about. I had to get on with it.

I was so lost in these thoughts that I almost walked into someone. I was vaguely aware of a figure, stooped like Mrs Mackenzie had been, but over a waste bin, and poking about in its contents. I managed to avoid him and was going to step round him when I recognised Newspaper Norman.

'Hi, Norman!' I said.

If you saw Norman you'd think he was just another old

wino dossing on the streets, occasionally rescued by the Salvation Army, cleaned up, fed, kitted out and five minutes later back to his scruffy unwashed self. Norman is certainly grubby enough. He has long hair and a beard, unwashed and uncombed. He wears a dirty raincoat of the sort that used to be known as a flasher's coat, over striped pants from a morning suit and a pullover full of holes. But you'd be wrong. Norman isn't just another old down-and-out looking for a pile of paper to make his bed that night or seeking to earn a few pence from returned copies or waste paper. Norman is a great British eccentric.

Hearing me say his name, he looked round crossly, still hunched over the waste bin, but seeing who it was he straightened up and replied graciously, 'Good morning, my dear.' He then glanced up at the sky and asked, 'Or is it already afternoon?'

I told him we were well into afternoon and heading towards evening. This early in the year the light was fading by five.

'Good heavens,' said Norman. 'How time flies.'

He sounded and looked, with the striped pants, like a butler who'd lost his post without references after being found *in flagrante delicto* with a parlourmaid and was now in sadly reduced circumstances. 'I haven't finished yet,' he said. 'I haven't got the *Guardian*.' A peevish note entered his voice.

Every day Norman set out with a plastic bin bag to collect up discarded newspapers; hence his nickname. He didn't want just newsprint in bulk. He wanted one fairly clean and absolutely complete copy of each title. He included everything: the broadsheets, the tabloids, the local press. He set out early each morning, roamed the railway termini (good places, he'd told me, for discarded papers), bus shelters and

parks. Top of his list was a copy of *The Times* in which no
one had done the crossword. When he'd got them all, he took
them home and filed them. Well, filing is too grand a word.
He packed them tidily in boxes. The ground floor of his house
was stacked with boxes of newspapers, all date-marked with
felt-tip pen. The first floor was let out to tenants. The tenants
probably worried about sleeping above all that combustible
material, but Norman was their landlord, and the tenants were
generally the sort of people who didn't want to draw attention
to themselves. The house, from the outside, looked about to
fall down. Norman had inherited it from his parents. He'd
lived there all his life. If what might once have been a hobby
had grown into an obsession, so what? Norman was a man
satisfied with his lot.

Only not so satisfied at the moment, owing to the absence
of a copy of that day's *Guardian*.

'Hari may still have one at the shop,' I said.

But at this Norman looked sly and pointed out that he'd
have to pay for it, wouldn't he, then?

We made our way down the street into the lengthening
shadows, side by side.

'You still living in that garage?' he asked me suddenly.

That's another thing about Norman. You'd think he has no
interest in anything but the national press. But he generally
has a pretty good idea of what's about.

I told him I was.

'I've a back room available,' he said. 'Very nice. Looks
out on to the garden. A room with a view, as you might say.'

I'd seen Norman's garden, full of long grass, tangled
bushes, an old privy festooned with ivy and inhabited, he
claimed, by an owl, broken domestic appliances and rats. I'd

also glimpsed from time to time some of Norman's other tenants as they crept furtively back and forth. The company of the rats would have been preferable. I thanked him and declined the offer. He wasn't offended. We parted company at the corner of the street. Norman went in further search of the *Guardian*. I went back to the shop.

Hari was in the storeroom and Ganesh was alone, resting his forearms on the counter and reading *Personal Computer World*. His long hair was secured with an elastic band but a bit of it had escaped and hung down by his cheek. He was studying all the technology on offer intently and would have made a good model for someone like Rodin if he'd wanted to knock out another *Thinker*. Ganesh hasn't actually got a computer, in case this obsession of his with computer magazines should make you think otherwise. The only technology around the place is the lottery ticket terminal and the till. But Jay, his brother-in-law, is seriously into the Internet and Ganesh is feeling a bit left out. He looked up.

'Where've you been all day?' he asked

'I had a bit of business to attend to,' I told him with dignity.

Ganesh looked disapproving and heaved a sigh. 'If you think I don't know what you're up to, Fran, you're wrong.'

I must have looked startled, because I didn't see how he could know if I hadn't told him.

'You needn't look so scared,' he went on. 'I don't know exactly what it is, of course I don't. Because you're keeping all your cards close to your chest, aren't you? But it's something that will get you into trouble, and when it does, you'll come running to me to help you out of it.'

'I hate it when you're smug,' I told him.

'So I'm right!' he crowed.

'I didn't say that. I just said – forget it. If you want to know, I went down to the housing department.' He had raised his eyebrows, so I shook my head and added, 'No luck.' He grunted. 'Gan,' I ventured, 'has Rennie Duke been around here again, like this evening?'

He shrugged. 'Haven't seen him.'

'Have you seen a car like his?'

'No. How could I, stuck in here?' This was accompanied by a glower towards the back room, from which came scraping and rustling noises, indicating that Hari was busy about some kind of stock-taking exercise. Ganesh had probably been manning the fort most of the day.

I told him I'd see him later. I went through to the back room. Bonnie jumped up from her cardboard bed and went bonkers welcoming me. Hari greeted me more sedately from the top of his stepladder. I scooped up the wriggling Bonnie and made for the yard door and my garage home before Hari could ask me any questions, like, how much longer was I going to be there. How was I to know? It was beginning to look like indefinitely.

In the circumstances I had decided it might not be the best thing to eat with Hari and Ganesh in the flat that evening. However, Ganesh, who pretty well always guesses how my mind is working, came down to the garage when they'd shut up shop at eight, and suggested we went out for a bite to eat. We ended up in Reekie Jimmie's baked spud café because it was near at hand, certainly not because Jimmie's baked potatoes were anything your average gastronome would want to write about. The best you could say about it was that it was warm in there. In fact there was a real old fug, what with the odours of cooking and hot greasy dishwater, to say nothing of the smell of the fags Jimmie nipped out to smoke in the corridor behind the counter area, the smoke from which seeped in through the half-open door. That evening he had on offer the usual four fillings: vegetarian (baked beans); chilli (baked beans with a token amount of meat); cheese (rubbery); tuna with sweetcorn (a lot of sweetcorn and very little fish). Gan asked for vegetarian and I had the tuna, even though all that sweetcorn tended to give me wind.

'Haven't seen you in a while, hen,' said Jimmie reproachfully, ladling beans over a blackened spud.

We muttered excuses and carried our potatoes to the far corner, which took us out of Jimmie's orbit but put us directly under the piped music.

'When are you thinking of going to see your mother again?' Gan asked. 'Only I've got to let Dilip know if I want to borrow his car.'

'Perhaps tomorrow,' I said. I could at least let her know that I'd an address for the Wildes. Pity it was so far away. This was an exercise requiring time and money, and I was short of both.

We made conversation on a variety of subjects, skirting round the one uppermost in my mind and Gan's suspicions that I was getting into something over my head, as usual.

Business had slowed. Jimmie left his counter and drifted towards us. He wore checked chef's pants and a whitish jacket. His hair must once have been red but had paled to a speckled grey and hamster ginger. Rumours about Jimmie were numerous, but you couldn't check any of them. He was said to be an ex-bank robber, to have two wives and several children in Scotland, to have played professional football, and, the most unlikely, to be a criminal mastermind who used the spud café as a front. This I found hard to believe, because he spent most of his time in the café, and if you had any money, would you do that? I suspected the rumours were started by Jimmie himself just to keep the punters coming in.

He seated himself uninvited. 'All right?' he enquired.

We took this as wanting to know if the food had been satisfactory and assured him it had. Well, it had been as good as we'd expected it would be, which was not very, but then you couldn't say it had failed expectations either.

Jimmie leaned forward to impart a confidence. 'Spuds have gone out of fashion, you know, hen. Right, aye?' He nodded towards Ganesh.

Ganesh, appealed to as an authority on the capital's eating habits, said cautiously, 'Depends.'

'No, no, you take it from me. I've been thinking of turning this place into a pizza joint, you know?'

At the thought of the same spud fillings spread on pizza bases, I probably blanched. 'There are a lot of pizza places about, Jimmie,' I said. 'At least this place is – is different.'

'Aye, but that's because they're popular!' he returned wistfully. 'That's what the public wants. I thought, mebbe paint the place up, make it look a wee bit Eye-talian. Hang some of those fancy bottles on the walls. Table service. You wanting a job?' This was aimed at me.

I said I was always wanting a job. I didn't think he was serious, so there was no harm in going along with his plans. We all have dreams.

'Right then,' he said, getting up. 'I'll remember.'

I didn't sleep very well that night. The sweetcorn was intent on reminding me why I usually avoided it. I don't know why I chose it. No one but myself to blame, as usual. But then, cheese or baked beans can play havoc with the digestion as well. If you want a good night's sleep, don't eat at Reekie Jimmie's.

I dozed off eventually, even so. Bonnie woke me in the early hours, as she'd done before, growling softly. She was standing near my head. I put out a hand and it touched her. The hair on her spine was rigid. She gave my fingers a quick lick, just to let me know I wasn't the object of her growling, then rumbled threateningly again.

A car had turned into the blind driveway where the garages stood. Perhaps one of the other garage owners? The engine was switched off. But I heard no squeak of neighbouring garage doors opening. I listened hard. Someone was walking up and down outside. Not running as on the previous occasion I'd heard someone there. Just walking, pausing, walking on. At last, before my locked doors, the footsteps stopped.

I sat up, swung my legs to the floor, scooped up Bonnie and clamped a hand on her muzzle.

I was just in time. A faint tapping was heard at the door. Bonnie wriggled and uttered a muffled squeak. I whispered, 'Shh . . .' She froze.

The tapping sounded again, louder. I heard a voice, a man's voice. It was muffled, but I could have sworn it called my name.

This was all wrong. Anyone who knew I lived in the garage probably knew I came and went through the back door into the yard. I never used the main garage doors. Besides, who'd want to talk to me now, at this time of the night, or early morning? Not having any windows, I couldn't tell what time it was. I put hearing my name down to nerves. In the circumstances, I was ready to imagine anything. It was probably no more than one of those lost souls who'd taken the turning into the blind roadway and was wandering about, looking for a way out. I was getting fed up with this. Perhaps Gan and I could nail up a board reading *Garages Only.*

Then the door shivered as an unknown hand rattled at the catch. In my arms, Bonnie felt as though she was about to burst out of her skin with frustration. Neither of us had imagined that.

The footsteps moved away. I heard a car door slam. I waited for the engine to start up but it didn't. I couldn't work this out and I didn't like it. For a long time I sat there, with Bonnie on my knees, listening and waiting. She, too, waited and listened. Then she stiffened. I couldn't hear anything new, but she had. I strained my ears. Was that a footstep? Or just a piece of debris blown in by the wind and rattling its way past all the garages? There was another sound, sudden and unexpected, a kind of yelp. I wasn't sure it was even human. It could have been a human voice, cut short. Or it might have come from some kind of animal, hunting out there in the gloom. There were several feral cats around the area. It could even have been Norman's owl. Without warning, making me almost jump out of my skin, a car horn blared a brief, shocking fanfare, splitting the night air. It was followed by a scraping noise and a clunk. Someone, something, was panting. And then, whatever it was, or had been, was gone.

How I knew it had gone I couldn't tell you, but I knew it had, and Bonnie knew it, too. I released her. She dropped to the ground and ran towards the closed double doors. But there she stopped, and barked a couple of times in an experimental way, before beginning to whine and scratch at them. I switched on the garage light. The fluorescent tube buzzed and flickered into white light. Bonnie, by the doors, turned to look at me enquiringly. Then she scrabbled some more at the doors, whined and looked back at me again.

I told her to wait and struggled into my clothes. Then I opened the small door into the shop's back yard and peered out. It was still dark but there was a distinct lightening on the horizon despite the raindrops starting to fall. I looked at my watch. It was almost five and the temperature was pretty low. Bonnie abandoned her attempt to dig through the main doors and pattered past me through the back door out into the yard. A sudden patch of yellow showed as someone put on a light in the flat over the shop. A distant dustbin lid clattered to the ground, almost certainly dislodged by one of the cats. Bonnie barked and I told her to shut up.

The curtain at the lit window twitched and I saw the outline of Ganesh's head and long hair. He could see me, too, in the lit doorway of the garage. He disappeared, and a few minutes later the back door of the shop was opened.

'What are you doing?' he asked, coming out into the yard. He was unshaven and had pulled on jeans, a sweater and old trainers. He blinked blearily at me through a thick fringe of black hair.

'I woke up early,' I said.

'Making a habit of that, aren't you?' he asked. He ran his fingers through his hair in an attempt to tidy it. 'It's cold and wet out here,' he grumbled.

I followed him into the shop and put the kettle on. He leaned against the doorjamb of the washroom, watching me, his arms folded.

'OK,' he said. 'You don't fool anyone. Not me, anyhow. What's going on?'

'Someone was out front by the garages,' I told him.

'So? People go to work.'

'No, I mean, wandering about, tapping at the doors of Hari's garage, trying the handles. I think he called my name. Bonnie heard him and woke me.'

Ganesh glanced at the nearest window. It was still darkish out there despite the street lighting.

'Right,' he said. 'I'll get my jacket and we'll go and take a look.'

'He's gone now,' I protested.

'He might have left some trace or other behind. Come on, the papers will be here soon.' He was struggling into a leather jacket.

We went out of the front of the shop after collecting a torch from the storeroom. Gan locked the shop's street door behind him. It was tipping it down now. Rain beat disagreeably into our faces. The pavement glittered beneath the street lights, and as the drops hit it, the force sent them bouncing up like tiny fountain jets so that we walked through a mass of dancing spray. We scurried, hunched in our jackets, to the access road to the garages. A car was parked just inside it, a Mazda.

I muttered, 'Oh, no, Duke!' That sad apology for Philip Marlowe was definitely dogging my footsteps after his chance success in Wimbledon. I felt like steaming over to the car and, even if Rennie wasn't in it, leaving a nasty message taped to the windscreen.

Gan, sensing my mood, put a restraining hand on my arm. 'Hold on, it mightn't be his. There are hundreds of them around.'

The lighting by the garages was certainly so poor that the colour of the car was unidentifiable, just dark greyish. A good detective, back in Wimbledon, would've made a note of Duke's registration number, but I'm still learning. Gan's words made me hesitate, but not for long. My eyes had adjusted to the gloom and I was sure that someone was sitting in the driver's seat, and sure in my own mind who that person was. Giving Rennie the slip in Wimbledon had been pretty useless, seeing as he knew where to find me.

Gan was stamping his cold feet and muttering. Huddled together against the icy wind, trickling wet fingers of rain finding their way under our collars, we consulted bad-temperedly.

'It's Rennie Duke,' I said, shivering. 'It's got to be. Let me go over there and give him an earful.' I wasn't just angry, I was worried. The last thing I needed was that perishing little creep hanging about.

'There are other Mazdas,' persisted Gan doubtfully from somewhere inside the upturned collar he held together in front of his mouth.

'I tell you, it's him. I feel it in my bones. And if I stay here much longer, it'll be pneumonia I feel.'

'What on earth would he want? And why choose to call on you in the middle of the night?' Gan abandoned his grip on his collar to fold his arms and tuck his hands into his armpits.

I said I didn't know. Privately I could guess. Duke's appearance in Wimbledon the previous day meant he'd sniffed out some clue to my mother's secret, from sneaking a look at the letter or otherwise. True to form, he was acting on it. But why had he been parked so obviously in the garage area? He couldn't have intended to tail me surreptitiously as I left. If it had been him rattling at the door during the night, it looked as if the little squirt really wanted to talk to me. To what purpose? Did he believe I'd team up with him? That I'd even tell him anything at all? That I was that daft?

'You're right, we'll go and ask him what he's playing at,' said Gan. 'I'm not hanging about out here any longer!'

I couldn't have stopped him and I didn't want to. I was curious too. Ganesh marched up to the car and, stooping, tapped on the window. I joined him and, crouched shoulder to shoulder, we peered inside.

Through the rivulets streaming down the glass, we could see the driver as a dark outline. He appeared to be asleep. His head was propped on the back of the seat. A sheepskin cap was tilted over his nose, obscuring his face.

'That's Rennie's hat,' I whispered through chattering teeth. 'I told you it was him.'

Ganesh rapped loudly on the car window again, but the slumped figure didn't stir. Ghostly fingers seemed to run lightly up my spine. In the pit of my stomach I was getting a sick, tight feeling.

'We need that flashlight,' I said. My voice sounded dull and flat.

Ganesh said, 'Stay back, Fran. Let me take a look.'

He took out the torch and made his way to the driver's side of the car. The beam of the torch lit up the interior so that even from where I stood, I could see everything clearly in a frozen diorama, even the mascot dangling in the middle of the windscreen. The scene was dominated by Rennie Duke's partly collapsed form, propped up in the driving seat. Even in the thick jacket, it looked frail. His sheepskin hat at its rakish angle suddenly seemed a pitiful gesture of bravado. His hands were both raised against his chest, the fingers spread out in a clawing gesture, and round his throat, just visible above the collar of his jacket, was a dark line. The ends of the knotted cord which had choked the life out of him were lying on his shoulder.

Ganesh switched off the torch. His voice shaking, he said, 'I'll phone the police.' He moved towards the entrance to the driveway, then turned. 'You coming or staying here?'

I husked, 'I'll stay here, in case anyone else comes. You won't be long, will you?'

'No, only as long as it takes to ring the cops and get Hari down to take care of the papers. And then,' added Ganesh, 'neither of us will have very long before the cops come, so you d better get your story straight, Fran, whatever it is.' He paused. 'Is there anything you want to tell me now, quickly, before the law gets here?'

'No,' I said.

I fancied he looked relieved. I couldn't blame him. I'm not sure ignorance really is bliss, but it makes life much easier when you've got the police grilling you. Hiding what you know is a whole lot harder, as I'd soon be finding out first hand.

Chapter Six

At first, when the police arrived, they were all efficiency and reasonableness. They checked the car and its silent occupant, radioed for back-up and suggested we might like to tell one of them all about it back at the flat over the shop while the other stood guard at the scene of crime.

Ganesh said his uncle wouldn't like it. The police looked glum. One of them blew on his hands and rubbed them forlornly. He had as much chance of generating heat as a Boy Scout with a couple of sticks and a pile of wet twigs. The rain had eased but it hadn't got any warmer. We all stood in the grey dawn light in the lee of the garages and the poor shelter it offered. Gan and I were shaking like leaves. Being forced to stay out in the rain could easily turn the law against us – rather sooner than they'd turn against us anyway. I imagined the cosy flat. Then I imagined the hysterical Hari. Gan was right; the flat was out. I suggested tentatively we might at least go to the shop.

'Don't be daft, he's down there himself by now,' said Gan.

Fortunately, he then remembered he had the key to the main garage doors on him. So he opened them up to a series of protesting groans which fitted the scene like a Greek chorus.

'Don't use the garage much?' asked one of the coppers. Alert type. Should go far.

Ganesh mumbled something about not running a van at the moment. We all squeezed through the gap into my temporary home.

Until then, the coppers had seemed to assume that we'd found the body when coming to the shop's garage at the start of the working day, and they were happy enough with that. They were even sympathetic.

'Nasty shock,' one had said.

But when they twigged that going to the garage wasn't part of Ganesh's morning routine, and even more when they saw my camping equipment, things changed. They not only became suspicious; they got that look of furtive triumph on their faces that coppers have when they think they have stumbled on an illegal activity.

One asked, 'What's all this?' in policemanly tones. He might just as well have said, ''Ello, 'ello, 'ello . . .' He pointed his biro at my bed, the heater and Bonnie's bowl. 'What's going on here?'

I explained I was living there. It didn't go down well.

'What, here, in a garage?' He stared at me in disbelief.

'It's a long story,' I told him, 'but I'm between accommodation.'

Bonnie, in the yard, heard my voice and began to whine and yelp at the back door. 'And that's my dog,' I said. Bonnie scratched frantically at the door in support. I knew better than to let her in. She doesn't like uniforms. Her previous owner had slept rough. To Bonnie, uniforms mean being moved on.

'Where do *you* live?' they asked Ganesh.

'I told you, over the shop with my uncle.' Ganesh had a

mulish look about him. He was embarrassed. It was a toss-up whether he was blaming Hari, blaming me, blaming Duke, or blaming the police. I had a feeling it would end up being me.

They stared from one to the other of us and decided to start with the tax-paying citizen.

'As you're a resident, sir, it's possible you might recognise the dead man. Do you feel you can take a look? He might be a user of one of the other garages here.'

'I've looked already,' said Gan. 'I'm not looking again.'

'And?' The cops were waiting.

It was a pity he'd asked Ganesh. If he'd asked me I'd have said I didn't know him from Adam and put an end to it. But Ganesh is honest and said yes, he had met the deceased briefly. He understood the dead man's name to be Clarence Duke. He wasn't an owner or renter of one of the garages. He believed him to be a private detective.

All this time I was signalling to Ganesh to shut up. The more you tell the cops, the more you give them to go on, the deeper in schtuck you are. Don't go thinking that the more helpful you are, the more the fuzz will trust you. Oh no, their minds don't work that way at all. They just assume that if you know anything at all, you know all there is.

I was also uneasily aware of a ripple of excitement emanating from one of the constabulary as Ganesh spoke. PC Plod now scuttled back to the car and peered in again.

'Gawd,' he called out, 'he's right. It's Rennie Duke.' He turned back to his colleague. 'You know, that bent shamus. What's the poor little sod doing here?'

They stared majestically at poor Ganesh. 'May we ask if you were having dealings with this private detective, sir?'

'I haven't had dealings with him,' said Gan crossly. 'He

99

called in the shop asking about someone and left me his card.'

But they knew they were on to something. 'You wouldn't happen to remember the name of the person he was asking about, I suppose?'

I knew Gan was going to blurt out that it was me, and I was thinking desperately of some way of stopping him when an interruption came. The scene-of-crime operatives had arrived, spilling out of a van laden with all kinds of paraphernalia. A car brought a cross-looking individual with a medical bag. It's been my bad luck before this to be on the spot when murder investigations have got underway. You might even say I'm an old hand. I knew the doctor was there to pronounce Rennie dead. They don't leave these things to chance. Even if they've only got half a body, a doctor has to declare it lifeless. This one, having officially signed Rennie off, left. The pathologist would be along later.

The SOCOs were busy now. Blue-and-white tape was tied across the entry to the garages to bar access. A screen was put up round Rennie's car. Flashlights popped. Another medical figure appeared on the scene, a plump gent with baggy eyes, the patho. He clambered into a one-piece protective suit and wombled his way out of sight behind the screen.

Ganesh and I asked if we might go. The cops were unhappy about this. 'CID will be here in a minute,' they told us.

That was what I was worried about.

During all this activity, other people who garaged their vehicles in this row had begun to appear and were not happy at being denied access. Our two uniformed men went over to explain and placate them. They didn't do very well. People had to get to work. They wanted their cars. One or two might even have had items in their garages they didn't want the cops to see, and feared a search. Explanations about messing up the scene of crime rolled off them like the proverbial water of a duck's back. Word had got out on the street. A crowd of curious onlookers had started to gather. More uniformed coppers arrived. One of the original ones returned to me and Gan, looking harassed.

As he did so, a car drew up and a couple of plain-clothes types, one a woman, got out and began to force a way through the noisy crowd. The copper muttered, 'CID's here.'

The male detective was ordering the crowd to disperse, which it began to do unwillingly. The woman joined our group in the garage, hands thrust into her pockets and shoulders hunched against the cold. She fixed me with a disapproving look.

'Well, Fran, I can't say I wasn't hoping not to see you again!'

It was Inspector Janice Morgan, whom I'd met before. Though not without the usual faults instilled in them at police college, she had on that occasion turned out to be the most sensible copper I'd ever come across.

My first feeling was of immense relief. The person I'd been dreading seeing arrive was my old foe, Sergeant Parry. But Morgan had a different sergeant with her, one I didn't know. He had left the dispersing crowd and was standing a little way back and taking in every detail of my domestic arrangements with mean little eyes.

'It wasn't my idea,' I said. 'The feeling's mutual, if you see what I mean. No offence. I didn't arrange this.'

Morgan gave me a funny look and went outside. One of the uniforms followed her. We watched her walk over to the screen around Duke's car. When she came back, she called over one of the original uniforms, who began to fill her in on the details to date. 'Local shopkeeper' and 'homeless person' were the phrases I caught. I wanted to correct him. I wasn't homeless. I was just living in temporary accommodation. Other people might think that's homeless, but to me, being homeless is having no roof at all. There's a big difference, believe me.

Morgan returned to Gan and me. 'I think,' she said, 'we'd all be more comfortable down at the station.'

'We don't have to go to the station,' I said mutinously. I'd been through it enough times to know the rules.

Ganesh spoiled it again by insisting, 'We can't go back to the shop. I told you, Hari will have kittens. He'll have them anyway when he hears I'm not available for work for an hour or two.'

I thought 'hour or two' was being optimistic but I didn't say so.

Morgan eyed him. 'You told the officer that Duke had called at your shop. Would this other person, Hari, also have met him?'

This time Gan was really tempted to lie. I could see it in his face. But he admitted that yes, his uncle had seen Clarence Duke.

Morgan said that in that case, she would need to talk to Uncle Hari at some point. Ganesh entered into an involved explanation of Hari's nerves, but it didn't get him anywhere. They let him lock up the garage and go back to explain to Hari that he wouldn't be there for a bit. I called after him to put Bonnie in the storeroom. I heard him mumble crossly but I was confident he'd let her in, even if she did bark at him and try and grab his trouser leg.

He came back a few minutes later and said, 'I've told Hari there's been an accident.'

They put us in the back of their car and drove us to the station.

Once we got there, they split us up, true to form. The atmosphere was no longer sympathetic. I was shown into an interview room by a desk officer oozing synthetic civility, which was worse than outright sarcasm, and offered a cup of tea. I accepted. It was going to be a long morning, even if Gan didn't think it was. The tea arrived in a plastic cup. It looked like creosote and smelled pretty much like it too. I was assured Inspector Morgan wouldn't be long and left to brood.

But brooding wasn't a good idea. I ought to have taken the chance to have a good clear think. However, after a disturbed night and an early start to my day, my brain felt as though I'd been hit with a sandbag. I also felt depressed, and not just because finding a corpse before breakfast does lower the spirits, but because besides all my other problems, I now had this giant one to contend with. What I really needed was some shut-eye. I arranged the chairs so that I could put my feet up on one and prop myself against the wall, folded my arms and closed my eyes. I might as well get five minutes' kip as sit here sunk in gloom.

I did doze off, and was awoken suddenly by Morgan's arrival. I nearly fell off my chairs.

'Sorry to disturb you,' she said drily.

I put my feet to the ground. She took away the chair I'd rested them on and wiped the seat off with her handkerchief before returning it to the far side of the table and sitting down.

She looked much as she had on the first occasion we'd

met. Her dress sense hadn't improved. I've never known a young woman dress in such a middle-aged way. She was wearing a dreary grey suit over a pale-blue jumper I suspected she'd knitted herself. Her hair was what I suppose you'd call bobbed. She had little make-up. She looked like a character in an Agatha Christie adaptation. All she lacked was a string of pearls. I decided to break the ice. She and I went back some way, after all, and I remembered her domestic problems, as they'd then been.

'How's whatshisname, Tom?' I asked. 'Did you get back together again?'

She shook her head. 'We're divorced. He calls from time to time but I put the phone down. Mostly.'

So nothing had changed there.

'Actually,' she said, 'I'm supposed to ask the questions, Fran.' She paused, looked me critically up and down and sighed. 'So you're living with Mr Patel and his uncle now?'

'In a manner of speaking,' I told her cautiously. 'I'm sort of dossing in their garage.'

'Does he charge you rent?' she asked indignantly.

'No, he thinks it's temporary. He's helping me out.'

She cast her gaze to the ceiling. 'Honestly, Fran, I really thought you'd have made it to something better by now. I thought you had it in you. You're not a no-hoper like some. But things seem to be as bad if not worse. I thought that old chap, Monkton, was keen to help you?'

'He was. He did. He found me a flat. I was flooded out.' She was still giving me that reproachful look, so I went on the attack. 'Look, don't blame me, right? Blame the ruddy water board. The council won't house me. I'm out of a job at the moment. Unless I win the lottery, I don't have a lot of choice.' Getting stroppy with the cops doesn't usually help, but I was cheesed off. Anyone would think I went round hunting out awkward situations and then putting myself squarely in the frame as a sort of masochistic exercise.

I added defensively, 'I don't *like* being in police stations.'

She didn't reply that I had the knack of finding my way back to them like a homing pigeon. Instead she snapped, 'I'm not always keen on being in them either. I particularly don't like long, dreary mornings spent listening to improbable yarns spun by jokers who think they're smart and can run rings round the poor old plods. I don't like clever clogs who conceal evidence. I don't like the same person always being around dead bodies.'

'Oi!' I interrupted. 'I didn't kill him.'

'Did I suggest you did? Well, you don't want to be here, and believe me, I'd rather not be here. But we're both stuck with it, so we're going to have to make the best of it, aren't we?'

The door opened and the sergeant I didn't know came in. He was a pale little chap with thin fairish hair and acne. His eyes were still mean.

'We're going to record this, OK?' she said. Spotty switched on the machine on the table. 'This is Sergeant Cole,' she went on, introducing him to the machine rather than to me. 'And for the record, I'm Inspector Morgan.'

'I don't like it being recorded,' I sulked. 'Why can't he take notes like in the good old days?'

'Know a lot about police procedure, do you?' asked Cole in a weedy voice.

I gave him a glare which turned his acne scarlet, safe in the knowledge that tape-recorders can't register dirty looks.

Janice Morgan began again, briskly. 'Tell us all of it, Miss Varady. Had you also met Clarence Duke before this morning?'

'Yes,' I admitted.

'Fine. So tell us how, why and where. Because I need to know how you – and not anyone else – came to find him dead in his car right by where you're presently living. Don't tell me it's a coincidence. I don't believe in them, not this sort. Don't leave any of it out and don't be creative. We've been through this routine before, you and I, on other occasions. You know you'll have to tell us in the end. Save both of us time, why don't you?'

'Look,' I said, 'I met the guy once and I spoke on the phone to him once.'

'It looks as if he might have been keen to speak to you again,' she retorted. 'He was waiting outside your garage at five in the morning.'

'That's an assumption,' I pointed out.

'I think it's a fair one. We'll go on it, anyway, for the moment. What did he want to see you about?'

'It's private business and has nothing to do with his death.' I wasn't giving up without a struggle.

'If we decide the information has nothing to do with his death, we'll discard it. But right now, we need to know.'

Obviously I had to tell her about my mother. But what I hadn't got to tell her, couldn't tell her in any circumstances, was about my search for the Wildes and Nicola.

'I think I told you my mother walked out on us when I was seven,' I began. She nodded, frowning slightly. She suspected I was about to send her after a real red herring. 'Well, in a way, she's walked back in again,' I went on. 'I mean, not literally. She's dying. She's in a hospice at Egham. She asked Duke to find me and he did. She wanted to see me before she died.'

Whatever she'd been expecting, it hadn't been this, and I'd taken the wind out of her sails. She was looking at me incredulously. Even the puny Cole looked a bit startled.

'You can check,' I told them. 'I'll give you the name of the hospice and its phone number and everything. You ask for Sister Helen. After Duke told me about my mother, I went out there with Ganesh Patel to see her. Sister Helen will confirm it.'

Morgan said soberly, 'I'm sorry your mother is terminally ill.'

'Dying,' I corrected her.

'It's a word . . .' she began.

'It's the right word. You can be terminally ill for months. My mother doesn't have months. She doesn't have weeks. She doesn't need you lot crowding round her. Above all, she doesn't have to know Clarence Duke is dead. She used to know him. She hired him to find me. She doesn't need bad news. Check with Sister Helen but stay away from my mother.'

There was a silence. Cole fingered a pustule on his chin. Then Morgan began to speak again very slowly and carefully, as if picking her way through a verbal minefield.

'I don't like having to do this to you, Fran, at a time like this. I don't want to make you go over and over it. That's why I'm asking you, for your own sake, to tell me everything you know, now. Then we can let you go and you can go and visit your mother, which I'm sure you want to do.'

There was a hint of arm-twisting there. But Morgan hadn't quite got it right. Perhaps an excuse not to go and see my mother was what I secretly wanted. I felt a stab of guilt. Of course I had to go. She'd be waiting to hear how I was getting on with my search. But it was the search which made me so unwilling to go out to see her. If only she had asked Duke to find me just for my own sake. Because she wanted to see me and not because she wanted me to do something for her. I suppose, looking back, I was feeling resentful and perhaps a bit jealous of the unknown sister I'd been set to track down. I knew in my heart that it was love that was behind my mother's willingness to take the gamble of contacting the Wildes to find out about the baby she'd given up. I wasn't sure she had ever loved me as much. Perhaps I was being unfair. But that was how it looked to me.

'Fran?' Morgan was prompting.

'I've told you everything,' I said.

She drummed her fingers on the table and stared at me. 'You met Duke. What did you think of him?'

'Not much, a bit weird.'

'Weird?'

'Sort of creepy.'

'But good at his job, presumably, because he found you.'

'I suppose so,' I said uneasily, not sure where this was leading.

'Did you ask him how he found you?'

Now it was my turn to be startled. No, I hadn't, oddly enough, either through fear of what he might say, or for the shock of hearing my mother was alive and wanted to see me. It should have been an obvious question but I hadn't put it. But how *had* the wretched Duke found me?

I shook my head. 'I didn't think to ask at the time. I've no idea.'

'Suppose I could suggest to you the way he tracked you down?' She was eyeing me again, sizing me up.

I was even more uneasy, but I really did want to know, and said so.

'In his wallet we found a newspaper cutting from the *Camden Journal*. It was about your street being flooded just before Christmas. It gave the names of some of those who'd had basement flats and come off worst. Just a guess, but possibly your mother saw that in the local rag, figured there could only be one Fran Varady, and cut it out. She gave it to Duke and asked him to seek you out.'

'Makes sense,' I agreed, but my mind was running on. Belatedly my brain had woken up and was now throwing out ideas like sparks from a Catherine wheel. Amongst other things, I was miffed that Morgan had known all along about my being flooded out, but had still made me explain it to her.

'So he spoke to you and told you about your mother?'

I nodded.

'And he phoned you?'

'No, I phoned him. I had told him I'd let him know if I'd go and see her. That's what I did. He gave me the address. That was the last time I had anything to do with him.'

After all, you couldn't count seeing him in his car lurking near Mrs Mackenzie's house.

'You had no idea he was waiting outside the garage in his car?'

'No.'

'Did you hear anything?'

'I did hear a bit of a rumpus out there during the night,' I confessed.

She hissed. 'You see? I have to drag every bit of information out of you, Fran. It's like drawing teeth! When? What time? What did you hear?'

I told her I didn't know what time. During the night. 'I didn't get up and put the light on and the garage has no windows.' I'd heard a funny noise which I thought might have been an animal, and a clunking sound which, yes, might have been a car door, and panting. Yes, panting! Of course I didn't blooming well go and look! What am I? Crazy? It wasn't the first time I'd heard noises during the night outside. I'd heard some a couple of nights before, someone running. It happened all the time.

'People take the wrong turning,' I said. 'It's a blind alley but they don't know.'

'This time was different,' she said quietly.

I didn't reply. I knew what she meant. This time what I'd heard was Rennie Duke being murdered. I felt very cold and knew I was in shock.

'How exactly did you come to find the body?' She sounded matter-of-fact, as if finding bodies happened all the time. It was beginning to feel as though it happened all the time to me.

'I went to the shop to give Ganesh a hand with the morning papers. I told him someone had been messing around outside the garages and we went to check it out. You know, someone might have had the idea of breaking into the shop that way, or thought Hari stored things in the garage, the sort of things worth nicking.'

'And you recognised Mr Duke straight off?'

'Not straight away. I saw it was a Mazda car. We looked in. We thought the driver was asleep at first. It wasn't until Ganesh tapped on the window . . . Look, I don't know what he was doing there, all right? If I knew, I'd tell you. I'd like to know myself, so if you find out, tell me. I'd appreciate it.'

'End of interview,' she said suddenly. Cole switched off his little machine. 'You're going to be living in that garage for the foreseeable future, Fran? We're going to be able to find you there?'

'If Hari doesn't chuck me out now,' I said gloomily.

'If you change address, you let us know straight away, right?'

'Sure. I'll let you know which doorway I'm sleeping in. Can I go now?'

They let me go. Ganesh had already left and was probably back at the shop trying to explain to Hari what had happened and why the cops were going to be round to see him at any minute. I didn't like to think what sort of a state Hari would be in by the time I got back.

I was getting into a bit of a state myself. One big fat fact had detached itself from all the others and was running round and round in my head. Inspector Janice was absolutely right in saying it couldn't be coincidence that Rennie Duke had been waiting outside my garage home. I knew that. He wasn't to know I didn't use the main doors. He'd expected me to emerge that way in the morning and was ready to jump out and nab me. I no longer had the slightest doubt he'd been the one tapping at the doors during the night and rattling the catch – something else I hadn't told Morgan about. He'd wanted to talk to me in the middle of the night when no one else would be about. He'd wanted to talk to me urgently. He'd kept obbo outside, and as he waited, probably dozing in his car, someone had crept up on him and killed him. The way I worked it out, Rennie had been tailing me and someone else had been tailing

Rennie. Oh yes, definitely tailing Rennie. This hadn't been a mugging. I knew that because of something else Inspector Janice had told me. They'd found the newspaper clipping in Rennie's wallet. A man who still has his wallet hasn't been mugged.

I wondered whether Rennie had had any idea he was being followed. In his line of work, he ought to have been able to spot that kind of thing. Was that why he'd sought me out at dead of night? Gambling that whoever was watching him had to sleep sometime, and night was a safe period to contact me?

I couldn't answer that one. The big question was, now that Rennie Duke was out of the picture, was the mysterious other person going to come after me?

If he was, I'd find out very soon.

Chapter Seven

I'd had no breakfast, unless you counted the tarry tea, and there was a sinking feeling in my stomach. My way home led me past Reekie Jimmie's. I wondered if Jimmie would condescend to do me beans on toast, as an alternative to a spud, provided I asked nicely. I ought at least to be able to cadge a coffee. But when I got there, the door was locked and a notice hanging in it read *Closed for Refurbishment*. Jimmie wasn't letting the grass grow under his feet. He'd really meant it about that pizza place.

There was a movement inside. I peered through and caught a glimpse of Jimmie himself, fag glued to his lip, stacking the furniture in the middle of the floor. I tapped urgently. He looked up, waved the smouldering cigarette at me in acknowledgement, and came to unlock the door.

'Come on in, hen,' he invited.

I slipped in and Jimmie, after a quick look up and down the street in case a horde of customers demanding food threatened to follow on my heels, relocked the door.

'Want a coffee?' he asked.

'Please. I was hoping you'd be open for business. I've been down at the copshop and haven't had any breakfast.' I sounded wistful.

'Why didn't you get the boys in blue to give you some breakfast? They do a good bacon and eggs down there in the canteen.'

How did he know this? 'Do me a favour,' I pleaded. 'Do I want to sit down there eating with the fuzz?'

Jimmie took the point. 'Come on through. I'll fix you a sausage sarnie. Could do with one myself.'

That was more like it. In Jimmie's dingy back room, in a cloud of nicotine, we munched hot greasy sausage sandwiches with lashings of mustard. They were better than anything Jimmie had ever served in the café.

'You ought to put these on the menu,' I told him.

'They're not Eye-talian,' he replied deadpan. He was taking all this seriously.

Jimmie managed to smoke and eat at the same time, taking alternate bites and drags.

'Having a wee bit of trouble with the polis?' he enquired sympathetically.

Feeling my lungs seize up and wondering if I'd collapse over the table at any minute, overcome by smoke inhalation, I told him Gan and I had found a dead man in a car parked by the garages. News of the discovery would reach Jimmie soon anyway. I didn't tell him we knew the corpse's identity.

Jimmie took the information in his stride, commiserated with me over my bad luck, and turned to the matter uppermost in his mind, transformation of the premises.

'The idea I've got is to paint the whole place red and white. The staff can wear white shirts and red waistcoats. I'm going upmarket, you know, attract a classier type of punter. Put the prices up.'

'Staff?' I exclaimed, not very politely.

'I told you,' he reminded me. 'I offered you a job. You accepted. I'm counting on you.'

'Did I? Oh yes, so I did. Does this mean I'll have to wear the red-and-white outfit?'

'You'll look bonny,' said Jimmie firmly. 'Wearing one of those full skirts with coloured braid stitched round the hem. The Eye-talian peasant look.'

I asked him if he was sure Italian peasants dressed like that.

'More or less,' he said confidently. 'All those folk costumes look the same. I've got a contact down at the market who knows someone who'll run up the costumes cheap. I've got a load of other ideas. At weekends, I'm going to have live music.'

This was pushing the boat out. 'A band?' I asked incredulously.

He shook his head. 'A band would be way too expensive. Just a feller playing the accordion, wearing a red waistcoat like the rest of you.'

'You've got someone lined up for this?'

'A friend of mine,' said Jimmie. 'For fancy fingerwork, you can't beat him. He's just done a wee spell inside so he's looking for a job, a legit one.'

'What was he inside for?' Perhaps I shouldn't ask.

'He and a mate worked the racecourses,' said Jimmie. 'You know, lifting wallets.'

Fancy fingerwork indeed. As tactfully as possible, I suggested to Jimmie that there might be disadvantages in employing a known dip.

Jimmie reassured me. 'It's all right, hen. He's given all that up. He lost his nerve. You've got to have the nerve for that sort of thing. He could still lift the wallets but then he started dropping them when he passed them to his partner. You can't have that, can you? I mean, a runner's no good to a relay team if he keeps dropping the baton, is he?'

Fair enough. But I couldn't help feeling all this was becoming an obsession for Jimmie. Nobody can keep that level of interest up for ever. At least, Jimmie couldn't. He was a man who'd made a lifestyle out of doing the minimum. I just hoped it wouldn't, as Grandma would've warned, all end in tears.

I put my head round the shop door nervously. Gan was moping about by the till. There was no sign of Hari. I went in.

'They let me go,' I said, obviously. 'Where's Hari?'

'Where do you think? Upstairs drinking herbal tea and having a nervous breakdown.' Gan scowled at the ceiling.

'He's going to want me out of the garage now, isn't he?' There was always the room Norman had offered me, even if it was rather like proposing to stay at the Bates Motel. The owner of that had been called Norman, too. How many bad omens flocking in from the left did I need?

Tentatively, I mentioned it to Ganesh, who retorted that I couldn't possibly lodge with Newspaper Norman. I'd get raped.

'By Norman?' I asked. 'I don't think he's interested.'

'No, not by Norman, by all the other psychopaths he's got living there. You're safer in the garage.' Gan heaved a sigh. 'It's not Hari you've got to worry about. It's the rest of the family. Once they get to hear of this, they'll all be here.' He paused. 'I phoned Jay. I thought he'd be the best person to tell them what's happened here. He wasn't too happy about it but he said he'd do it.'

'How's Usha?' I asked. Usha was Ganesh's sister and Jay's wife.

'Fine. Fingers crossed, expecting a baby.'

'Good news, then.'

'We could do with some,' said Ganesh grimly.

'It seems to me at least,' I told him, 'that it would be a good thing if I kept out of the way for a bit. I don't mean skip out. Inspector Janice would go bananas. I mean, just not be here too much.'

This was paving the way for my absence the next day, when I intended to go out to Kew. Gan didn't know about that, but I hadn't forgotten my promise to my mother. 'This afternoon,' I went on, 'I'll go to Egham, to the hospice.'

'I can't get time off to drive you,' Gan said. 'I can't leave Hari. The old chap's in a terrible state. Morgan said someone would be round to interview him this afternoon. I've told him all he's got to say is that Duke came into the shop and asked for you. That's the one and only time Hari saw him. But you know Hari. He keeps saying we are all under suspicion.'

I could imagine it. The way the police mind works, it might be true, at that.

'Then I'll definitely keep out of the way. Don't worry, I'll get the train out to Egham.'

I set out for the hospice shortly after this conversation, via Waterloo, as I'd told Gan. When I got there, I took a bus up the hill. It dropped me near the hospice. The rain had stopped but the day was dull. It had rained out here earlier too, and water dripped from the rhododendron bushes as I turned in the hospice gates.

I was thinking about my mother and what I was going to

say to her and not paying much attention to anything else, and it nearly cost me dear.

There was a sudden roar of engine and crunch of tyres on gravel. A car sped down the drive towards me, causing me to leap for my life into the bushes. I had a brief glimpse of the driver, a man in his thirties or early forties with a pale, set face and eyes staring ahead of him. With a screech of rubber on tarmac he turned right and belted off. I hoped the idiot would encounter a speed camera. I didn't think he'd noticed me at any time, on the drive or sprawling in the greenery. I disentangled myself and wiped trickles of water ineffectually from my jacket. Perhaps the Wacky Racer had just made a difficult visit to a hospice patient and his mind was all over the place. He could still kill someone, driving like that. He'd nearly killed me.

I carried on up the drive and made my way into the hospice. I tapped at the office door just inside the lobby. Someone called out for me to enter.

Sister Helen was standing by the window, looking out at the drive. She appeared flushed and not as in control as when I'd last seen her. She looked round, saw me and said, 'Ah, Fran.'

I saw the mask of composure slip neatly back into place. Working here, it was something she'd had to cultivate. I admired her for doing such a difficult job, but she was looking at me in a speculative way which made me wonder what was in her mind. As it was, I had something on mine.

'Someone nearly ran me down,' I told her indignantly.

'That,' she said, 'would be Mr Jackson. I saw him leave.'

She paused as if I would have some comment to make about this. When I didn't, she indicated a chair. We both sat down.

'You didn't recognise the car?' she asked. 'Or see the driver? The name doesn't mean anything to you?'

I shook my head. 'I saw his face. I didn't know him.'

She made a noise like 'tsk!' and frowned. After a moment she appeared to make up her mind and said, 'Your mother's been sleeping most of the day. I'll go along and see if she's awake in a moment. Perhaps we could have a word first.'

I didn't like this but I couldn't refuse. I asked, 'What about?'

'Well, Mr Jackson for a start, though you say you don't know him. I was hoping you might. Fran, I know something's worrying your mother. It's been on her mind since she first arrived here. Before Mr Duke found you I thought it was that she feared he wouldn't – or that you wouldn't come even if he did. Now she seems so eager to see you again, but it's not the usual kind of eagerness. It's as though she's expecting you to bring her some kind of news.'

I shifted on my chair and must have looked guilty but I said, 'I can't explain that.' Which, as far as it went, was true. I wasn't free to explain. If she took my words to mean I was ignorant of the cause of my mother's nervy state, so much the better. I wasn't sure she did. She was too sharp. I thought she probably understood that I knew but wouldn't tell.

'We get all kinds of people calling here,' she began now. 'Usually they've been in touch first, or the person they're visiting has told us about them. Mr Jackson just turned up about half an hour ago, wanting to see Mrs Varady. When I asked if she was expecting him, he said no, but he was an old friend. So I asked who had told him she was here. But he was vague about that and distinctly jumpy. I told him Eva was asleep and suggested he wait. He did sit in the lobby for a few minutes, fidgeting all the time. Then he went outside and called someone on a mobile phone. I couldn't hear the conversation, of course, but I could see him through this window. He looked very agitated, even quite shocked. When his call was over he just jumped in his car and drove off without coming back to tell me he was leaving. I'm not happy about any of it. I was very relieved to see you. I thought you might be able to explain some of it.'

'I don't know Jackson,' I said. If that was his real name. I doubted it. Another unknown bobbing about in the equation. Wonderful.

'Sister,' I said, 'I do have some news for you but it isn't good. It's about Mr Duke. He's dead and it's in the hands of the police.'

She stared at me with her clear gaze, which seemed able to see right into my head. 'You mean it's a suspicious death?'

I nodded. 'But my mother mustn't know he's been – that he's dead. I've explained to the police about her but they might come round, wanting to talk to her, even so.'

'We can handle that,' Sister Helen said, and I felt comforted. Morgan and Cole wouldn't get past this defence easily. She rose to her feet. 'I'll just go along and see if Eva's woken up.'

My mother was propped on her pillows. She looked tired and more frail than when I'd last seen her. She held out her hand wordlessly. I took it and sat by the bed.

'I went to the address you gave me, in Wimbledon.'

She turned her head, watching, saying nothing.

'The Wildes don't live there any more.'

I felt her hand twitch in mine. Now, I have a confession to make. It had occurred to me, sitting in the train on the way there that afternoon, that I had a cast-iron excuse for putting an end to this chase after the Wildes right now. All I had to say was they'd moved and I hadn't a clue where they'd gone. But now I knew I couldn't lie to a dying woman.

'I've got another address, from a neighbour. It's in Kew. I hope I'll be able to go there tomorrow.'

'Thank you,' she said.

We sat quietly for a while, hand in hand. 'Is it difficult for you to take time off work like this?' she asked suddenly.

'I haven't got a job at the moment,' I told her. 'But I've got one lined up, in a pizza parlour. It's a new place, or will be, when it's finished. The owner's got ambitions for it. I'm going to have to dress up like someone in the chorus of *The Gondoliers.*'

She managed a faint smile. 'You'll look very nice, I'm sure.'

'I'll feel a bit of a prat, though. Anyway, it doesn't matter. I've got plenty of time at the moment to go to Kew.'

'Is Mr Patel with you today?'

'No, he does have a job and he couldn't get away.'

She nodded. 'You'll need some money, all this running around on my account. I'll ask Sister Helen to give you twenty pounds. She keeps a sort of kitty for each of us for odd expenses. I'm sure there's twenty pounds in mine. I don't have any expenses.' After a moment she went on, 'I should have known that, shouldn't I? About your not having a job. I should have asked you that sort of question last time you came. I didn't ask you anything about yourself I was so keen to get Miranda's story off my chest. I wanted so much to hear you say you'd do it, do what I wanted.'

She was still calling my sister Miranda. In her mind, Miranda would always be her baby. She knew that baby had taken on a new identity, but a corner of her mind wasn't accepting it. I had an uneasy feeling that what she was trying to do was turn the clock back. No one can do that.

'Don't worry about it.' I could see she was tired and struggling to concentrate. 'I'll come back when I've been to Kew,' I promised. 'We'll have a talk then. With luck I'll have good news for you.' I stooped and kissed her forehead. Her skin felt soft and papery.

She raised a hand to touch my cheek, her palm resting against my flesh as lightly as a feather. 'Call Sister,' she said. 'I'll tell her about the twenty pounds.'

I thought Sister Helen might question me about the money, but all she said as she handed it over was, 'It isn't necessary for your mother to know everything, Fran. We'll keep Mr Duke's death from her and you'll know if there's anything else.'

I set off back to London, realising for the first time that even if I was successful in tracking down the Wildes, I might not find what Mum was expecting. If I didn't, what should I do?

That evening a guy I knew from my drama studies days called Marty came round. He'd heard I was looking for a place to live and he knew of a squat in Lambeth. There might be a place for me, no promises.

I went down there with him so that he could introduce me and tell them I was an OK person. It was a big old house with a damp problem not disguised by an interior decoration top to bottom in lilac paint. The youth who opened the door to us had the pale skin and staring eyes of the confirmed junkie. As he lifted his arm to point up the stairs, his sleeve slid back to reveal the bruises and angry red puncture marks. Any squat I've lived in has always operated a no-hard-drugs rule. From behind one door came the sound of a first-class row between a couple who had the technique of veteran scrappers. Any minute now it would become physical. From behind another door a baby wailed with the sad hopelessness of instinct. It knew things weren't going to get a lot better than this.

As it happened, I was too late and the spare room had already been taken on by someone. I wasn't altogether sorry. As we left, the junkie at the door asked if we had any spare dosh. Marty retorted, did we look as if we had?

Outside Marty apologised for bringing me on a wasted errand. I told him not to worry and bought him a pint because he'd meant well.

'The last time I was there,' he said, still worrying about it, 'it was a really nice place. It's gone downhill a bit.'

Like me, he had his standards. Also like me, the stage didn't appear to be providing him with much of a living. He had a tatty beard and the unhealthy look of someone who eats all the wrong food. However, I was wrong in thinking he had no plans in that direction.

He cleared his throat. 'I was going to look you out anyway, Fran. I've got this, um, project.'

He looked both proud and embarrassed. I asked what it was.

'You remember Freddy, the landlord at the Rose pub?'

'I do indeed,' I said. 'And if you're thinking of doing a turn on that stage he sets up, you'd better be ready for anything. I've seen the audiences he gets.'

'Old Freddy's a bit stage-struck,' said Marty, defending him. 'He fancies himself as a promoter.'

'Freddy fancies himself, period.'

'Are you going to listen or not?' Marty asked, hurt by my cynicism. 'I'm offering you work.'

'I'm listening!' I told him.

'Well, he hasn't just got that stage downstairs. He's got a big room upstairs and every Christmas he puts on some kind of a show for his regulars. One year he had a panto. Last year he had an old-time music hall. This year he wants to put on a play.'

Marty sighed. 'I was hoping I could persuade him to let me put on one of mine. I've written several. But no, he wanted something they'd recognise and like. He reckons they'd like a mystery. To cut a long story short, he asked me if I could do a stage version of something with Sherlock Holmes in it. And I said,' Marty drew a deep breath, 'I'd adapt *The Hound of the Baskervilles*. Freddy was pretty keen. All his regulars have heard of that. Most of them have seen the old film on telly. I've started on the script. I thought you might like to play either of the female roles, preferably the main one.'

'Of course I will,' I said at once. 'So long as I don't have to get into a dog outfit and play the hound.'

'I'm going to have a real hound,' he said smugly.

'Marty,' I pointed out, 'trained animals cost the earth. They come with handlers.'

'Don't be daft, I can't afford that sort of animal. Irish Davey's going to train his dog. It looks the part.'

I knew Davey's dog and yes, it did. It was huge, a mix of breeds, all big. It had shaggy black fur and it dribbled a lot. It was also unpredictable and I doubted it was house-trained. I mentioned this.

'All it's got to do,' said Marty, 'is run across the stage at the climax of the play. Just go from one side to the other. How difficult can it be to train a dog to do that? Davey will be there to take care of it.'

I had my doubts but Marty was our producer. Let him sort it out.

'Freddy's got some Victorian-style costumes left over from the music hall. We can cobble the rest together ourselves. We divvy up the profits between us. Freddy's going to charge three-fifty a ticket. His regulars won't pay any more. It eats into their beer money. As soon as I've got the script finished and assembled the rest of the cast, we can all meet up and read it through.'

We parted company. I went back to my garage home, wondering if my urge to strut my stuff on the boards had led me to abandon reason. The regulars at the Rose formed the kind of audience which in ancient times watched the lions eating the Christians. They were hooked on inflicting pain. But I was trying to put in enough paid work to claim my Equity card, so I couldn't be choosy.

The garage looked welcoming and cosy and, above all, private. I wondered again if I was losing the ability to put up with communal living.

I strolled into the shop the following morning and, under the pretext of making some tea, managed to filch the A – Z guide again and take it into the washroom. I located the Wildes' road on it and slipped the book back on the shelf, I thought rather neatly.

'I saw you,' hissed Ganesh, accepting the mug of tea. 'If you keep on borrowing that A to Z I'll make you pay for it. It'll get shop-soiled. What are you up to now?'

'Curiosity killed the cat!' I chirped.

'Killed Rennie Duke, more likely. Try remembering that.'

Hari appeared from the storeroom. He looked as if he hadn't slept a wink all night. His hair was dishevelled and he'd gained so many extra lines on his face it was as wrinkled as an old apple.

'A man murdered on my doorstep,' he said gloomily. 'The police here in my shop interviewing me. All my life I've been an honest man. How can such a thing happen?'

I said I was really sorry, as if I'd had anything to do with it.

'What was he doing there, this is what I want to know!' moaned Hari. With what could only be described as grim satisfaction, he added, 'We shall all be arrested. You will see. I am right. All of us, taken away in Black Marias. Everyone watching. I must warn the family to have someone ready to take over the shop when it happens.'

'Go on,' muttered Gan. 'Go and get yourself into whatever scrape you've got planned. It can't be worse than being stuck here all day with him!'

Chapter Eight

Kew is a nice place, if it's peace, quiet and civilised living you want. By the time the Tube gets there, it's been running overground for quite a way, and there was even more greenery by the track than I'd found on my way to Wimbledon. Eventually we reached Kew Gardens station and I wasn't really surprised to find it looked just like one of those old red-brick ones Hercule Poirot caught his trains at. About six people, all wearing sensible walking shoes, got off the train with me and promptly disappeared. I left the station, passing by a pub and through a small shopping area of upmarket florists, speciality food shops and nice cafés. In the summer I supposed this place would be buzzing with keen gardeners and tourists, but unlike Wimbledon's get-up-and-go feel, Kew has an air of life taken at a slower pace. I ignored the signs for the Botanical Gardens and was soon alone in a complex of quiet streets.

The Wildes' house was halfway down a curving sweep of gracious red-brick villas. I didn't like to think what these houses cost. All the ones in this street were separated from the pavement by large forecourts and wrought-iron railings. The front doors were sheltered by porches held up by columns with Corinthian capitals. They had large square bay windows, offering discreet impressions of designer furnishings within. These kind of surroundings make me uneasy. At the entry to the street was a notice announcing it was a Neighbourhood Watch area. To me, it might just as well have proclaimed *Abandon Hope All Ye Who Enter Here.*

It's not just that this isn't my lifestyle. (I like to think my life *has* a style, by the way, despite Ganesh's criticisms.) The point is, people who do enjoy this level of living also enjoy other things, like money and influence. They're pally with magistrates and judges and solicitors and senior cops. Any complaint made by them is taken seriously. In a conflicting version of events, say, my version and any version given by one of them, I knew whose account authority would believe. I was wearing the decent outfit of blazer, sweater, jeans and zip-sided boots I'd worn when visiting Mrs Mackenzie. I still felt like a fish out of water. I also wished I had my puffa jacket, because it was a chilly day. I braced myself, thought of uplifting examples like Joan of Arc and that bloke who walked out of Scott's tent in the Antarctic, and sought out the Wildes' number.

The house was much like the others. The ornate capitals of the porch were whitewashed and all the other paintwork was fresh. The bay window was veiled with blinds made out of some sort of natural fibres. There were earthenware pots standing outside the door, ready for planting out when the weather permitted it. It looked a really nice place. I stood outside for a while and wondered if anyone would be at home. It was just after eleven. Coffee-break time. Now-or-never time.

I walked up to the front door and rang the bell. I hadn't decided how I'd begin. I thought it safer to play it by ear.

There's nothing worse than having a story all prepared and right at the outset something happens to make it inappropriate and you find yourself completely thrown. The funny thing was, although I'd been sick with nerves all the way there, once I rang that bell, the nerves steadied. Now I was doing a job and I meant to do it well.

The door opened. The woman standing in front of me must have been in her late thirties, but in build she could have been a child of twelve. Only her face and skin told me this wasn't Nicola herself. I'm not tall, but she only came up to my shoulder. She wore jeans which I'm sure she must have bought in the children's department. A pink knitted sweater, too long in the waist and sleeve, made her look as if she'd been bundled up by an overprotective mother. She had short, curling mid-brown hair, a snub nose and slightly protuberant blue eyes.

I heard myself asking doubtfully, 'Mrs Wilde? Mrs Flora Wilde?'

'Yes.' The voice at least was adult, firm, a little aggressive. She thought I was here to sell her something. She began to close the door, ready to shut me out.

'My name is Fran Varady,' I began.

I think if I'd physically hit her it couldn't have been worse. She stumbled back away from me, putting out her tiny hands on which the wedding ring looked incongruous. Her mouth had fallen open and worked soundlessly. The blue eyes popped at me in terror. The door swung open and I could see her, standing in her tidy hallway, looking as if her whole world was about to be swept away. She even stretched out her arms to either side in a futile protective gesture.

'It's all right,' I said quickly. 'Don't get the wrong idea. If you'll just let me explain, you'll see there's nothing to worry about.'

She whispered, 'Please go away. I don't know who you are. I don't want anything.'

'I'm not selling. You know I'm not, Mrs Wilde. I've brought a message from my mother. But please, don't be alarmed. She's dying. She's not seeking to – to disturb anything. She just wants you to know how grateful she is for everything you did for her some years ago.'

Ganesh had been absolutely right. I had got myself into something I should have stayed well clear of. How had I imagined, how had my mother imagined, that I could walk into these people's lives and not have the effect of an earthquake, shattering the foundations of their world?

'I don't know your mother,' she said, obstinate now.

'Eva Varady.'

'I don't know an Eva Varady. You've got the wrong house. The wrong Wildes.'

'Look,' I said sympathetically, because I did feel a louse, 'she told me all about it, but you really don't have to worry. The last thing I want to do is rock the boat. My mother would like to know that – that your daughter is well and – and everything . . .' My voice died away.

Flora had regained some composure. The blue eyes had lost their expression of fear and now stared at me as hard and dead as glass eyes in a dummy's head. 'I don't know what all this is about, but I suppose, at the bottom of it, it's money. Though I don't know how you think you're going to get any from me.'

'No!' I was horrified. But of course she thought this was a build-up to blackmail. 'Mrs Wilde, will you let me explain to you about me and my mother? It would make things clearer.'

An elderly woman walking an overweight fox terrier passed the house, calling out a greeting to Flora.

Flora returned it automatically, but the idea that neighbours might see me arguing with her on the doorstep inspired her to change her attitude.

'You can come in,' she said in a clipped voice. 'Provided you don't bother us again, you can have five minutes to tell me just what you're up to. Then you either go or I call the police.'

There was a touch of desperation in her voice, and I thought I knew what lay behind it. The Wildes couldn't afford to call the police or any other authority in connection with my errand. I wasn't supposed to be there. This wasn't supposed ever to happen. If an outsider, in or out of uniform, once asked me, 'Why are you here?' and I told him, the fat would be in the fire. Suddenly everybody would be wanting answers.

She led me into the kitchen but I doubted I was to be offered any coffee there. I guessed this rear part of the house had been extended, making a large, airy room with a view of a garden which would be nice in warmer weather. Right now it had a winter barrenness about it. Shrubs had been pruned down to brown stalks. Wet leaves from nearby trees were strewn in a decaying carpet across the lawn and on the nearby flower-beds, themselves bare of growth. The only thriving thing was a windmill washing line with a couple of tea towels pegged on it. They flapped in a desultory way. There was a bird table but no sign of any birds, though someone had put a bread crust on it.

Inside, the kitchen was a cosy contrast, with a touch of *Homes and Gardens* in its Cotswold-type pine fittings and bunches of dried flowers. The predominant tones were muted blues and russets. Flora indicated I should sit at the table and took a seat opposite me. In her big pink sweater and with her doll's head, she reminded me of a tea cosy Grandma Varady had had, a china lady's body over a knitted skirt.

I guessed Flora had just returned from a shopping expedition. She'd unpacked her bags but not yet put anything away. The table between us was littered with grocery items, a lot of them organic and none of them containing more than a modicum of fats or sugar. Even the crème fraiche was half-fat, and honestly, what's the point of that? There were packets of pre-washed salads, waxed cartons of freshly squeezed juices (no additives), a loaf of wholemeal bread and a packet of Ryvita. A few tins had crept in, but they contained things like chickpeas. This was a household which took healthy eating seriously. That was how Flora kept her doll-like dimensions. No one had ever cooked a chip in this kitchen. I wondered if they ate meat. I couldn't see a sign of any. I thought wryly that had I rung the doorbell half an hour earlier, very likely Flora wouldn't have returned and I'd even now be on my way home.

'You do know who I am, don't you? Really?' I asked encouragingly, giving her a chance to come clean.

Flora tilted her chin and fixed me with her brittle blue stare. 'I've no idea who you are. There's no reason why I should believe anything you say, and even less why I should care.'

I was forced to stumble on. 'At least you know my mother, Mrs Wilde, I know you do. You haven't heard from her in years but please, let me bring you up to date, explain why I'm here.'

'Go on,' she said discouragingly. 'I suppose I can't stop

you. I repeat, it won't be of any interest to me. You're wasting your time and mine.'

I let that go, even though I was beginning to fear I was. 'I don't know how much you knew about my mother when you met her some years ago,' I began, 'but she had just left my father – and me. I was seven then. We didn't hear from her again. We didn't know where she was or even if she was alive. That's important, right?'

She didn't reply. She knew how to use silence as a weapon.

I was getting annoyed. I hadn't wanted to come here. It hadn't been my idea. Flora was in a situation she didn't like but, heck, so was I! Why couldn't she make this easier for both of us?

'Yours isn't the only life she's walked back into, you know,' I said. 'She walked back into mine too. She had a private detective friend track me down.'

Flora twitched at the words 'private detective'. Her lips moved but no words came out and she pressed them firmly together as if to prevent any escaping.

'He's out of the frame now, so you don't have to worry about him,' I said hastily. 'But he found me and I agreed to go and see my mother because she hasn't got long and is in a hospice. This one.' I showed her the same piece of paper I'd shown Mrs Mackenzie and Ben, with the hospice name and phone number.

Flora barely glanced at it. 'I still don't see this gives you any valid reason for coming here.'

'Mum asked me to come,' I said. 'You're not supposed to refuse the request of a dying person. It's a difficult thing to do, anyway. *I* couldn't refuse her. I didn't want this job she gave me. But I'm doing it because it matters more to her than anything, right now at the end of her life, that she make contact with you, even if it's only through me.'

'I can't think why,' she said coldly. 'I can't think why she should want to do that.'

'Mrs Wilde,' I began, 'I know what happened and why. I understand. Your baby had sadly died and—'

'No!' She spoke so violently that I was silenced. She stared at me for a moment than appeared to make up her mind. 'No, she didn't. My baby didn't die. Eva's did.'

'W-what . . .' I babbled.

'Oh, for goodness' sake!' she burst out. 'You say yourself you hardly know your mother and yet you seem to have accepted everything she's told you. Of course I remember her. I've spent years trying to forget her, thank you! She had a baby at St Margaret's but it died and she took it very badly. She even went dotty for a bit. She was convinced her baby was alive but had been switched with a dead one by the hospital for some reason. I mean, how barmy can you get? She took it into her head that our baby was hers. We had to move house to get away from her. I can't believe, after all these years, that she's still persecuting us. I can only suppose that, in her present condition, her mind is wandering again and she's taken up the old fancy. Naturally, I'm sorry she's dying.'

No, she wasn't. She couldn't hide the surge of relief in her voice. I was badly shaken and didn't know what to believe. It was plausible. What *did* I know of my mother?

Yet something in Flora's expression made me hesitate to accept her version. She was watching me now with a kind of triumph. Because she'd whipped the carpet from under my feet? Or at the thought that the biggest threat to her family was about to be removed permanently?

Her look had become calculating. 'Go and tell her you've spoken to me, if you must,' she said. 'If it will make her happier at the end. You have, I suppose, to indulge her. Tell her, if you like, that we're all very well. However, there is absolutely no need whatsoever for you to come again, or to try and contact any of us again. I might say, too, that in future, should the occasion arise, perhaps you ought to be a bit more careful before you start agreeing to carry out dying requests.'

She'd hit the nail on the head there, whatever the truth of the matter.

'Fine,' I said. 'I'll tell her.' I stood up to go, and as I turned, I saw behind me on a dresser a photograph of the type schools have taken of pupils. It showed a fair-haired girl in a uniform shirt and a tie. 'Is this—?'

I'd barely got the words out when Flora moved, darting past me to the dresser, seizing the picture in its frame and slamming it face down. Her face had contorted with rage and now it was my turn to step back in alarm.

'If you go anywhere near my daughter,' her voice was low and shaky, but there was so much pure rage in it the effect was twice what it would have been if she'd shouted, 'I'll kill you.'

I don't know what I could have replied to that, but in the event, I didn't get a chance. I was totally unprepared for what happened next. I shouldn't have been. I've mixed in some pretty rough company in my time, the sort that prefers fists to words. But Flora wasn't like that. Or I thought she wasn't. That pretty little doll-like creature? In this nice middle-class home? All that organic food?

She swung a haymaker that caught me in the midriff and

knocked the breath right out of me. I just folded up in agony on the floor. She was boiling with fury and began kicking me. Fortunately, past experience and an instinct for self-preservation came to my aid and I grabbed her foot, hanging on to it for grim death.

'Let go!' she shrieked.

Not bloody likely, as someone else said. So she could kick my head in?

She grabbed something from the table, one of the groceries, a tin. She began swatting at me with that. I managed to get to my knees as the blows rained down, still hanging on to her ankle, though instinct made me want to throw my arms over my head. I shoved hard with my shoulder at her knees. She went down with a crash.

Freed, I scrambled up and gripped the table for support. 'What do you think you're doing?' I gasped. 'Are you bonkers or what?'

'Get out!' she spat at me from the floor. Her pretty little face was contorted and unrecognisable. Spittle flew from her mouth. 'Get out, get out, GET OUT!'

I got out. There are too many handy weapons in a kitchen and I wasn't going to wait around until Flora put her hand on one.

Well, that's it, Fran, I told myself on my way home. Mission accomplished. As far as it was accomplishable. I hadn't seen Nicola but I'd glimpsed a picture. I had a message from Flora that the family was well. I'd seen the house Nicola lived in, and very comfortable it was too, in a nice area. All of that ought to satisfy my mother. Oughtn't it?

I certainly hoped so. My head was still ringing from being clouted with healthy eating products, and my diaphragm yelled protest at me every time I breathed.

I was back in Camden and nearly at the shop, looking forward to sitting down with a mug of tea, when a car drew up to the kerb beside me. The window rolled down.

'Miss Varady?' called an official voice. 'We've been looking for you. Inspector Morgan wants a word.'

The station tea hadn't improved since my last visit, nor had Morgan's dress sense. She wore a navy jacket teamed with a droopy navy skirt and looked like a health visitor. I was still convinced she bought her clothes from those ads in the newspapers which invite you to buy one skirt and get the second half-price, all direct ex-factory prices.

'Where were you this morning?' she demanded, not beating about the bush.

A warning bell jingled, or rather, given the state of my aching head, clanged. 'I've got to go out sometime,' I said. 'I'm not a prisoner in my own garage, am I? I should have thought you could've guessed I'm flat-hunting. I've been asking round about a new place.'

'Is that how you got that lump on your forehead?'

I touched my forehead. Something there felt like half a boiled egg and growing.

'Oh, that,' I said nonchalantly. 'I walked into something in the dark, in the garage. Hari's got a lot of junk in there.'

She uttered a sort of disbelieving growl. 'Well then,' she said. 'Any luck?'

'What with?' My brain wasn't functioning as well as it needed to.

'With the flat-hunting.' She gave me a mirthless grimace imitating a smile.

'Oh, that. No.'

'Well, you can't go on living in that garage!' she said sternly.

'That's what you brought me in here to tell me?'

That gained me another wintry smile. She folded her hands on the tabletop between us and contemplated me for a moment or two. I knew she was working out a change of approach so I was more than half prepared for it when she began, 'You have problems, Fran, and I recognise they're serious ones. But believe me, you're not the only one finding life hard going.'

'I never thought I was,' I countered. 'But knowing everyone's got something bugging them doesn't help me. You're going to tell me how tough it is for you, aren't you? I don't want to sound unsympathetic, but as far as I'm concerned, so what? I deal with my troubles. You deal with yours.'

'I'm a police officer,' she returned drily. 'The one thing I've learned not to expect is understanding or sympathy from the general public. Most don't have the slightest concept of how hard we have to work to keep the peace and solve the crimes in an area the size of metropolitan London, with that density of population. They don't think of the harrowing scenes of crime we attend, the decomposing bodies we have to view, the truly horrific tales of abuse we hear, the distraught relatives we have to reassure or console.'

I'd actually heard this argument before, and the obvious question it begged was: so why do you persist with this career?

She was ahead of me. 'I can see it in your face. You're thinking, if she can't stick the heat, she ought to stay out of the kitchen. I *can* stick the heat, Fran. What I can't stick, and

I know I've told you this before, is being messed around. I don't have the time to spare for that.'

She sat back and frowned. 'You know the one thing that always gets to me in TV cops series or crime novels? Mostly the detecting officer only has one case on his desk. He spends the entire time chasing down one villain. If only! Rennie Duke's murder is my biggest case at the moment. A murder's got to take priority. You've got very little time in a murder case. Three, four days tops. After that you're chasing a cooling trail. So I've no choice but to put the pressure on.'

'So put it on someone else, not on me,' I grumbled.

'You're what I've got. Perhaps I should be concentrating on someone else. Perhaps you'd like to tell me who that person is? No? I thought not. Put it this way: until you do, or until you tell me whatever it is you're hiding – no, Fran, please! Do us both a favour. I know there's something.'

I closed my mouth.

'So, until that happy time, you, Fran, are the object of my concentrated attention. And if you can't stand the heat, you know what to do to turn it down, or even off altogether, right? You might also bear in mind that I don't have unlimited patience and that there's such a thing as obstructing police enquiries. Please remember that also calling on my attention are a couple of armed robberies, a ram-raid, a nurse who's gone missing and a case of arson which didn't result in a death only by some miracle. OK, I'm not on my own, I'm part of a team. But even so, there are only so many working hours in any day. Every Joe Public who comes through the door thinks his problem is the most important, even if it's a lost cat, and the police aren't doing enough. Have you got the message, Fran?'

'I've got it,' I told her. 'You've made it clear. I'm not thick.'

'No, you're not. Which is why I begrudge having to take the time to explain all this to you when you're smart enough to suss it out for yourself! It's also why you're sitting here now. I'm giving you a chance to review your evidence to date. I understand if, under stress of circumstances, something may have slipped your mind when we spoke before. Finding a body's not nice. But I'm sure you've been thinking it all over in the meantime. So, is there any little thing? Best to clear the air.'

In her own way, she was playing fair. She'd worked out that I was sitting on information somewhere along the line. She was practically doing somersaults giving me a chance to speak up. She was the only copper I knew who'd have been that decent and it really gave me grief that I couldn't take the hand she was metaphorically stretching out.

I told her I had nothing to add to my previous statement. Then, struck by a thought, I asked, 'Have you lot been out at Egham bothering my mother?'

'Calm down,' she urged. I must have sounded pugnacious. 'No, we haven't spoken to her. We did check that your mother was in the hospice. You would have expected that, wouldn't you? The senior staff member to whom I spoke was adamant that your mother is in no state to be interviewed. It seems a doctor's signed statement to that effect was ready and available. That's a bit odd, isn't it? Almost as if she was expecting us. She has since faxed us a medical report and we have to accept it.'

Good for Sister Helen.

'But you, Francesca, are certainly in a state to be questioned, and believe me, I'm going to keep firing questions at you until I'm satisfied you've got nothing else to tell me.'

'I can't stop you,' I told her. So long as she left Mum alone, that was all that mattered. Although I wasn't sure how fit a state I was in just at that moment, I was still confident I could handle anything she lobbed at me.

'When did you last see your mother?'

Didn't some old misery in a Puritan outfit ask a similar question of a kid in a silk suit standing in front of a table?

'Yesterday afternoon,' I told the latter-day female Roundhead interrogating me. 'And yes, I did warn Sister Helen that you might turn up. I don't care about your investigation. My business is to protect my mother.'

'My business is to solve a murder,' she countered.

'Mum didn't have anything to do with that. How could she?'

Morgan studied me, murmured, 'Hmm . . .' then asked, 'How is she?'

I told her that my mother was hanging on.

Morgan said, 'I really am sorry, Fran. I don't like badgering you at a time like this, but, as I said, I've got to run down any lead. That means you.'

'I can't tell you anything about Rennie Duke,' I said wearily. 'I hardly knew the man.'

'Then perhaps I can tell you something about him,' Morgan said pleasantly. 'He had been in business as a private detective for some years and we knew him quite well. We had nothing against him. He had been warned a few times for prying a little too enthusiastically on behalf of clients. He was twice charged with illegal use of surveillance equipment, but in the end there wasn't enough evidence and the charges were dropped. In fact, over-enthusiasm was Rennie Duke's main fault. There were never any official complaints. But noticeably, clients seldom used him twice, and it wasn't because he hadn't done as they wanted. The local solicitors stopped using him, and private detectives get a lot of work that way. No work coming in from the legal trade meant Rennie probably couldn't be too fussy about the clients he did get. But as I said, even the dodgier ones shied off after one experience. No one could ever quite put a finger on what was wrong with Rennie,' Morgan mused. 'Perhaps there wasn't anything and he was whiter than the driven snow.'

'He was a creep,' I said. 'Even I could see that. But it's not a crime, is it?'

'No, Fran, it's not a crime. But murder is, and—' Morgan leaned towards me and I couldn't prevent myself drawing back defensively – 'nobody and nothing is going to get between me and solving this one. Just bear it in mind, would you, Fran?'

'Will do,' I promised. 'Can I go now?'

'Of course you're free to go, Fran. You came here entirely voluntarily.'

Ho, ho, ho. I trudged out and went to find a chemist who'd sell me some arnica.

Chapter Nine

In the meantime, no matter what else pressed on my attention, there was another ongoing problem, that of my lack of accommodation. It was hardly fair on Hari, with the police hanging round, for me to stay on in the garage. It was taking advantage of his generosity and cruelly ignoring the damage to his tattered nerves. I don't sponge off people in any way. I never have. I stand foursquare on my own bootsoles. I'd told Morgan I was flat-hunting and I ought to do something to back that up. I turned aforesaid boots reluctantly in the direction of Newspaper Norman's home sweet home.

It would, if Norman had bothered to get the place done up, have been a highly desirable residence. I felt sorry for his neighbours, all of whom had kept their places in shape. It was a mid-Victorian terraced house with a flight of steps up to the front door and another down to the basement. Once it had been painted white, but over the years most of the paint had peeled like a bad case of sunburn. What hadn't peeled had turned grey. The door had been painted black, but that too had cracked and flaked. Someone had removed the brass letterbox so that only a waist-high rectangular slit remained through which the wind must whistle and through which, if you felt like it, you could look into the hall. Or anyone inside could look out.

It was dark already despite the early hour, and I was pretty sure Norman would be home, sorting the day's gleanings. Someone was home, at least. There was a light on the first floor and one on the ground floor to the left of the front door, filtering through faded curtains. The basement, which had a separate entrance, was also occupied.

I rang the bell. After a minute or two I heard sounds of movement. Shuffling footsteps reached the door and stopped. I stooped to the letter-hole and said, 'It's me, Norman, Fran.'

A voice at the level of the hole said, 'Just a tick, dear.'

The door creaked open and a blast of fetid air hit me. Norman stood in front of me, now wearing an At Home outfit of red jogging pants teamed with an ancient velvet smoking jacket with moth-eaten quilted silk lapels.

'Come about the room?' he asked, before I could say anything. He stood back and waved me past him. 'Very sensible. It hasn't been snapped up yet but it will be.'

The hallway was cold and damp. The walls were covered with faded flowered wallpaper on which hung several pictures in Edwardian taste, including a reproduction of *The Monarch of the Glen* in an ornate gilded frame, caked in dust. The odour of boiling vegetables oozed from a room at the far end, presumably the kitchen. Through an open door into the lighted room on the left, I could see stacks of newsprint. It was everywhere, spilling from cardboard boxes and stacked in heaps, covering every surface and half the floor.

'Follow me,' invited Norman.

Ganesh was right. I had to be mad.

'I don't offer my rooms to just anyone,' said Norman,

preceding me up the creaking stairway. 'I have to take a fancy to them.'

Help! Perhaps I should just turn and run right now. The stairway smelled of mice. I've lived in old buildings and I recognised it at once. Mice, I've been told, lack a muscle to control the flow of urine. They wee all the time.

We'd reached the landing. Four doors gave on to it, one to the left, one to the right and two straight ahead. Norman produced from his pocket a ring of keys of the sort gaolers carry, selected one, and stretched out his hand to a door in front of us. Before he could open it, the door to the right flew open and the hairiest man I'd ever seen stepped out.

Despite the chill in the place, he wore only a singlet and jeans. He was unshaven and his thick black eyebrows grew right across his brow in an unbroken line. More black hair sprouted across his shoulders, down his arms, and burst in a forest from his chest. It grew right up his throat. His bare feet were thrust into flip-flops and even his toes were hairy. Even from where I stood, I caught a whiff of acrid sweat. He pointed a finger at me and demanded in hoarse, heavily accented tones:

'Who she?'

'It's all right, Zog,' said Norman. 'It's only a nice young lady come about the room.'

Why not just describe me as a nice toothsome morsel? Zog was staring wildly at me from beneath his beetling brow.

'You're not to worry about Zog. It's just that strangers upset him. He's frightened of the immigration,' whispered Norman. 'He keeps thinking they'll track him down. He's a timid soul. The other night he came in late in a terrible state. Someone had pulled up in a car next to him as he was walking home. I dare say the driver was lost and only wanted to ask for directions, but poor Zog took to his heels. He was in such a panic he ran into the blind entrance to those garages you live in. That made things worse, of course. He got out of there and raced home here, shaking like a leaf.'

Well, that explained one thing. Now I knew who'd been outside the garage a couple of nights before Rennie Duke. If you've come into the country in the back of a lorry, you've got a lot to be scared of, and you must have been pretty desperate to start with.

'He was coming home from work,' Norman continued. 'He works nights, cleaning. He feels safer then. He doesn't go out much during the day.'

'Don't worry!' I told Zog, but he twitched violently at the sound of my voice and looked as if he was going to pelt down the stairs and away. Hurriedly I asked Norman to tell him I was myself the child of an immigrant family and definitely sympathetic.

'There, you see,' said Norman. 'That's why you'll get on all right here. You hear that?' he added in a raised tone to Zog. 'You and the young lady have a lot in common.'

Well, I hadn't actually said that.

Zog grunted, scratched his chest hair and shambled back into his room.

Norman unlocked the door ahead of us and switched on the light, which glowed with all its forty-watt strength from a worn flex in the middle of the ceiling. No lampshade. Naturally.

'Fully furnished,' said Norman, gesturing widely to encompass the room's fixtures and fittings.

Yes, it was. It had been furnished in his parents', if not grandparents', day. I guessed much of it stemmed from the late 1940s. The carpet was worn to the backing threads. There was a double bed with head– and footboards constructed of flat slats, so that the sleeper lay as if between a couple of picket fences. The mattress sagged in the middle and was stained ominously. I couldn't help wondering about bugs. The bed stood high enough off the ground for you to keep a cabin trunk underneath if you wanted to. Rashly I peered underneath and saw a sea of fluffy dust and a receptacle with a handle, painted with roses.

'Norm, you have got a loo?' I asked in horror.

'Bless you, dear, of course. It's just next door in the bathroom. But you've got your own washing facilities.' He pointed at a cracked washbasin hanging from the wall.

'Fire escape?' I ventured. I couldn't ignore all that newspaper downstairs.

'No problem,' said Norman confidently. 'You can always climb out the bathroom window and drop down on to the roof of the lean-to. From there to the ground it's no more than eight feet.'

And two broken ankles.

I looked round despairingly. The rest of the furniture comprised a small wardrobe, a dressing table with an oval mirror and two hardbacked dining-room chairs. There were pictures on the walls up here, too. One showed children in black stockings and Holland pinafores, picking wild flowers. The other showed a sinking ship in mountainous seas with people clinging to spars. A girl with flying golden tresses was nobly rowing to their rescue in a tiny boat. A small brass plaque told me it was entitled *The Lighthouse Keeper's Daughter.*

'Could probably find you an armchair downstairs. Put it

over there by the window. Pity it's dark and you can't see the view.' Norman padded to the window and peered into the night. 'The sash is broken but I'll fix it.'

I didn't need to see the view. I'd seen enough.

'Terms by arrangement,' said Norman discreetly, coughing into his hand.

I couldn't refuse outright. Norman, in his own way, was trying to be helpful – and get himself a reliable tenant. Besides, I mightn't find anywhere else. Yet I balked at acceptance. Surely there must be something, somewhere? I went through the actions of a seriously interested applicant. I turned the tap in the sagging washbasin. The pipes coughed hollowly at me and a trickle of rust-tinged water ran out. The plughole was clogged with hairs and gunge. It whiffed a bit. I tugged open one of the dressing-table drawers. A knob came off in my hand. Having wrestled the drawer open, I then couldn't shut it.

The close inspection was making Norman nervous. He removed the drawer knob from my hand with a tetchy 'Gently!' and thrust it back into place.

'There we are, then!' he said brightly. I was still looking round, so he decided on a diversion. 'Nasty business over your way.'

It took a moment for me to realise he meant the murder. My surroundings exerted a horrid fascination which blotted out all else. 'Yeah,' I said. 'It was.'

'Know him, did you? The dead feller?'

I concentrated on Norman with an effort. 'Why do you ask?'

His gaze eluded mine. 'Thought you might have known him. After all, what was he doing down there, parked by those garages? Dead end, that, ain't it?'

'He took a wrong turning,' I said. 'Like Zog.'

I didn't want to discuss it and Norman knew I didn't. In his crafty way he'd speeded up my departure before I wrecked the remaining fixtures and fittings. Nevertheless, on the way out, he insisted on showing me the bathroom. The promised fire-escape route through the window here was facilitated by the fact that the catch was broken, and despite the icy temperatures outside and the lack of heating inside, the window with its cracked frosted glass in a mouldering wooden frame was wedged permanently ajar. The huge old enamel bath stood on four lion's paws and was rusted round the plughole and so eaten away elsewhere it brought to mind bodies being dissolved in acid. The cold had perhaps led to the cracking of a pipe running along the wall from the loo which was leaking into a pile of surplus newspapers stacked underneath in a festering yellow heap. Even Norman seemed to feel he should offer reassurance.

'I'm going to get that fixed, too. Sidney up in the attic is very handy with tools.'

I didn't ask where Sidney had learned to be handy with tools. Probably cracking safes.

I didn't want to hurt Norman's feelings, but no way could I live here. I'd rather doss in a doorway. I said I'd let him know. He seemed surprised.

'Don't take too long about it,' he advised.

I've never been so glad to be out of a place in my life. Standing on the wet pavement, breathing in the evening air and listening to distant traffic noises, I felt like one of those prisoners who climbs on stage at the end of *Fidelio*.

The shop, when I reached it, was a haven of normality. Hari was selling the *Evening Standard*, Ganesh was restocking the cold drinks cabinet, Bonnie snoozed on her cardboard bed in the stockroom. I could've kissed them all.

The next morning, I took the train out to Egham and toiled up the hill to the hospice. The bump on my forehead had subsided and I'd taken the precaution of buying some concealant and covering up the purple bruise which had come out overnight. I would have to keep it covered. I didn't want Ganesh asking me about it, quite apart from my mother. If she noticed.

'How is she?' I asked Sister Helen.

'Quiet,' she said. 'Sleeping a lot. Last night she talked about you.'

I must have looked startled, because she smiled.

'She's very happy to have got in touch with you again.'

'Sure,' I mumbled, then asked, 'what did she say, about me?'

'That it was nice to see you managing so well and that you'd got a new job lined up. She hoped you'd come again today and keep her up to date with events, whatever they are.' She twitched an eyebrow.

I didn't respond to the unspoken invitation. I knew the events my mother waited to hear about. She hoped I'd come with news that I'd seen Nicola. I felt ridiculously disappointed. Aloud, I thanked Sister Helen for keeping the police at bay.

'We're here to make things as easy for your mother as we can,' Sister Helen said calmly. 'Naturally, she mustn't be harassed.'

She gave me a steely look and I understood she meant I wasn't to upset my mother either. The fact that she thought I might do that was in itself suspicious. I wished I knew how much Sister Helen herself knew. I got the funny feeling she was holding out on me in some way. But it was no good hoping she'd let on. Even if my mother had told her anything, she'd consider it akin to being under the seal of the confessional, and she wouldn't go blabbing it out, not to the police, not to me, not to anyone.

I told her I understood the rules.

They'd moved Mum's bed. It was over by the window so that she could see out into the garden at the rear of the building. It was milder out today, and the sun shone weakly. I didn't know why they hadn't put it there before.

'Look Fran,' she said when she saw me. 'I can see the birdbath from here. The starlings all push and shove one another trying to get in. It's quite funny.'

I sat on the edge of the bed and looked across her, out of the window, at the birdbath. There was a blackbird in it at the moment, ducking his head under the water, thrashing his wings, having a wonderful time. Water droplets flew everywhere.

'I've been out to Kew,' I said. 'It's where the Wildes live now. I saw Flora Wilde.'

My mother caught her breath, and colour flooded into her pale cheeks. She put out her hand and grabbed mine. 'I knew you'd do it, Fran.'

'Hang on,' I said awkwardly. 'She wasn't very pleased to see me. I tried to explain. I told her about you – being here. But she was scared. I mean, you can see her point of view.'

But that was just what my mother couldn't or wouldn't see.

'Oh, but she doesn't have anything to fear,' she said in that infuriatingly confident way. 'I just want to know what

Nicola, as I must call her, looks like. In my mind, you know, I still call her Miranda.'

Inwardly I groaned. She just didn't want to know about any obstacle to the beautiful idea she'd had to send me hunting for my half-sister. I felt a twinge of resentment again. She wasn't giving any thought to Flora or to me or to how much trouble could be caused. She'd just got this thing in her head about my seeing Nicola. The words 'in my mind' stirred unease in me. Was this really all just in her mind, as Flora had said? Had she transferred Miranda's name and identity to another baby, not hers at all? Was the thirteen-year-old out there in leafy Kew my sister or not?

I took a deep breath and described the house in Kew to my mother. She was pleased it was so nice. Then I told her I'd spotted a school photo and described that. That really cheered her up. But it didn't satisfy her.

'You're so near, Fran. You've almost seen her. You can't give up now,' she beseeched me when I ventured to suggest that perhaps my mission had been accomplished.

'This is dangerous, Mum,' I insisted. 'The more I ask around, the riskier it all gets.'

'How?' she asked sulkily, turning her head from me to stare defiantly at the garden and the now deserted birdbath.

'You don't want Nicola to know the truth, do you?'

She was silent. My heart sank. 'Mum?' I asked. 'What *is* the truth?'

She turned, looking surprised. 'About what?'

I was miserably aware I wasn't to upset her, but if I was to go on with my task, I had to be sure.

'About Nicola. Is she really my half-sister?' My mother was still silent. I felt as if I was walking in treacle. I struggled on. 'She isn't Flora's child? You are – you are quite sure about that?'

'Is that what Flora's said?' she returned. 'I know my own baby, Fran.' She put out a frail hand and stroked my cheek. 'Find her for me, Fran. Speak to her.'

'About what?' I was horrified. This wasn't what she'd originally asked of me. 'You said you just wanted to know what she looked like.'

She gave me a strange look, like a child who's trying to manipulate an adult into some course of action which it knows a straight request won't bring about. Or was it a child who'd committed some transgression and was trying to shift the blame? I wished I knew.

'It would be nice to know what her voice was like.' She gave me a wheedling smile. 'To know some words she'd actually spoken. I can't see her, Fran. I can't talk to her. You can.' She sighed and closed her eyes. 'I'm tired now. I think I'll have a little nap. Come again.'

I knew I was being played like a fish on a line, but there wasn't a thing I could do about it. I told her I'd be back, and left.

Sister Helen wasn't around when I passed the office. I was rather pleased about that. I wandered down the drive with my hands in my pockets, planning my next move. I should, I supposed, at least have another shot at going to Kew. I could hang around and I might catch sight of Nicola. Flora needn't see me. I'd be careful. I'd be very careful. Next time she might come at me with a knife. I still couldn't believe it had happened. Flora had looked so – so frail and dainty, like a bit of Dresden china. That'd teach me to make assumptions.

'Yeah, yeah,' I muttered. 'Even if Flora doesn't get me, someone will. That's Neighbourhood Watch territory. If a stranger hangs around there, it'll be noticed. Someone will phone the cops.'

I'd reached the end of the drive. There was someone there, a man. He stood with his back to me, staring at the road. But as I reached him, he turned round. He stepped forward and to one side, blocking my progress. The pale face and straight dark hair, brushed back flat from a high forehead, were somehow familiar.

'Miss Varady?' he asked politely. 'I was hoping you'd come today. In fact, to be honest, I was counting on it.'

'You,' I said, identifying him suddenly, 'nearly ran me down in your car the last time I was here! Why don't you just get out of my way?'

'But I didn't know it was you,' he said. 'I'm sorry if I caused you a fright. Not, of course, that I'd aim to run down anyone,' he added hastily. 'I'd had some bad news and wasn't paying sufficient attention, I admit. If I had known it was you I'd have stopped, because we really do need to talk.'

'Do we?' I said discouragingly. 'Not that I can see.'

'My name is Jackson,' he said. 'And all I want is half an hour of your time. I think you can guess what it's all about.'

Chapter Ten

'I don't want to talk to you,' I said, attempting to step round him.

He barred my way. 'I really think it's in the best interests of everyone.' His voice was soft but determined.

'I don't even know who you are, and a surname certainly doesn't tell me,' I said sourly. 'So how can I tell if it's in anyone's interests or even know what the hell you're talking about?'

'I'm an old family friend of the Wildes,' he said. 'I'm acting on their behalf.'

'You're a lawyer?'

He gave a tight little smile. 'Hardly likely, is it?'

No, it wasn't. The Wildes wouldn't want the law in any form interfering in their particular problem. But there was another profession, not the law, but travelling parallel to it . . . and occasionally around it.

'I hope,' I said with sinking heart, 'you're not another private eye.'

'Good Lord, no!' he exclaimed, as if I'd made an indecent proposal.

'That's something, then. Go on,' I told him. 'Let's have it. What's the message?' I might as well hear what he'd got to say.

'Not here,' he said quickly. 'We can be seen from the building. That matron or whatever she is, I could do without her watching us.'

I told him that no way was I going anywhere with him. Specifically I wasn't getting in a car.

He rubbed his chin and studied me. 'All right, fair enough. You're suspicious. Of course you are. Look, a little further up the hill is Royal Holloway College, part of the University of London. It's got extensive grounds. What do you say we walk up there and stroll round the grounds. You look like a student. No one's going to question you if you wander round showing a visitor, me, the layout.'

Reluctantly, I agreed. I have to say, I had a shock when I saw the college. It was a monster of a place, all red brick and white decorative bits like icing. The whole thing appeared to be modelled on one of those French chateaux. There were funny little turrets, balustrades and oddly shaped windows everywhere. Jackson and I walked through the gates and, turning right, began a slow perambulation around the place. There were plenty of other people about and no one took any notice of us.

Jackson could see I was fascinated by my surroundings. 'It was built by a pill-manufacturer turned banker turned philanthropist by the name of Thomas Holloway,' he said. 'Aided and abetted by his wife, Jane. He intended it to be for middle-class women students. There were plenty of institutions looking out for the poor, and the daughters of rich families could look out for themselves. Holloway targeted the in-betweens.'

'There seem to be plenty of men around,' I said.

'They've had male students here as well for some time.'

He seemed to know the place well. But we were getting away from the purpose of our being there at all.

'Miss Varady,' he said, 'I know you went to see Flora Wilde. It really wasn't a good idea. Now you've seen her, you'll know that she isn't very robust.'

I opened my mouth to tell him that the not very robust Mrs Wilde had floored me with a single well-directed punch. But I decided to let him talk on uninterrupted.

'The Wildes are devoted to their daughter,' he was saying. 'Nicola is a very bright, happy girl. She's gifted, musically gifted. She has a brilliant future ahead of her. Any parent wants to protect a child. You can imagine how determined the Wildes are to protect Nicola, and especially as the threat in this instance is based on a completely false premise.'

'What?' I snapped.

His voice was soothing, like before the nurse sticks a needle in your arm. 'Eva Varady is given to flights of fancy. Naturally, she's your mother, and your instinct – and your wish – is to believe her. So you haven't questioned whatever story she's told you. I'm suggesting to you now that perhaps you should. Have you any idea how much trouble you can cause by following the wishes of a woman who has always been very unstable?'

'No one's suggested my mother is or ever was off her rocker,' I interrupted angrily. Other than Flora Wilde, who wasn't exactly an impartial observer.

'There are degrees of being, as you put it, off one's rocker,' he was saying in a judicious way. 'Eva Varady had a baby. It died. It's enough to unbalance anyone. Mrs Wilde was in the same hospital at the same time. Somehow Eva took it into her head that the babies had been switched. She's pursued the Wildes ever since.'

So he was going to repeat Flora's story. She must have told him that was what she'd told me.

'So you say,' I replied angrily. 'Well, in my opinion, if anyone is wonky in the top storey, it's Flora Wilde!'

He flushed. 'Listen to me, Miss Varady. You've got to stop all this. Whether you like it or not, what I've told you now is the truth. That's why you've got to stop trying to do whatever Eva Varady asked of you. Eva's crazy, she always was. Do you really want to destroy the happiness of an entire family, ruin Nicola's life, because of the ramblings of a dying woman whose mind was always scrambled?'

'I'm not going to ruin Nicola's life,' I said, meeting his gaze. 'She's my sister, isn't she? Why should I do anything to harm her?'

He flinched. 'She is not your sister! How many times do I have to tell you? Can't you get it into your head, or are you a fruitcake, just like your mother?'

'And are you asking for a bust nose?' I snarled. I'd had it with this bloke. He was seriously annoying me.

'All right!' He held up his hand placatingly. 'Perhaps I shouldn't have said that. But you're making this very difficult. It's so important and you are being, frankly, irresponsible. Can't you see it?'

In fact, I could see that what I was doing might be construed as irresponsible. What I couldn't do was get my mother to see it. He'd noticed my indecision, probably because I hadn't come back with a lippy reply.

'The Wildes have asked me to ask you not to go to the house again, or to try and contact Nicola directly. Can I tell them you agree?'

When I still didn't reply at once, he urged, 'Miss Varady?'

The anger was breaking out in his voice. He couldn't hold it all together for much longer. I was glad we were in a public place. This was one very jumpy man and I really didn't want to get into a scrap with him, for all my fighting talk.

'I don't like being called Miss Varady much,' I said. 'I'm usually called Fran.'

'Well, then, Fran—' he began.

But I interrupted. 'And your name?'

'My name? Oh, my first name, I see, it's . . .' He hesitated.

'Don't bother,' I told him. 'I know it. It's Jerry, Jerry Wilde.'

I thought he might deny it. I think he thought about it. Then he shrugged his shoulders. 'All right, I'm Jerry Wilde. I thought it would be better if I told you another name, but I suppose you were bound to guess.'

We'd turned the corner and were at the back of the building, where steps ran down from a balustraded terrace. I leaned back on the balustrade and stared up at the fascinating but crazy building before me. The architect seemed to have run amok.

'Whose idea was it?' I asked.

'To say I was Jackson? My own.'

'Actually,' I said, 'I meant, whose idea was it to build this place looking like this?'

He glanced carelessly at the pile. 'Holloway's. He visited Chambord in the Loire Valley and wanted the same sort of thing, but when the building was well underway, he made a trip to Cambridge and took a fancy to the Gothic architecture there. So he came back and told the architect to add Gothic bits. Must have nearly driven the poor guy mad. He also had a sanatorium built in the area, same kind of thing.'

Two girls and a young man came clattering up the steps

from the grounds below. We waited until they'd gone round the corner of the building.

'Just now,' I said, 'you used the word "frankly". But this Honest Joe business doesn't wash. You tried to give me a false name. You gave the same false name to Sister Helen when you made an attempt to see my mother. You didn't get to see her because she was asleep. You waited for a while, then went outside and made a call on a mobile phone. Then you left in a heck of a hurry, nearly knocking me over. I fell in the rhododendron bush.'

'You're very well informed,' he said coldly. 'And I've explained, I didn't see you. I'd had some bad news.'

'Sister Helen saw you. That's why I'm well informed. Why were you coming to see my mother? What did you want from her? Don't tell me you were there out of concern for her. You've made it all too clear how you feel about her. And here's another thing. The way you've been talking, you've made it sound as though you're here because I went to Kew and saw your wife. But you were trying to get to see my mother before that. So what's going on? How did you know my mother was in the hospice?'

'Will you promise me that you'll stay away from my family?' he almost shouted.

'I don't make deals with people who hold out on me.'

For a moment I thought he might do as Flora had done, take a swing at me. His fists clenched. But he remembered someone could be watching us from one of those many windows.

'I heard that someone was asking about us,' he said quietly, head lowered. 'Did you and your mother think I wouldn't?'

'I suppose Mrs Mackenzie told you,' I said. I should have

expected that either she or Ben would get in touch with the Wildes and warn them about me, and allowed for it. I hadn't. My mistake.

'I don't know what she was thinking of, giving out our address like that,' he grumbled. 'She must be going gaga.'

'Not a bit of it!' I snapped. 'She realised it was an emergency.'

He snorted. 'It became an emergency after she put you on to us! Of course, I knew that behind it all must be Eva Varady.' He looked depressed. 'I thought we'd seen the last of her. It's been a nightmare since Dorothy contacted me. I didn't want my wife to know. She's a very nervous person, delicate. I wanted to sort it out myself and told Dorothy not to breathe a word to Flora. I hoped you'd get in touch by letter first. I watched the mail. I rushed to answer every phone call. I didn't imagine you'd just turn up on the doorstep like that. You've ruined everything and you don't care one bit. You and Eva both. You just don't want to know how much damage you've done.'

He looked up then and there was hatred in his eyes. But I was wondering just how far he'd been prepared to go to protect Flora, to keep her from knowing the hunt for Nicola was on. Enough to take out Rennie Duke?

I thought my reply out carefully. 'I promise I won't call at your house again. I promise that if Nicola does find out the truth, it won't be because I've told her.'

'Truth!' he shouted at me. A girl walking past turned her head curiously. Wilde paused, flushed and added in a low, husky voice, 'I've told you the truth and you can't or won't accept it! My little girl is not your sister! Stay away from my family! If you don't – if you don't, I'll make you wish you had and you'd better believe it! Don't underestimate me, Fran Varady.'

I watched him stride away around the corner of that brainstorm of a building. My mind was in a whirl. I didn't want to believe him because I didn't like him and I didn't like his dinky little wife. But that wasn't reason enough for him to be lying. After all, what did I know about my mother and her state of mind? For all I knew, she might have been having some kind of nervous breakdown when she left home, ditched Dad and me. Perhaps her child *had* died. Perhaps the notion that Nicola Wilde was really her baby had been just the fancy of an unhinged brain. Now that she was dying and on medication, had that fancy returned to haunt her – and through her, to haunt me?

I came nearer then to deciding to tell Ganesh all about it than at any time. I thought about nothing else during my journey home, and by the time I got back, I'd all but decided to take Gan into my confidence. I desperately needed to talk to someone. I even went to the shop, to ask him if we could go down the pub when they closed up so that we could discuss something. But when I went in, someone was there ahead of me.

'Ah, Fran,' said Janice Morgan. She was leaning against the counter with her hands in the pockets of yet another dreary jacket. I was in my usual jeans, boots and puffa jacket. I suppose I hadn't the right to criticise anyone else. But Morgan must have the money. She didn't have to shop at Oxfam like me. I set aside these thoughts. Right now wasn't the moment for me to be worrying about Morgan's dress sense. She'd really meant it about keeping up the pressure on me. However she was turned out, she was a copper and a good one.

Ganesh was on his own. Where Hari had got to I hadn't a clue, nor how long Gan had been fending off the inspector. He looked like a drowning man just coming up for air for the last time. His expression, when he saw me enter, was that of one of the shipwrecked characters in that painting of Norman's, seeing the lifeboat heading their way. I half expected him to raise a hand and shout 'Ahoy!'

'I was just asking Mr Patel if he knew where I could find you,' said Morgan amiably.

'You found me!' I said, avoiding Ganesh's accusing eye. I was now thoroughly fed up. While I felt the need to confide in someone, it certainly wasn't, and wouldn't ever be, the police. 'I'm not volunteering to go to the station with you. You made your pitch yesterday. Nothing's changed since then as far as I'm concerned.'

She managed to look reproachful and innocent. 'I've not come to take you in again. I thought I'd just drop by and have a word informally, while I was on my way home. This is in my own time, Fran.' She managed to make it sound as if she was doing me a favour.

I didn't buy it. Everyone wanted to talk to me, even off-duty coppers, and everyone wanted something.

Ganesh asked nervously, 'Do you want to go up to the flat? Only my uncle is up there sorting out some orders, and he—'

Morgan declined the offer, to Ganesh's obvious relief. 'No, no. Fran and I will go and have a cup of tea somewhere. Right, Fran?'

I told her I'd been to see my mother and was tired, but it didn't do any good. I was wasting my breath. I trailed out of the shop in her wake.

* * *

She took me to a little place she knew which turned out to be a fancy cake shop with a café in the back. She was playing Grandma Varady's trick, softening you up with chocolate torte. I went along with it because I had no immediate plan of action, and just drifting with the tide until I saw what was bobbing along next seemed the best idea.

'I don't come here too often,' confided Morgan. 'The temptation is too great.' She stuck a fork in a lump of pastry the size of half a brick.

'Yeah,' I mumbled. My chocolate cake was all right, not as good as Grandma's. Still, I wasn't going to turn it down. On principle I acted cool for a moment or two, drawing lines in the frosting with my cake fork, until the empty feeling in my tummy asked what the heck I was wasting time for. I tucked in.

'There have been some developments in the Duke murder case,' she went on chattily, as if we'd been talking about shopping.

'Like what?' I mumbled suspiciously through cake.

'We've been checking Duke's business records.' She glanced up and waved the fork at me. 'He was a methodical chap, kept proper files, all his receipts, tax returns. Makes our work easier. We went through the lot but didn't turn up anything immediately interesting. However, we'd handed his computer over to our experts to see what they could find in that. They found the draft of a letter, addressed to a Mrs Elvira Marks. Now, Mrs Marks doesn't warrant any cross-reference in the paperwork and Duke's wife denies any knowledge of her. That seemed odd to us, Rennie being such a tidy-minded chap.'

I put my cake fork down on the little marble-topped table, leaned back in my chair, crossed my arms and sighed. It was a bit of a pantomime but I couldn't for the life of me see where this was leading, and I was tired. I should have known I'd have to pay for the cake in some way before I even got halfway through it.

Morgan gave me a look which told me she was about to produce a rabbit from a hat. The cake had begun to lie on my stomach like lead. I knew I was never going to be able to finish it.

'Especially as he'd asked Mrs Marks if he could go and see her for a little chat in respect of Mrs Eva Varady.'

The cake in my stomach gained a pound in weight and seemed to have swelled to double its dimensions. I hoped I wasn't going to throw up. Just what I didn't need, another complication. I kept quiet, waiting for the punchline.

'So we went to see Mrs Marks,' said Morgan briskly. She'd managed to finish her strudel and pushed the plate to one side. 'The name means nothing to you, I suppose?'

I told her it didn't mean a thing. What was more, I wasn't Madame Rosa, the crystal-ball gazer. 'What you need,' I said, 'is a good medium. Then you and Sergeant Cole and her can sit round holding hands and get in touch with Rennie himself. Ask him all these questions. Get him to rap on the table. How am I supposed to know what he was up to? He was a private detective. Just like you, he must have been working on more than one case.'

'Probably,' said Morgan. 'Glad you're remembering that, Fran. But this has to do with this one. Now, it may be painful for you,' Morgan's tone told me she didn't care if it was, 'but can we go back to the time your mother left home?'

'No,' I said. 'It was fourteen years ago and you have to be on a fishing expedition. You're stuck. You've tried grilling me. Now you're feeding me with coffee and cake, hoping I'll kick-start your investigation. I can't. My mother went, just disappeared out of my life. I went to bed one night and she was there. I got up in the morning and she wasn't. I was seven years old. No one told me anything, only that she'd gone away. For a long time, I believed she'd died.'

'When you discovered that she hadn't died, did you have any reason to suppose your father or any other family member was ever in touch with her after she left?'

'If he was, he never said. I don't think he was. He was too broke up.' I didn't want to talk about this. It wasn't Morgan's business. The police always think they have the right to know everything.

She carried on as if I hadn't objected. 'So you must have had a lot to talk about with your mother during your recent visits. After all this time, catching up, finding out about each other, getting to know one another—'

I interrupted. 'What is this? A rehearsal for *The King and I*?'

Morgan said firmly, 'Your mother had asked Duke's agency to find you. She clearly wanted to set the record straight, make it up to you for all the distress she'd caused you way back then.'

I thought I could now see the way the wind was blowing. They couldn't question Mum, but they reckoned Mum had talked to me, unburdening herself of all the things on her mind. The worst of it was, they were right. But I wasn't going to tell them so.

'She's not up to long talks.' I met Morgan's gaze. 'My

visits only last minutes. That's how long she can manage. Some of that time, I just sit there holding her hand. I tell her things like about the job I've got lined up in a pizza parlour. That's about it. Why don't you just tell me who Mrs Marks is and put us both out of our misery?'

'Didn't I say?' She gave me a bland look. All around us people were stuffing their faces. Cups clattered. Spoons chinked. Voices rose and fell in a warm wall. 'Mrs Marks is a registered child-minder. She's cared for a number of babies over the years. They come and go. Some stay longer than others. Mrs Marks is getting on but she's always enjoyed her job and she's got pretty well total recall of all the children who've been in her care. It seems that about thirteen years ago, or a little less, Mrs Varady brought a baby girl to the crèche, under a month old—'

'What?' I exclaimed, so loudly that several heads turned. I didn't care. So Flora and Jerry *had* both been lying! My mother wasn't now and never had been crazy. She'd left the hospital with a live baby and the Wildes' child had died, just as she'd told me. I felt elated, no other word for it. I hadn't been on a fool's errand out there at Kew. I hadn't been acting on the word of a sad, deluded woman. Mum had told me the truth, and the Wildes had lied, both of them, through their teeth. I wanted to shout out *I knew it!* I just managed not to.

Nevertheless, Morgan had realised something was going on she hadn't anticipated. She looked less confident. 'Did you know your mother had had another child?'

'How should I know what my mother did after she left?' I pulled myself together. I could blow it if I didn't watch out. 'Why don't you just go on telling me?' I suggested. 'You seemed keen to do that.'

She gave me a fishy look. 'Well, Mrs Marks was a little unsure about taking on a child so young, but the mother was desperate. She needed to go to work. She had no one else to care for the child or support her. Mrs Marks remembers the child's name, Miranda, because, she says, it was so pretty. But then, after only a few weeks, Eva Varady removed the child. She had decided to give her baby up for adoption. At least, that was the reason she gave.'

Morgan's voice hardened. 'Now, the odd thing is, so far the relevant social services department hasn't been able to turn up any record of this child, Miranda Varady, being put up for adoption. So we checked hospital records, and yes, Eva Varady gave birth to a baby girl, who, if she is still alive, would be going on for thirteen years old now. So, Fran, you see my problem? In addition to investigating the death of Rennie Duke, it turns out I'm also looking into the case of a missing baby.' She sat back. 'Still got nothing to tell me, Fran?'

'Nothing,' I said. 'Not a damn thing. But thanks for the cake.'

I walked home, putting the new information into place. The euphoria at knowing the Wildes had lied had faded, and now a bleak picture was forming. Morgan hadn't spelled it out to me, but she didn't have to. The cops thought baby Miranda Varady was dead. They suspected Mum was responsible. Desperate women, finding themselves alone, and often suffering post-natal blues into the bargain, had done such terrible things before. I could have put matters right with a single sentence: *If you check out the Wilde family, you'll find Miranda is alive and well, but she's now Nicola Wilde.*

Had I spoken the words? Of course I hadn't. But I needed to see Mum again urgently and set her on her guard. When it had only been the death of Clarence Duke they were investigating, they'd been prepared to accept my mother was too ill to be interviewed and unlikely to be involved. If they believed she'd had a hand in the death of a child, no matter how many years ago, they weren't going to be so easily put off.

Increasingly the truth about Nicola was becoming impossible to hide. Perhaps, for my own protection, I might finally be forced to speak up. I couldn't forget that of the people who knew that secret, one of them, my mother, would soon no longer be around. Another had already left the scene: Duke, who'd been on the trail. Why else would he have wanted to talk to Mrs Marks? That left me, and I didn't need an interview with Jerry Wilde to be told that the knowledge I had was dangerous. My mother had handed me a ticking bomb.

I couldn't see my mother until the next morning. In the meantime, I could follow up the lead Morgan had given me – though she wouldn't be seeing it like that.

I fished in my pocket, fingers searching for a vital piece of card, praying it hadn't fallen out. I found it and drew it out. Clarence Duke's business card. Time to make use of it.

Chapter Eleven

The address on the card led me to a flat on the top floor of an old-style low-rise council block. It was nightfall by the time I got there, and the whole area was so poorly lit I found myself peering at the ground to see where I was setting down my next step. The asphalt surrounds were cracked and holed, the debris had been blown by the wind into small heaps against brickwork. I was particularly worried about discarded needles lying unseen in the shadows. If you step on one of those, it can pierce straight through any thickness of bootsole into your foot before you've had a chance to realise what's happening.

Inside the block, lit by a cheerless neon glare, the lift was out of order. I toiled up the grubby staircase, with its graffiti-strewn walls, and stepped out on to the balcony which ran the length of the building past the front doors of the flats on this level. Out here it would always be draughty, but tonight the wind cut like a razor through my clothing as I sought the right number. It was at the far end, its blue-painted front door protected by a metal grille. The wall by the door was splashed with virulent green paint, the letters GR followed by a wavy line downwards and a splodge, as if the artist had been disturbed. Either Rennie had made enemies in his time as a PI or the neighbours were a little rough. The surroundings made it obvious that detection hadn't paid Rennie very well. He may have found blackmail a necessary evil to supplement his slender means. I contemplated the scrawl. Private investigators did make themselves unpopular, and so did blackmailers. Perhaps Duke's death had nothing to do with me, my mother, the Wildes or any of it. The man had probably had more enemies than you could shake a stick at.

There was only one way to find out. I rang the doorbell. After a few moments, the door opened and a welcome tidal wave of heat engulfed me. A woman appeared in the lighted hallway, staring sullenly at me through the security grille. She was a thin bottle-blonde, wearing black leggings and a sweatshirt. There was a whiff of booze about her which seeped out on the warm air. She squinted at an unfamiliar caller and the smudged scarlet outline of her lips turned down.

'Yes?' she asked discouragingly.

'Mrs Duke?' I'd caught sight of a wedding ring. 'Can we talk? My name—'

She slammed the door, cutting short her own abusive refusal.

I leaned on the bell. Eventually she couldn't stick it any longer and the door flew open again. I was quite glad of the grille between us at that moment. She looked pretty mad.

'You a bloody journalist?'

'No,' I told her. 'I'm Fran Varady. Rennie was keeping obbo on me when—' I sought for a tactful way to say *when the little squirt got croaked.*

'When we found him,' I substituted. 'Me and a friend of mine. We called the cops.' I pulled out Rennie's card. 'Look, he gave me this the first time I saw him.'

'Hang on,' she said. She unlocked the grille and stood back.

I squeezed past her into the hall. She closed the grille and the front door, but not before giving the green lettering on the wall a disdainful kick with her trainer toe.

'Neighbourhood's going downhill,' she said. 'Kids mostly. Pinch anything not nailed down. They want the money for drugs. Vandalise the place too, if they could. Just out of spite, you know? Because Rennie was a private investigator, they thought he might be a grass too. Stupid . . .' She broke off at this point and led me into a small sitting room.

It was ferociously overheated. A gas fire in the hearth sent out rays hot enough to toast a crumpet from the doorway. The radiators were also belching Saharan temperatures. From chilled I went to sweltering in an instant.

'Do you mind if I take my coat off?' I asked, feeling the sweat break out on my body.

She shook her head. 'Whatever you like. Siddown.'

She sat down herself, shook a cigarette from a crushed packet and put it to her lips. An ashtray on a coffee table held a pile of lipstick-stained butts. There was a glass on the table too, and a gin bottle. Two supermarket own-brand tonic-water bottles, one empty, one half full, lay on the carpet.

Yet the room, though untidy, wasn't a dump. The furniture and carpets were clean. The three-piece suite in blue velvet-type material looked quite new. A row of carefully dusted flamenco dolls pranced across the mantelpiece, and in the hearth stood a pottery cat wearing a pink bow. Its glazed green eyes crossed slightly. The television flickered in one corner but it was unlikely she'd been watching it. Her eyes had a bleary look compounded of booze, grief and sleeplessness.

'Want a drink?' she asked. 'I'm going to have another.' She lit the cigarette and, with it dangling from her lips, got up to rummage in a cabinet for another glass. I took the opportunity to grab the remote and turn the volume on the television down low so we could hear one another without the constant interruption of synthetic enthusiasm from overpaid presenters. (A job I'd like, by the way.)

She turned back holding the glass. 'Run outa ice,' she said. She was doing her best to be a good hostess. 'I've got half a packet of cheese straws but they've gone soft.'

'No problem,' I assured her.

She slopped gin into the glass, filling it to nearly a third, and added a splash of tonic. She pushed the mix towards me and poured a similar one for herself.

'Cheers!' she said, raising her glass with its lipstick-stained rim. Her mascara was also smudged. She looked a mess.

I returned the toast and sipped cautiously. The gin ripped down my throat and I burst out coughing. When I'd stopped, eyes watering, she'd nearly finished hers.

'I'm sorry to come and bother you at a time like this,' I began hoarsely.

'Every bloody person's been bothering me,' she returned morosely. 'Cops, tabloids, chap in a dog-collar. Don't know where he came from.'

'The police are bothering me too,' I told her.

She sympathised. 'It's a bugger, isn't it?'

I agreed that it was.

'I used to tell Rennie,' she said, 'to give it up, all of it. It's a risky business. But he always said it was the only business he knew. What else could he do? And we did all right out of it. Made a decent living.' She glanced round the room. 'I know it's not much, but lots of people have got less, haven't they?'

I had, for a start. It seemed I'd been wrong about Rennie's business not turning in a profit. But did his wife know where all the money came from? Morgan had told me what a good record-keeper Rennie had been, and that, to me, smelt fishy. If you keep that watertight a set of books it's because you think someone might want to ask questions. I'd be willing to bet that somewhere was another set of accounts that no one but Rennie saw. Whether his wife did or didn't know about Rennie's less legit side, the odds were that now he was dead, she'd swear he'd been the next best thing to an uncanonised saint.

'We always had enough money to pay the bills, go out for a drink on a Saturday night. Took a holiday most years. Had the odd bad patch, of course. Bound to. But it was all right, like Rennie said. Only, we were both of us getting older. "You can't run fast enough no more, Ren," I told him. He just laughed. But I was right, wasn't I? Someone caught up with him. Always thought it might happen. Well,' she frowned, 'thought it might but sort of didn't believe it would, you know?' She looked even sadder. 'We had the money saved up to go to Ibiza this year. Now it will all go on Rennie's funeral. They cost a lot, do funerals, but I want to give him a decent send-off.'

I muttered again that I was sorry. I was intruding on her grief, but maybe she needed someone to talk to.

'Mrs Duke,' I asked, 'you seemed to recognise my name. Did Rennie tell you about me?'

She squinted at me through a rising column of smoke. 'You're Eva's girl, right?'

'Yes. You know my mother?'

'Used to know her. Haven't seen her in years. She worked

for Rennie for a few months. It was when I had my hysterectomy and couldn't do anything, couldn't even lift a kettle, let alone tramp round the streets doing house-to-house. I worked in the business too, you see. Sometimes you need a woman operative.'

'But Rennie told you all about me?' I persisted.

'I guessed you must be Eva's kid. She'd got hold of Rennie and asked him to find you. He told me about that. He said he had found you. He was good, was Rennie.'

'Do you know why he was still watching me? Even though he'd done the job?'

She shook her head. 'Didn't know he was doing that. Knew he was busy about something or other. He didn't always let on what he was up to. We were husband and wife, but not business partners. Any work I did for the business was strictly as an employee. Rennie said it was best for tax reasons. But really, he liked to run things, he liked playing his cards close to his chest. He used to say that what I didn't know couldn't do me any harm.'

She gave a snort of bleak amusement. 'I suppose in his own way he was trying to protect me. I knew he sometimes rooted around on his own account if he got interested in a case. The clients, they never tell you more than they've got to. But Rennie, he didn't like loose ends. Always wanted to dot the i's and cross the t's. It didn't do any harm, though I used to tell him he was a nosy blighter. "That's right, Susie," he'd say. "Got a nose for other people's secrets."'

That was something he'd told me himself, something I should have realised was likely to affect me. I wasn't sure his talent hadn't done Rennie any harm in the end. I leaned forward. 'Did he tell you anything at all about Eva? Other than that she'd asked him to find me and he had? Please try and remember. Had he talked to anyone about her?'

'I don't know.' She shook her head again. 'It's no use asking me. Like I said, he didn't tell me everything. The police took his computer and all the files, the lot. I suppose I'll get 'em back. They've kept the car an' all. It's really inconvenient. They say they haven't finished going over it. What do they think they're going to find?'

'Clues,' I told her. 'Perhaps the killer dropped something inside, or had special mud on his boots.'

'Yeah, right,' she said brusquely. 'Like in books.'

I persevered, getting to the point of my visit. 'Did Rennie ever mention a Mrs Marks? He wrote her a letter.'

'Didn't mention her to me. If he wrote a letter it'll be on the computer, most likely, but the cops have got that, I told you.' Her forehead puckered as she dredged up a memory from the fog that enveloped her brain. 'The police asked me about her, Mrs Marks. But I told them I didn't know nothing. They never give up, do they, cops? They keep on and on even when you tell them you can't help 'em.'

I had no argument with that. On the other hand, I was about to keep on and on, as she put it, myself.

'Susie,' I urged, 'is there anywhere else he might have made a note of Mrs Marks's address?'

'They took it all,' she said. I don't think she'd heard me. She'd become hooked on her grievance. 'Every scrap of paper they could find. Ferreting about in all the drawers and cupboards. I asked if they had a search warrant. They asked if I objected. They were trying to find Rennie's murderer, they said. Surely I wanted to help? Cheeky blighters. Fat chance they'll ever find who killed poor Rennie.'

A tear trickled down her cheek and her hand reached for the gin bottle. It was nearly empty. I was prepared to believe she had a stash of them. I neatly intercepted her and moved the bottle out of reach. She looked surprised but not angry, more resigned.

'Susie,' I began, 'I know this is a difficult time for you. You say you don't think the police will have much luck finding out who killed Rennie, but you'd like him found, wouldn't you, Rennie's killer?'

'They oughtn't to get away with it,' she mumbled.

'Quite right. I want to know too. You've done detective work, so've I. Perhaps together we can do better than the cops?'

For a moment she looked almost as if she were going to latch on to this with some degree of enthusiasm. But then she slumped in her chair and muttered, 'I'm not up to it. I suppose I'll have to try and keep the business going, but right now, I can't put my mind to it.'

'So let me try?' She shrugged, which I took as a yes. 'What about someone Rennie may have upset in the past? Someone with a criminal record or dodgy dealings? You know, someone who might have a bit of hired muscle.'

I was throwing out feelers here. I still felt Rennie's death was linked to me and my mother's quest, but it doesn't do to be tunnel-visioned in investigations. After all, the only way I could really be sure his death was down to Mum's secret was by eliminating anyone else with a grudge. In Rennie's case that would be a long job and well-nigh impossible to complete, but I could try.

She was doing her best to think, frowning and blinking in the spiralling cigarette smoke. 'Over the years, several people have reckoned Rennie crossed them. Some of the clients turned out bloomin' ungrateful, no other word for it. After all Rennie had done for them, too.'

This tied in with what Morgan had told me of Rennie's relationship with his clients. Did Susie really have no idea that he might have had a lucrative sideline or two?

'Anyone more ungrateful than most?' I coaxed. 'Anyone recently?'

Chances were, if someone like that was involved, it'd be someone Rennie had dealt with in the near past. People living on the edge of the law generally don't let grievances fester. They settle them asap.

'Things have been quiet recently,' she admitted. 'Rennie was getting worried about the work not coming in. I don't think anyone was after him. Not during these last six months or so.'

I regretfully shelved that possibility, always an outside chance in my book. I had another idea. 'Is there anyone Rennie worked for more than once? Someone with an ear on the street, perhaps? Someone who might be interested in helping to track down his murderer?'

She looked a bit despondent at that and said that Rennie had had few friends. Then she perked up. 'There's Mickey Allerton. Rennie did a couple of jobs for him. He ought to be grateful. Doesn't mean he will be, though. Still, he's got the sort of contacts you mean.'

He might also have a sense of justice. Not the type dispensed by the law, but street justice. 'Where can I find him?' I asked.

She told me Allerton owned a club in Soho. The Silver Circle. 'Stage show, strippers, that sort of thing. Private membership though any punter can join at the door if he gets past security and Mickey don't object to his face. Got a lot of high-rolling foreign guys there, don't want their names known or faces seen. He's mostly there over lunchtime. They're busy then.'

I could check it out, provided I got past the heavy bound to be on the door. Meantime, there was Susie to consider.

'Susie, have you had anything to eat?' I asked. She couldn't go on knocking it back on an empty stomach.

She looked vague. 'Can't remember. I suppose I must have done.'

'I'll fix you a sandwich.' I got up and made for the kitchen, which was behind the sitting room and communicated with it through a serving hatch.

Susie might be well supplied with the stuff in bottles but she didn't have much in the grocery line. Some bread in a bin looked stale. A lump of cheese in the fridge was beginning to show signs of mould. There was a box of hamburgers in the freezer compartment but no buns. I scraped the mould from the cheese and made a toasted sandwich under the oven grill. It hadn't been cleaned since the last use, and as it heated up, the smell of burnt fat permeated the kitchen. Susie wasn't a slattern, I'd seen that. But Duke's death had knocked her all of a heap. I kept an eye on her through the hatch while I grilled the sandwich, and saw with dismay that she had indeed opened another bottle.

I took the sandwich to her and put it on the table. Then I gently removed the bottle from her hand. 'Eat up. You've had enough of this stuff. You'll have a hell of a head in the morning. I'll make some coffee.'

Luckily she did have coffee and some milk. When I went

back, she was chewing the sandwich in a half-hearted way.

'Have you got anyone who can come and stay with you for a bit? A friend? A relative?' I asked. I was really worried about her. I liked her. She'd loved the poor little runt. There was no accounting for taste.

'Got a sister in Margate,' she said.

'Can't you go and stay with her for a few days? A bit of sea air would do you good.'

She shook her head. 'She's got kids. They do my head in. Rennie and I couldn't have any, not after my hysterectomy. I didn't mind too much. But I think Rennie did. Rennie liked kids. Not the ones who come and write filth on our wall and spray paint on the window, of course. But little kids, you know, in buggies. He liked kittens and puppies too. He was sort of sentimental. He bought that.' She pointed at the pottery cat. 'Only got it down the market. Still, it's nice, isn't it?'

I nodded. I'd seen worse pottery cats. But something she'd said had set my mind running off in a new direction. Rennie had liked kids. The Dukes were childless. Rennie had tracked me down for Mum without charging her any fee. For old times' sake? Or because he'd wanted to find a lost child and reunite her with her mother? In the same way, had something Mum said given him the idea that she had more than one lost child? Had some altruistic impulse set him on the trail which had led him at least as far as Mrs Marks? Or had he just been dotting the i's and crossing the t's as Susie described. I hadn't known Rennie and now I never would. It was a downer, all right.

I put the gin bottle back in the cabinet. 'Promise me,' I said, 'you won't knock back any more of the hard stuff tonight. Go to bed. Get some sleep. You look all in.'

'Yeah,' she said. 'I know I'm in a helluva state. I'll be okay.'

I took the plate and the glasses back to the kitchen and rinsed them under the tap. I opened a couple of cupboards and found the one where the crocks were stored. Tidily I carried the things across, and as I did so, my eye fell on the telephone fixed to the wall nearby. What's more, when I closed the cupboard door, I saw, tacked up by the phone, one of those laminated cards you write notes on and wipe clean with a damp cloth. My old optimism returned. It was scribbled all over, but a diligent search revealed, written at the bottom, the letters EM followed by a phone number. Eureka! As the guy said when he found the bath water was too hot or something.

I went to the hatch and called through it. 'Susie, do you know anyone with the initials EM?'

She thought and shook her head. 'Don't think so.'

Right. Gleefully I copied down the phone number. Morgan had removed all Duke's records, but she and her minions had missed this.

Outside the block of flats kids were racing round on roller blades. They nearly knocked me over. I yelled at them. They took no notice. In a gloomy corner, someone was breaking into a parked car foolishly left there by its owner. I pushed my hands into my pockets and walked quickly away. Sartre wrote a play about a lot of people stuck in a place with a bunch of others they can't get on with and can't leave. It turns out to be Hell. Something like this place, I thought. Still, I was leaving here with a couple of leads, and no one could say my journey had been wasted.

I didn't want Ganesh to know what I was up to. So the

following morning I decided not to ask to use the shop phone to ring the number I'd cribbed from Susie's kitchen board. I'd nip down the road and hope to find an unvandalised kiosk.

Before I could do so, however, Ganesh appeared in the garage and asked, 'Where did you get to yesterday evening? Were you with that woman copper?'

I could have lied and told him I had been, but I don't lie to Ganesh. I filter the truth sometimes, when necessary, or refuse to answer, but I don't lie.

'No, only for about an hour. She bought me tea and cake. After that I was just out and about. Why?'

'We didn't see you all yesterday!' he said accusingly. 'Not until you waltzed in late afternoon and out again with Inspector Morgan. I waited up. I thought you'd call by and tell me what she wanted.'

Waiting up late for me, when he had to get up so early the next morning, had been a sacrifice. My not turning up had made it useless. No wonder he was grumpy.

I countered with, 'What is this? Have I got to report in, or what?'

'Don't give me that. You're always in and out of the shop. You usually turn up for a coffee at some point in the day if nothing else – or lately, to sneak a look at the A to Z! You weren't here yesterday evening. So where were you?' He sat down on a packing case and folded his arms with the air of a man who wouldn't go without getting an answer. 'You know,' he went on, 'you're getting really furtive. I don't like it. Don't you trust me?'

'Come off it, of course I do.'

'So tell me what's going on. Starting with yesterday evening.'

I know Gan well enough to realise that I had to give him some sort of explanation. So I told him the truth, that I'd been to see Susie Duke.

'Why?' he asked suspiciously.

'Give her my condolences. Be polite.'

Gan unfolded his arms and stabbed a finger in my direction. 'Don't come the sweet innocent with me! You've been playing detective again.'

I told him I didn't play at detective. I reminded him that I had, on previous occasions, detected for real with some success.

'Don't get big-headed about it,' he retorted. 'You've been lucky. Luck doesn't last for ever. It runs out. Duke's did, and he was a proper professional. I suppose you think you can find out who killed him?'

'Gan,' I said, 'I *have* to find out who killed Duke.'

'I don't see why,' he replied. 'Or if you've got a reason, you're not telling me what it is.'

'He died out there!' I flung out my hand to indicate the area before the garages. 'He was waiting for me. I know he was. He wanted to talk to me. He was scrabbling at the door during the night but I didn't open up. If I had, he might be alive today. What did he want? Who wanted to stop him? It all makes me very nervous.'

'*You* make me nervous,' said Ganesh. 'Honestly, Fran, I just can't trust you an inch. I never know what you're going to do next.'

'Believe me,' I told him, 'it's better that way.'

He stomped off back to the shop. I felt really bad about not confiding in him. I knew his feelings were hurt. Yesterday, I'd been ready to tell him everything, and had it not been for

Morgan, would've done. But overnight I'd got over my weakness, as I now saw it. I'd started on this alone and I'd see it out alone. God willing, as Grandma Varady would've piously added.

I went out and managed to find a public telephone that was in working order, though plastered with pictures of girls offering their services with assurances that everything was real. But it isn't, and any woman working like that has some pimp taking most of the dosh. It makes me mad.

I knew I was through to the right number as soon as someone answered. In the background I could hear children's voices and the discordant jangle of a toy xylophone. 'Mrs Marks?'

'Speaking.' She sounded harassed.

'My name is Francesca Varady. I'm the daughter of Eva Varady. I think—'

She interrupted. 'The police have been here already, asking about Eva. I couldn't tell them anything. I looked after the baby for a couple of weeks, no more. It's nothing to do with me.'

'Please,' I begged. 'Can I come and talk to you?'

'I'm busy,' she snapped. 'I run a crèche.'

'Ten minutes,' I said. 'I won't be in the way. I'm good with poster paint.'

That was a lie. My infant encounters with poster paint had generally ended with more of it on my clothes than on the paper.

'Come this afternoon, around three thirty,' she said. 'Several of the kids will have been picked up by then. It'll be quieter. But you're wasting your time.'

'Great. Can I have your address?'

She gave a hiss but told me the address before hanging up with a clatter of the receiver that made my eardrum zing.

After I'd arranged to see the child-minder, I set off for Waterloo station. I had to get out to Egham to see my mother and warn her that officialdom was taking a hand in things. I also had somehow to put Sister Helen on the alert without spilling the beans. There's nothing like making life difficult for yourself, and just to add insult to injury, I discovered that the zip of one of my nice new boots was knackered. I had to put on my old lace-ups, and as I was doing that, one of the laces broke, which made it too short, and I could only lace halfway up the ankle. As a result my lower right leg moved freely in the unlaced leather, whereas the left one was tightly supported. It gave me a lopsided gait.

'She was a little poorly during the night,' Sister Helen told me. 'But she's awake this morning and anxious to see you. Brightened up quite a bit. It is your coming to see her which keeps her going, you know.'

In a sense. It was the hope that I'd find Nicola which kept her going. But my resentment at that was fading. I was slowly coming to terms with it. News that my mother hadn't been doing so well since my last visit, however, worried me.

'Jackson's not been back?' I asked.

Sister Helen shook her head.

'Look,' I told her, 'I don't want to upset my mother, but there's something I've got to mention to her. Things might be getting a little sticky. You see, the police might come back, and next time they could insist on seeing her. I know you've kept them at bay until now and I'm really grateful. But I know the cops, and they're not sensitive souls.'

She was listening to this, head tilted, eyes thoughtful. 'Has all this anything to do with Mr Duke's death?'

'Tangentially,' I admitted. 'I may have to tell her he's dead, if I can find a way. It's better she hears it from me than from the police. But that's not what I've come to talk to her about. It's a – a family matter.'

'If you feel you must mention it to her, whatever it is,' Sister Helen said in her calm way, 'then you will. It's for you to decide. However, she has a choice too. Her choice might be not to discuss it. If that is what she decides, then you must accept it. We can always ask questions. We don't always get answers. It's a fact of life. Eva mustn't be harassed. After all, that's what we're both trying to stop the police doing to her, isn't it?'

I told her once more that I understood the rules. As I set off towards my mother's room, I heard Sister Helen speak again.

'Fran? You know, nobody's perfect, and no one becomes perfect because he or she happens to be dying. We love people in life as we love them in death, with all their imperfections. That is what love is about. Without sacrifice, love is nothing.'

'I know,' I said. 'I do love her, and I have to believe that in her own way she loves me, no matter what happened years ago. I can't tell you I'm completely happy in my own mind about it, but I'm getting there.'

My mother put out her hand to me in greeting. I took it and she gave my fingers a weak squeeze. Her bed was still by the window but today the clerk of the weather was supplying drizzle and the panes were streaked, obscuring the view.

'Mum,' I said, 'I want to do what's right. You want to do what's right, don't you?'

'I am,' she replied. 'I'm putting things right.'

'No, you're not.' I tried to keep my voice gentle and not to let the frustration show. 'You're stirring things up.'

She answered in the slow, considered, confident way which I had learned meant she wouldn't budge. 'I'm making them right for me.'

Sister Helen's voice seemed to echo in my ears. This was what she'd been trying to tell me. My mother was one of those people who are incapable of seeing anything in any way other than from their own internal viewpoint. Everything, for such people, is judged by how it affects them, never how it will affect anyone else. Even love is judged by this benchmark. My mother took comfort in the fact that by doing her bidding in searching for Nicola, I was showing love for her. She couldn't see how desperate I was for some token from her. It didn't mean she didn't care about me. It was just that there was a pattern to her thinking and she was in the middle of it. Me, Dad, Grandma, the Wildes, Nicola, everyone else in her life, had always turned slowly round her like a model of planets circling the sun.

I knew now what she wanted of Nicola. Not to know what she looked like. Not to know what sort of things she did or liked. What she wanted was Nicola's love. She was asking me to get it for her, and I couldn't do that. No one could.

I'd never get her to see it the way I did, and there was no point in trying. However, for all the weakness of her body, I was confident that my mother's mind was tough. I had to tell her about the police's discovery, and that meant mentioning the subject I had spent all my time with her trying to avoid.

'Rennie Duke,' I began awkwardly.

She blinked, and I noticed her eyelids were lashless. The look in her eyes was furtive. 'What about him?'

'I think he may have been asking around about you – about the time, years ago, before you knew him, after you left Dad.'

She drew her knees up beneath the coverlet and wrapped her arms round them in a curiously foetal gesture. 'Then you've got to stop him, Fran.'

Me again. But as it happened, this time someone had already done the job. I omitted that detail and went on, 'It's like this. Duke's stirred things up a bit. He's found Mrs Marks.'

Now she looked frightened. 'Impossible! She's old. She can't still be around. You've got it all wrong, Fran. Mrs Marks? Even if he has found her, she wouldn't remember me.'

'I don't know about that. All I know is, others may be getting interested in baby Miranda Varady.'

'Why?' She was bewildered. 'Who?'

'Duke may have tipped off the police somehow. They may come here, wanting to know what happened to your baby.'

I thought she'd panic. I was even ready to ring for help. But oddly, at the word 'police' she looked more relaxed. 'Oh, the police,' she said. 'I'm not worried about them.'

'You're not?' I asked in surprise.

'Bless you, darling. Of course not. What can they do to me? They can't make me answer any questions. They can't arrest me. They can't haul me off to gaol.' She gave a little gurgling laugh. 'They can't do anything to me, Fran.'

I had no answer to that. I sat silent. She stopped looking amused and frowned.

'But Rennie's different. Rennie's got to be stopped.'

'He won't do any more harm now,' I said, unthinking.

Her eyes were suddenly bright with intelligence. 'Rennie's dead, isn't he? Something's happened to him.'

So, in the end, I'd let the cat out of the bag myself, clumsily. But there wouldn't have been a kind way to break the news. She must have counted him as some sort of friend. 'He had an accident,' I told her.

I wondered if she'd ask what kind, and was ready to plump for traffic. But she didn't ask. She didn't seem particularly surprised. She had known him and his little ways, after all.

She just leaned back on the pillows, her fingers picking absently at the front of her nightgown. 'Poor Rennie,' she said. 'I knew I couldn't trust him. But he can't hurt me now.' And she smiled.

It chilled my blood.

When I got back from Egham it was one thirty and I had two hours to go before my meeting with Mrs Marks. I could, if I put my best foot forward (wonky boot allowing), get over to Soho and try for an interview with Mickey Allerton. Susie had said he was at his club over lunchtime. I might just catch him.

The Silver Circle was in a narrow side street, jostled on one side by a restaurant and on the other by a sex shop. The club's façade was tastefully picked out in black and silver and bore the legend *Members Only*. A gentleman with a flattened nose and a suit too tight for him stood in the doorway, moodily watching a couple of pigeons pick at something spilled on the pavement.

I drew a deep breath and walked up to him. He said nothing,

only looked down at me as if I was another pigeon. I explained politely that I'd like a word with Mr Allerton if he was in his office.

'We're not hiring any new girls,' said the doorkeeper.

'I'm not after a job,' I explained.

He studied me dispassionately, top to toe. 'Just as well, you ain't got the figure for it.'

'Never mind the personal remarks,' I told him. 'Can I see Mr Allerton?'

'What about?'

'I'm making some enquiries. I'm a sort of private detective.'

'What, you?' He seemed mightily amused by this.

'Yes, me!' I extricated Rennie's by now well-worn business card. 'We've done work for Mr Allerton in the past.'

He glanced at it. 'Cor blimey, what's the world coming to? Don't make no difference. He ain't here.'

'Can I leave a message, then?'

'No. I don't take no messages. Not part of my job.'

I might have given up at that point, but just then a taxi drew up. The doorman's manner changed in an instant, alert as a perishing gun dog. He dived forward, scattering the pigeons, to open the cab door. A beefy, well-dressed guy in a camel overcoat, with thinning fair hair expensively styled, got out and paid off the cabbie.

'All right, Harry?' he enquired of the doorman.

'All right, Mr Allerton,' Harry assured him, albeit with an uneasy glance at me.

I nipped forward smartly. 'Mr Allerton? My name is Fran Varady and I'd be really grateful if you could spare me five minutes.'

'You haven't got the figure for it, love,' he said kindly.

At this rate I'd end up with a really poor self-image. 'I'm not after a job,' I said.

'Sing? Do a novelty act?'

'No! Mr Allerton, I'm a sort of private investigator.'

'Gawd,' he said. 'They say when the coppers start to look younger it's a sign of old age. I don't like to think what it means when kids like you turn up and claim to be private eyes.'

'Five minutes!' I said loudly and clearly, holding up the fingers of my right hand.

'Hop it!' growled Harry, seizing my upper arm painfully.

But Allerton was grinning. He must have had a good lunch somewhere. 'You've got bottle, I'll say that. What are you investigating, then? Oi, don't tell me a missing girl. I don't employ anyone under age, and if they're old enough, then it's up to them if they don't want their families knowing what they do.' He jabbed his finger at me.

'Rennie Duke's death,' I gasped, wincing from the pain in my arm.

He stopped grinning. 'All right,' he said. 'Come in and tell me why you're so interested. Not that I've got anything to tell you. But call me curious.'

He walked past the incredulous doorman, who let me go reluctantly. I trotted after his boss.

The vestibule was gloomy and the entry into the clubroom itself was covered with heavy velvet drapes. From the far side of them oozed a fug of smoke, booze fumes and perfume. Someone was playing the piano. From high in one corner, the CCTV camera kept an accusing eye on new arrivals. A very pretty Oriental girl leaned on the reception desk. From the look of her, I wondered how honest Allerton had been about not employing anyone under age. Behind her, coats hung on hooks, and in front of her was a stack of printed forms, I guessed membership applications. I wondered what they cost. She also snapped to attention when she saw Allerton. He gave her a brief nod of acknowledgement, then turned left down a narrow corridor, me at his heels.

We fetched up in a tiny office. It contained a desk with a swivel chair and another chair for visitors. Three screens flickered silently, showing three different scenes: the foyer, the bar and stage, and another area I guessed was the rear of the place. In the bar, half a dozen slumped male figures watched a girl in thigh boots and a handful of sequins do a kind of gymnastic dance on the stage. Her heavily painted face expressed nothing, her eyes fixed on some place far off, another world. It looked as beautiful and dead as the face on an Egyptian mummy case. She wasn't dancing for them, she was dancing for herself and some unseen and quite different audience.

'It's art,' said Allerton, following my gaze.

'No it's not,' I retorted. I hadn't meant to argue with him and set him against me, but I take the performing arts seriously.

Allerton's eyes had narrowed. 'You're not one of those feminist birds, are you? They turn up every so often, stick posters on my windows and pour instant glue in the locks.'

'No,' I said. 'But I was a drama student once.'

'Nice,' he returned without the slightest interest. He shrugged off his coat and sat at the desk. I wasn't invited to take the visitor's chair and remained standing awkwardly before him. I put his age at around fifty. As a younger man, he must have been handsome in a flashy way. Now he had the kind of striking looks, well-worn and battle-hardened, I'd seen on antique busts of Roman bigwigs. His very pale grey eyes were pouched in bags of soft skin. All his skin was as clear and supple as a baby's and I guessed at regular facial sessions. He probably detoxed regularly at health spas. But the eyes, in their paleness, were unsettling and reminded me of silvery fish-eyes. His nose was a good classical one, though, long and straight, his lips were thin, and a once square jaw had begun to acquire jowls, as yet no more than a sagginess spoiling the chin line. He looked like a man who was used to giving orders, who lived well, was careful in his choice of friends and in his business dealings. The sort of man even his enemies treated with respect. The sort, in fact, in whose presence I needed to tread very warily. I told myself to be extra polite. Grovel, if necessary.

'Rennie done one or two little jobs for me,' he said. 'His old lady keeping the business going?'

'For the time being,' I said carefully. 'She's not had a chance to make up her mind yet.'

He grunted. 'Right, let's hear it. I'm a busy man. Make it quick.'

I explained that my mother had left home when I was a kid, and later hired Rennie to find me. Rennie had subsequently turned up dead outside my abode (which I didn't tell him was a garage).

'So,' I said, 'the police keep bothering me. What I want to know is, has his death got anything to do with me or my mother, and if so, am I next on some killer's shopping list? Because if I am, I'd really like to know.'

'Doesn't explain why you're here,' he said.

'Look,' I urged, 'Rennie was a bit of a creep. We all know that. Maybe he upset someone? I just thought you might have heard something like that. It'd let me know if I'm worrying over nothing.'

'If I might have heard something?' He was looking amused. 'You're a funny little tart, you are.' The smile left his eyes. 'You'd better be on the level, darling, or I might get very cross.'

'You can check me out,' I said.

'You got my name from the widow, I suppose?'

I didn't want to get Susie into more trouble. 'She's very upset, she loved him.' I made it good, heart-breaking even. It bounced off Allerton.

'That's her problem. I paid Rennie well for the jobs he did for me. That's the end of it as far as I'm concerned. Sure, I knew he was dodgy, but he was never so stupid as to try anything clever with me. People don't.' The fish-eyes were at their most expressionless. 'So if Susie Duke has got any ideas about getting more money from me now, tell her to forget it. I'm not a charity nor an insurance company. Give her my regrets. I'm sorry he's gone. He was good, and it inconveniences me.' He was being honest about his feelings, at least.

'It's nothing to do with money, nothing like that. I'm not here on Susie's behalf, just my own. I'm worried about my neck,' I assured him.

'You'd protect your neck, darling, a lot better if you didn't go marching into places like this and bothering blokes like me. Didn't your mother tell you these things? Oh no, she didn't. You were saying she lit out when you were a nipper.'

He tapped his fingers on the desk and made a decision to revise his earlier statement. 'Perhaps I *am* interested to know who killed Rennie Duke. Very careless of 'em, whoever it was. So if I hear anything, I'll let you know. And if you get a lead, you'll let me know, right? Fair exchange, no robbery.'

I wasn't too happy with this arrangement, but promised I would do so if I could. He asked for a phone number and I had to give him that of the shop, explaining that they took messages and mail for me there, but were not in any other way connected. He scribbled down the number.

'We could get you a decent wig and an outfit, say leather, and make a hostess of you,' he said without looking up. 'Some of the members like something a bit different. You're different.'

'I'm an actor,' I said with dignity.

'Right, you said. Shouldn't that be actress?'

'We don't say that now.'

'Oh, don't we?' he mimicked. 'Don't they know the difference between fellers and girls in the theatre? We do in my business.' He gave me a sly look. 'Not a detective, then?'

'Both. I'm resting. I've got to do something while I'm resting.'

'I've employed lots of resting actresses,' he told me, probably truthfully.

'Not this one,' I said, but added politely, 'thank you all the same,' because I didn't want to offend him.

'Don't thank me,' he said. 'Just scram.'

I scrammed. A busty blonde in a leopard-skin jacket, leggings and stiletto heels tottered past me, greeting Harry on the way. One of the resting thespians was arriving for work.

Harry looked at her and then looked at me.

'Save it,' I said. 'You don't have to tell me again.'

Chapter Twelve

Mrs Marks's day nursery was run from the front room of her terraced home. The row of some dozen identical houses had been built around the turn of the century in red brick. An inset tablet between the upper windows in the middle of the terrace announced them to be called Ivy Villas. Lord knows why. There wasn't any ivy. There weren't any plants of any sort, unless you counted the blackened remains of weeds that had tried to grow between the glazed tiles of the tiny forecourts which stood between the houses and the pavement. This wasn't Kew. The owners had probably tired of putting out potted shrubs only to have them stolen. Some kept their dustbins in the forecourts instead.

Number four, Ivy-less Villas, did not have a dustbin and stood out from the rest by having a cornflower-blue door and distinctive decorations at its downstairs front bow window. Coloured paper butterflies and balloons were glued to the panes. Its window frames were painted the same blue as the door, and the stone window ledges were yellow. The doorbell played the sort of umpty-tumpty tune associated with nursery rhymes, just in case the caller still had any doubts about this being an infant-oriented establishment. I was a long, long way from the Silver Circle Club, in all senses.

The door was opened by a young black woman in a pink overall, holding a toy tambourine.

'Hi,' she said. 'You a new mother?'

'No,' I told her. 'I'm Fran Varady.'

'Hey, she's waiting on you.' I was ushered indoors.

In the front room, behind the paper decorations, I found a hive of industry. A pair of toddlers were methodically destroying everything within reach with plastic hammers. A plump little person wedged in a baby-walker zoomed merrily about the floorspace in a way which suggested he'd grow up to be a Formula One driver. Two little girls used toy rolling pins to flatten Plasticine. Their faces expressed grim intensity, and as they worked, they argued fiercely, illustrating the Chinese description of war as being two women in a kitchen. Amazingly, a young baby slept peacefully through it all in a cot in the corner. At the sight, I thought of Miranda, who'd spent a short time here in just such a way, perhaps in the same well-used cot, until she left to become Nicola Wilde. Mum had done her best for her, not dumped her on a hard-pressed neighbour for a couple of quid a week. This was a proper place and wouldn't have come cheap.

An elderly woman with greying hair regimented into permed waves, and blue plastic-framed spectacles, advanced to meet me. She eyed me up and down. I eyed her back and guessed she was rather older than she looked and was the type who stood no nonsense from infant or adult.

She had age on her mind, too. 'You're not the baby I looked after for Eva,' she snapped. 'You're too old.'

'No, I'm Eva's elder child. Mrs Marks, I really appreciate you seeing me.'

She looked round her at the infant-sized chairs and then

back at me, comparing my dimensions with the available seating. 'We'd better go in the back room. Lucille, keep an eye on things.'

'No problem,' said Lucille comfortably.

The back room was a tiny sitting room claustrophobically overfurnished and overprovided with ornaments. A caged budgie squawked at us as we came in. Mrs Marks indicated I should take a seat in an armchair protected by embroidered antimacassars, and plumped herself down in a matching chair opposite. Her spectacles glinted at me.

'Now I don't know what you want to know,' she began aggressively, before I'd had a chance to say anything. 'It was nearly thirteen years ago, must be, that Eva came to me with that baby. All of that. I told the police so.'

'Did you ever doubt the baby was Eva's own child?' I asked straight away, because we might as well get that one out of the way first.

'Of course not. She'd been breast-feeding but had to put the baby on to formula when she brought her here. It gave her some problems with her own milk. I recommended her Epsom salts. Usually dries it up pretty quick.'

Did I want to know this?

She was frowning at me. 'Is that what all this is about? The police wouldn't tell me why they were asking. Do they think Eva took a baby away from somewhere?' For the first time she sounded anxious.

'No. No, that's not it at all,' I hastened to assure her, and she relaxed. I went on to give her the carefully edited version I'd worked out on my way over there. 'As you might remember, my mother had to give the baby up for adoption. Now she'd like to trace her.'

Mrs Marks sat back and pursed her lips in thought. 'Is that why the private detective wrote to me? A Mr Duke, he was. I phoned him and asked what he wanted. He was cagey, didn't want to say over the phone. So he arranged to come and see me. But he didn't turn up and I didn't hear from him again. The police said they'd got my name from his computer. I don't hold with the things. My son-in-law is always on at me to get one. I ask you, what would I do with it? Seems to me if anyone can get hold of a computer and read all your private correspondence on it, it's a good thing to keep away from them. And what were the police doing with Mr Duke's computer in the first place? I asked the policewoman who came here. Pert little madam. Got nothing from her. They won't tell you what's going on. They never do. Is this Duke fellow in some sort of trouble?'

'Not now,' I told her. I'd been afraid that Mrs Marks would refuse to talk. Now I was worried she wouldn't stop long enough for me to get in my questions. 'He's well out of it now. Eva's – Eva's not got long. She's in a hospice for the terminally ill. She's got leukaemia.'

She tut-tutted. 'I'm really sorry about that. She was a nice girl, Eva. Got her life in a bit of a mess, I could tell that, but well, it's not unusual, is it? She could have gone on the social and not worked, just stayed home with the baby, but she had a little job on the till at the supermarket and she stuck to it. To me, that means she was made of the right stuff. I've always worked. Keep active and you keep young, that's what I say.'

All this was fine, but it didn't help me. There had to be something I could ask her, something that would point me in the direction of Rennie Duke's killer. So far I had a prime suspect in Jerry Wilde but that was all I had – suspicions. I had to find a connection between this lady and Jerry Wilde. In theory, Mrs Marks knew only that my mother had given the baby up for adoption. Yet Rennie Duke had apparently been working on the idea that she could tell him something which would lead him to the whereabouts of my younger sister.

She was getting impatient, glancing at the door, straining to hear sounds from the front room. 'Was there anything else?' She put her hands on the chair arms, ready to push herself up.

I struck out at random. 'Mrs Marks, do you know a Mr Wilde? A Jerry Wilde, or his wife, Flora? Have they been in touch?'

She flushed and I knew I'd hit a target. She shook her head vigorously. 'I haven't heard from anyone called Wilde. I don't know anyone of that name.'

'You're sure? Mrs Marks, it really matters.'

She didn't reply and stood up. I thought with dismay that she was about to show me out, but instead she went to check the scene in the playroom. When she came back, she closed the door with care and resumed her seat.

'You're really Eva's girl? You're not a policewoman? You know, plain clothes?'

'Have a heart,' I begged. 'No, I'm not a policewoman. Mrs Marks, the baby we're talking about is my sister, my half-sister. If you know anything, please tell me.'

'I'm not saying I know anything. But I will tell you, I wasn't ever really satisfied that Eva had given Miranda over to social services. Still, she said she had and I'd no real reason to doubt her, only that she loved that baby. I could tell. She was everything to her.' She stopped and looked at me. 'What's the matter, dear?'

I wasn't aware my feelings showed on my face so clearly. 'Nothing,' I said. 'Go on.'

'It's because I know she loved Miranda that I'm telling you this. Eva dying and everything, I understand she'd want to see that child again. You can turn your back on family all your life, but at the end of it, that's where you want to be, with your own. Now then, my daughter, Linda, she lives in Kew.'

There was no way I could control my reaction to that. I nearly jumped off my chair.

'That means something to you, does it?' said Mrs Marks drily. 'Then I'd better tell you the rest. I haven't told the police, mind you, and I'm not going to. I'd be obliged if you'd keep it to yourself, but I fancy you will. If you're looking for that child, you're doing it on the quiet, aren't you? I can tell.'

I admitted it.

'The people who come through that door . . .' She pointed towards the front of the house. 'The problems some of them have, you wouldn't credit it. I've seen it all. Still, it's a good little business if you like children. Linda wanted some job she could do from home and so she started up a crèche of her own, over there in Kew. She knew how to run one. She'd helped me out here. Just a couple of weeks after Eva took the baby away, I found myself with a free day, no children. So I took myself over to Kew to see how Linda was getting on with her little establishment. Only just starting up as she was, she'd got just one toddler and a small baby to mind. Well, when I saw that baby, you could have knocked me down with a feather. I felt in my bones it was Eva's. I asked Linda whose baby it was. She said someone called Wilde. She was looking after it just two mornings a week because the Wildes were busy doing up an old house they'd just bought. I told her it was the spitting image of a baby I'd been caring for. But Linda laughed and said that at that age, all babies looked the same.'

Mrs Marks paused. 'Well, she might think that but I never have. Still, I was in a bit of a pickle, as you might say. I didn't want to make any trouble for Linda, not with her just starting out. As a child-minder, your reputation matters. Any sort of bother and people don't come near you. I had nothing but my own fancies to go on. Suppose I'd spoken up, told the authorities, they'd investigated and found everything kosher? What then? I've have ruined Linda's business and then where would she be? Besides, when I thought about it, I decided that if the baby had been given by Eva to someone else, it was probably a family matter.'

I was puzzled. 'How do you mean?'

She gave me an old-fashioned look. 'It's how it was always done in the old days, dear, when I was young. You know, a girl would have a baby out of wedlock and it would be passed off as belonging to a married sister or even the girl's own mother. You'd be surprised how many women produced a baby suddenly, late in life, in those days! Nobody asked questions. We all understood. Believe me,' Mrs Marks gave me another dry smile and waved a hand in the general direction of the street, 'there are a lot of people walking round out there, probably most of them middle-aged now, who've called their grandmother "Mummy" and thought of their real mother as a sister or an auntie.'

'Someone must always know,' I argued. 'The rest of the family. The neighbours.'

'Probably. But they didn't say anything, that was the point. The family wanted to protect its own good name. The neighbours didn't want to damage a girl's reputation, spoil her chance of marriage to a decent boy some day. Who knows, perhaps some of them had a baby like that in their own family. Why open up a can of worms?'

'Why indeed?' I said dully. That was what I'd done, following up my mother's request.

Mrs Marks was saying, 'I dare say it's different now. Society is more tolerant. Girls keep their babies and no one thinks it odd. But I thought that maybe that was what Eva had done, given the baby to a married sister. So in the end, I said nothing.'

During the previous few minutes there had been noises from the front part of the house, strange adult voices, childish babble and movement, all suggesting the infants were being collected. Car doors slammed distantly. I could hear Lucille, the helper, organising things. Mrs Marks had been glancing from time to time at the window, where the light would soon be fading. She showed signs of restlessness.

'If you don't mind, dear,' she said, 'you'll have to go now. Lucille will be clearing up for me and I've got other things to do.'

I had forgotten it was Friday. I thanked her for giving me her time and telling me all she could. I advised her not to have anything to do with Wilde if he got in touch. 'And perhaps you ought to have a word with your daughter, warn her. If the police got to you, they may get to her, even if you don't tell them.'

I left, heavy-hearted. She ought to go to the police with her story for her own protection, if for nothing else. The weight of circumstantial evidence against Jerry Wilde was growing. If he'd killed Duke, it was because the detective was asking questions about Nicola. If he ever found out about Mrs Marks, then he'd see both of us as a threat to him and Flora. At the same time, the last thing I wanted was to lead the police to Linda Marks – I didn't know her married name, but that wouldn't hold the police up – and through Linda to the Wildes. This wasn't what Mum wanted and it wasn't what I wanted.

I cursed myself for ever agreeing to do as Mum had asked. Like Pandora, I'd opened a box and couldn't now get the lid back on again. Sooner or later, so it seemed to me, the police must join up all the dots and the outline would be of Nicola Wilde. They'd do it quicker if Mrs Marks told them her story. Even without her, eventually.

I felt I'd somehow let Mum down, that this was all my fault. I could've handled it all differently. I should've realised straight away that Rennie Duke was a loose cannon. It was all going pear-shaped and I couldn't make amends. But one thing I could do, must do. I had to arrange to see Jerry Wilde again, dangerous though it might prove. I had to tell him the police were looking for the baby he and Flora had taken on as theirs, though naturally I'd leave Mrs Marks out of it. I wasn't going to warn the Wildes for their sakes, but for Nicola's. The hunt was on officially now and threatening to blow my sister's world apart.

The problem was getting in touch with Wilde again. I knew where he lived but couldn't call at the house for fear of meeting up with Flora again. I couldn't write to him in case Flora opened the mail. I supposed he was in the directory but couldn't telephone because Flora or Nicola might pick up the phone. The only thing I could do was stake out his house and wait for him to come home, then dash out and waylay him.

Later in the year this would have been almost impossible.

Anyone hanging around, circling the block endlessly, lurking in doorways, waiting at bus stops without ever boarding a bus, would warrant a suspicious neighbour's call to the police. But at this time of year darkness fell early and would provide a welcome cloak for my stake-out. I recalled that a little further down the road from the house was a patch of grass and a wooden seat. If I sat there, hopefully no one would notice me, and I'd see Jerry arrive.

I dot-and-carry-one'd my way in my loose boot back to Kew.

The rush hour had already begun and the Tube was packed. Commuters streamed off it. I wondered if Jerry Wilde was among them and if waiting at the Tube station exit might be the best thing. But in such a crowd and in the poor light he could walk by me. Even if I stationed myself at the foot of the stairs to the over-track bridge, I'd miss him. I decided to stick to my original idea.

The drizzle which had begun that morning was still falling. It was bitterly cold. I found the seat in the Wildes' street and huddled on it, arms folded to keep the heat in and hands tucked into my armpits. Behind and above me trees rustled mournfully. The sodium streetlight gleamed on wet pavements. I was getting steadily soaked as water came at me from all angles, dripping from overhead branches down my neck, blown by gusts of wind into my face. Cars swept past, sending spray from overflowing gutters over my feet. Because the seat had been wet when I sat on it I even had the unpleasant sensation of wet drawers. I supposed this was all part of being a detective, but I'd decided by now it was an overrated profession. My only consolation was that, in weather like this, no one was out walking, like the lady with the fox terrier for example, and so no one was likely to ask what I was doing there. If anyone did, I'd decided I could always make up a story about being stood up by a boyfriend.

Up and down the street lights began to appear behind the expensive blinds and curtains. Occasionally, where curtains hadn't yet been drawn, they revealed comfortable interiors like a forbidden world of luxury conjured up by a genie. I could see the Wildes' house clearly. Lights were already on there so someone was home, but the blinds were drawn. Occasionally a fuzzy outline passed behind the blind but I couldn't tell who it was, not even if it was doll-like Flora. Images projected on to blinds by lamps tend to be enlarged and distorted.

I read a story once, I think it was a Sherlock Holmes one, where a cut-out figure in front of a curtain fools a watcher in the street that Holmes is at home. I can't see how that would work myself. The cut-out wouldn't move. Even just sitting, we move about a bit, even if we doze off. I've slept in chairs. It's not that comfortable. Your head lolls to one side or another. You shift about trying to get comfy. If the observer in the street was meant to think that was Holmes up there, wouldn't he wonder why the great man didn't tamp down fresh tobacco in his pipe now and then, or scribble a few words of the next little monograph on umpteen types of tobacco, or even decide to scrape away for a bit on the old violin? I tell you, it wouldn't work.

I didn't need reminding that I was pretty uncomfortable now, and wriggling about wouldn't help. I leaned back and tried to ignore my waterlogged state and how stupid I must look to anyone driving past. Perhaps they'd think I was drunk or drugged. Perhaps they'd call the cops on that account. I wished I had a headset so I could at least listen to some music. I began thinking about Norman's spare room and whether I could really live there. It wasn't Zog on the landing or Sid in the attic who put me off. I've shared living space with all kinds of people and most of them just want to be left alone. What worried me was all that combustible newsprint downstairs and Norman adding to it daily like some sort of demented squirrel.

Someone was coming, walking down the pavement towards me from the further end of the tree-lined avenue. The figure slipped in and out of view disconcertingly as alternately it stepped into the shadow of a tree then out into a dull pool of streetlight. As it got nearer, I saw it was a female figure, not tall, and bulked out with padded jacket and heavy bag slung over one shoulder. On the other side, she carried some kind of long, thin dark case. As she came nearer I saw it was a violin case and I thought of Holmes again. The girl was almost on me. She emerged from the darkness beneath a tree into the reach of the nearest lamp, and I saw her face lit with a pale fluorescent glow.

I couldn't stop myself. I just said, out loud, 'Nicola.'

I had no doubt it was the girl in the school photograph. She'd pulled up the hood on her quilted jacket but her long fair hair, lank with drizzle, spilled out. Beneath the jacket she wore a dark-coloured skirt, dark-coloured tights and sensible laced shoes. I guessed they formed part of some private school uniform. They don't change much. I'd worn much the same during my time in private education. I hoped Nicola was making more of her chances than I had.

She'd heard me and had stopped. Her eyes fixed me in a

puzzled but not cautious stare. She had the self-confidence which goes with being bright, pretty, loved and well-off. A little princess.

'Do I know you?' Her voice was equally confident, slightly accusing.

'No,' I said.

'You called my name.'

'No,' I repeated like a dummy.

'I heard you. You said "Nicola".' Now the accusation was open in her voice.

'No I didn't,' I denied. 'I coughed.'

She didn't buy it. She still stood there, glaring now at being contradicted when she was sure she was right.

'I've got a bad chest,' I said plaintively. 'I got it sleeping rough. Got any spare change?'

That settled it.

'No, I haven't!' she snapped. 'And if I did, I wouldn't give it to you!'

She strode away. I watched her cross the street to the Wildes' house and let herself in with her own key. I judged it politic to remove myself from my seat for a few minutes. She'd very likely tell someone at home about me. I got up and retreated behind one of the trees. Not a moment too soon. Nicola must have burst in with a tale of being waylaid by a beggar. The blind at the front window was pushed aside and a face stared out, Flora's, fixed and angry. Seeing the empty seat, she looked back over her shoulder at someone in the room. Nicola appeared, also peering into the night in the direction of the seat. She shrugged. They both left the window and the blind dropped back into place.

I waited a few minutes and then re-emerged, even wetter if

that was possible. I was glad Jerry hadn't come to the window. It indicated he wasn't already home. I was aware that I didn't even know if he commuted to and from work daily in a regular pattern. I could be wasting my time. He could work from home. He might all this time have been sitting in that cosy farmhouse kitchen, warm as toast, while I mouldered out here like Patience on a monument. But now I was encouraged to stick it out. He had to come, sooner or later. Mind you, I might get double pneumonia first.

In the meantime, I had plenty to occupy my mind. If it wasn't for Janice Morgan and her investigations into Mrs Marks, my quest would now be over as far as Nicola was concerned. I could honestly go back to my mother and say I'd seen and spoken to her. Even Mum couldn't insist on more. But Morgan and her thoroughness had put paid to that. Seeing my sister, speaking to her, had also put paid to any peace of mind I'd had left. I felt odd, a bit shaky. I told myself it was the cold but I knew it wasn't, it was emotion. She was real. She was flesh and blood, my flesh and blood. Had my mother ever considered what this moment would be like for me? But then, neither had I. I'd worried what it would do to Nicola, but never what it would do to me.

I continued to sit there for the best part of an hour. Every time a car turned into the street I got ready, hoping it would be Jerry Wilde, but it never was. My joints were setting stiff. I got up and walked up and down a bit. Cold was eating into my bones. I was hungry and thirsty and, perversely, wanted to spend a penny.

I was considering nipping behind the tree again for this purpose when headlights played across the road junction. Another vehicle turned into the street. It was travelling slowly, drawing up outside the Wildes' place. The driver climbed out. I was already moving forward, all discomfort forgotten. The street lighting played havoc with colours but the shape of that four-by-four and the glimpse of its driver were enough for me. I lurched across the road in my loose boot, calling, 'Hey! Ben! Ben Cornish! Wait!'

Chapter Thirteen

My reaction was the antithesis of good detective work. I should have noted the caller's identity and stayed where I was until Jerry turned up, as per my original plan. That I didn't do this was partly because I was surprised to see Ben and shouted out his name on an impulse, much as I'd called out Nicola's. But I fancy that subconsciously I knew I couldn't physically wait out there in the dark and wet for much longer. Moss would be growing on me soon. I had to make contact with Jerry some other way, and providence was offering me one. Besides which, I'm an amateur.

'Fran?' Ben was saying, staring at me in astonishment, as well he might. He had watched the approach of the dark booted shape hobbling towards him with a mix of fascination and horror. Now he could see who it was, things weren't improved. Drowned rats didn't come into it.

'Ben,' I begged through chattering teeth, 'we've got to talk. Please – don't ring the bell. I must talk to you first, before you see the Wildes.'

He hesitated for only a split second. 'Get in the car,' he said. 'There's a pub just up the road.'

I climbed into the four-by-four, and only as Ben pulled us

away from the kerb did it occur to my frozen brain to wonder what on earth he was doing there.

It was early in the evening for drinkers and he was able to park in the tiny car park to the side of the pub. As we made our way inside, he asked: 'Why are you limping? Have you hurt your leg?'

'No, just busted a bootlace,' I told him.

'Oh.' He held the door open for me, a gent. Inside it was blessedly warm and dry. Also welcome was the sign that read *Toilets*.

'Just a tick,' I said. 'Back in a minute.'

'What do you want to drink?' he called after me as I lurched away.

I called back that I'd like a coffee. Anything hot. It was the sort of pub which did coffee and food. I took a better look at it as I returned from my comfort stop. This was an upmarket watering hole for well-heeled local residents and tourists who'd come out here to visit the Gardens. It was spotlessly clean and all the tables shone. Each had a small brass disc with a number set into it, and above the bar was a VDU which showed what you'd ordered. All around the walls, a touch of culture, shelves of books. A quick squint at these suggested they'd been bought up as a job lot by the yard. There were titles covering every subject, from old romances of the Mazo de la Roche variety to out-of-date textbooks on physics and medicine. I wondered if anyone ever took one down and read it.

At this early hour of the evening, in any case, there was only a sprinkling of customers. The one or two who noticed me looked disapproving, as did the barman stationed beneath his flickering VDU. He had his name, Josh, pinned to his shirt and looked more of a yuppie than his clientele. Hey, Josh, I felt like saying, I used to live in Rotherhithe, where the regulars know who the barman is without it being stuck on his front with a sissy brooch. Nor do barmen there need a computer to tell them what you've ordered. They've got lightning-fast brains when it comes to totting up the score. They have proper names like Ron and Frank and they go in for weight training. They need to.

Josh's opinion of me clearly reflected mine of him. I was lowering the tone of the establishment. He might have asked me to leave had I not joined Ben, who was waiting for me, a bottle of lager in front of him. A cup of coffee at my place sent enticing steam curls into the air.

'Thanks,' I said, grabbing it. The doors opened to admit another couple. The girl wore a long fake-fur coat and her escort a City overcoat. They looked as if they'd just returned from a shopping trip to Harrods. Perhaps they had. The barman was all over them. They all glanced at me. Josh whispered. I was sure he was apologising.

'You look a bit wet. How long had you been out there?' Ben was asking. He was looking amused. I think he guessed at the silent duel going on between me and Josh.

I confessed it had been quite a while. I'd done my best while in the Ladies' to dry myself off in front of the hot-air blower and tidy up, but the improvement was marginal.

He didn't comment. He waited until I'd drunk my coffee and showed signs of returning to room temperature. Then he asked, 'Would you like to eat?'

I told him it was OK, but he didn't believe me.

'I think you should eat something.' His voice was quietly determined.

I gave in without too much argument. I was ravenous. The menu stood on the table and the list matched the establishment. I picked on the least fancily titled thing, the special hamburger and chips.

Ben went to the bar and ordered. I was rooting around in my pocket for money when he got back but he waved it away. 'No problem. Just tell me what's going on.'

He was asking the impossible. How was I ever going to be able to explain any of this to anyone? If I could've kept one step ahead of the game, I might have been able to handle things better. But I hadn't, not once Jerry knew I was on the trail.

'I should have realised, when I called on Mrs Mackenzie, that she'd phone the Wildes,' I said. 'That sort of screwed things up for me.'

'Aunt Dot was worried. She talked it over with me and I advised her to phone Jerry Wilde.' Ben paused. 'I phoned him myself, too, later. I gave him the address of the hospice. I reckoned if you were on the level' – Ben's gaze grew speculative – 'and the Wildes and your mother *were* old friends, Jerry would want to visit her. He certainly sounded pretty upset. Whether that was on account of your mother being so ill or not, I don't know. To be honest, I did think, when you called on Aunt Dot, that you were only telling us half the story.'

'I told you and your aunt the truth and as much as you needed to know,' I said. 'My mother's in the hospice. She did know the Wildes years ago. Yes, Jerry did try to visit her after you phoned, but she wasn't up to seeing anyone that day.'

'But there's more to it than that,' Ben said quietly.

'More, but I can't tell you.' I frowned. 'How well do you yourself know Jerry and Flora? I mean, when I visited your aunt, you didn't say you knew them at all.'

'You didn't ask me. I knew them quite well when I was a kid, when they lived near Aunt Dot. They didn't have Nicola then, and Flora made a bit of a fuss of me. I was about seven or eight. My parents—'

Again he hesitated at the mention of his parents. 'They were away a lot. I spent a lot of time with Aunt Dot and her husband, Uncle William. He's been dead a while. But I still keep an eye on Aunt Dot. She kept an eye on me all those years, after all. You should have seen her house then. It was full of those little dogs she used to breed. Every time the doorbell rang, they went berserk. Uncle William had his koi carp and other fancy fish for a hobby. He was a nice chap, an old-fashioned, home-loving nine-to-fiver.' Ben smiled. 'He thought a day trip to Boulogne was foreign travel enough for any man. He worked in an architect's office.'

That rang a bell. 'Is Jerry Wilde an architect, by any chance?' I asked. I was thinking how knowledgeable he'd been about Royal Holloway College. Moreover, if he was, it would have been a link between him and the Mackenzies, suggesting why Mrs Mackenzie had kept in touch all these years.

'That's right. They were a really nice couple and we were all sorry when, after Nicola was born, they moved away. Aunt Dot sent them a Christmas card every year, and I wrote "and Ben" after her name. Later I got too old for that sort of thing and started sending my own cards. Flora always sent an individual one to me, right from the start. When I was still at school, she sent funny ones. Now she sends the usual scenes of festive cheer. That's as far as it went until recently, when I started doing some research at the Botanical Gardens here at Kew, in the hothouses.'

'Best place,' I mumbled, thinking of my chilled wait.

He grinned. 'Best place for my research, certainly. Have you ever been there?' When I shook my head, he went on, 'You ought to pay a visit while I'm there so I can show you what I'm doing. Well, I thought, as I was in the area, that I'd look the Wildes up. I've called round there a few times since. It's been nice meeting up with them again, seeing how they are, how big Nicola's grown. I remember her as just a baby. She's a fantastic violinist, you know.'

I did know, because Wilde had been at pains to tell me, but I was spared having to discuss Nicola by the appearance of the hamburger, which arrived with plentiful chips and salad, carried by Josh. The burger looked great. Josh looked miffed. He set it down in front of me rather as he might have put down a bowl of Winalot in front of the family dog.

'Enjoy your meal,' he said starchily.

'Where's the mayo?' I asked. 'I like mayo on my chips.'

He didn't quite snarl at me. He fetched the mayonnaise in a dinky little bowl (no plastic sachets here), and dropped it down in front of me without another word. In addition to everything else, I had betrayed myself as a food philistine. However, I was embarrassed when I realised Josh wasn't returning with a second plate.

'You're not eating?' I asked Ben.

'Later.'

'With the Wildes?'

He nodded.

I was tempted to advise him to eat here first, remembering all that fat-free shopping. But I restrained my impulse in favour of good manners. 'Then I'm making you late. They'll be wondering where you are.'

'Don't worry about it. I was a tad early. Jerry's not due back for a bit.'

Just as well I had called off my wait. 'Ben,' I said, 'I need to talk to Jerry. The thing is, I don't want Flora to know about it, or their daughter. Flora would flip at the mention of my name. That's why I couldn't go to the house and was hanging about outside waiting for Jerry. He won't be too happy either. I know how dodgy it all sounds, but I can't explain it to you because it involves others and I'm just not free to do it. Can you just give a message to Jerry for me? That Fran wants a word, that's all. It's important. I can meet him in any public place.' I stressed the word 'public'. I wasn't going anywhere secluded with Jerry Wilde.

'And how is Jerry going to take it when I give him this message?' Ben raised a quizzical eyebrow.

'Not well,' I confessed. 'But he'll want to see me. Ben, believe me, I'm not making trouble for the Wildes. I'm trying to help them. Will you do it?'

He drew a deep breath and held it for a moment before slowly expelling it. 'All right. I'll pass the message on to him tonight. Have you got a phone number?'

I hadn't got any paper. Ben hunted in his pocket and brought out a miscellany of string, plant ties, pencil stubs, those little plastic markers you stick in seedbeds and, finally, some sort of bill with muddy fingerprints on it.

'Gardener's pockets!' he said ruefully. 'You name it, gardeners carry it round with them. You can write on the back of this.' He pushed the bill towards me, together with a pencil stub.

I wrote out the shop's phone number and explained that it was a newsagent's but that any message would certainly reach me, as they were friends.

'You ought to get yourself a mobile,' said Ben.

'Can't afford one.' I remembered something. 'Ben, when you get to the Wildes' place tonight, Nicola may say something about a beggar asking her for change near the house. It was me. I'm not a beggar but she wanted to know why I was hanging about there and I had to say something.'

He didn't comment on this and I didn't know whether he believed it. He'd begun stuffing all the bits and bobs back into his pockets. 'I'll have to leave you here to finish your meal alone, OK? I should get over to the Wildes' now. Oh, give me your boot. The one with the broken lace.'

I slipped my foot out and handed him my boot. Muddy, wet, old, it looked like one of those bits of abandoned footwear you see on canal banks, always the one, never the pair. I was wearing navy socks with white spots on them, but rain and pavement water leaking in had turned the spots grey. I hoped Josh couldn't see.

Ben pulled out the broken lace and threaded the length of twine from his pocket collection through the eyelets. 'Not beautiful, but it will get you home. At least you'll be able to walk straight.'

I thanked him. He said he wouldn't forget about the message for Jerry and would make sure Flora didn't overhear. Then he was gone. I relaced the boot on my ankle and finished my chips. As I left, the barman gave me a sneer which clearly said he thought I'd spun good-natured Ben some sob story to get a free meal. I called out a cheery goodbye and waved at him as if I were a regular, just to annoy him a little bit more.

I'd known that sitting about in the rain and cold wouldn't do me any good, robust as I generally am in adverse weather conditions. After all, I don't have central heating in Hari's garage, and in most of the squats I've lived in, you've had to sleep in your clothes in winter. But this time it got to me.

I slept very badly, tossing and turning on my narrow bed so that once I almost fell out. Bonnie got so fed up with the disturbance that she jumped off the bed and curled up nearby. I had a peculiar dream. I was walking up the drive to the hospice, but before I got to the door I saw Flora Wilde waiting to intercept me. She wasn't angry, but nice and smiling. She held out her hand to me and I almost took it, but then a woman I didn't know arrived on the scene. Her outline was indistinct and I couldn't see her face. Whoever it was, Flora stopped smiling and looked upset. When she turned back to me, her welcome had turned to accusation. 'You're responsible for this!' she said. I was denying it when I woke for the umpteenth time, cold and sweating together. For a moment I didn't know where I was, until Bonnie pushed her nose into my hand. I switched on the lights and made coffee on my little Calor Gas picnic stove, telling myself that I was *not* going to be ill. I'm a believer in mind over matter. I just wished I didn't feel so rotten.

A little after six I tramped up to the shop and asked Ganesh if he had any paracetamol.

'You look like death,' he said kindly.

In hoarse tones I informed him I was fine, just a bit headachy.

'For crying out loud, go upstairs and have a hot bath. Get Hari to give you some breakfast.' He pressed a pack of paracetamol into my hand. 'Don't take more than two in any four-hour period.'

'Thank you, Dr Quincy,' I croaked.

I didn't fancy any food, but the hot bath sounded like a good idea. I went upstairs, where Hari also informed me I looked very ill and suggested I see a doctor.

'Just a bit of a cold,' I assured him.

He told me colds were notoriously treacherous. They could turn to something worse before you knew it. He listed a variety of diseases which started with flu-like symptoms. He asked if I had any spots.

I told him I hadn't seen any but would check when in the bath. If I found any, he advised, I was to try rolling a glass over them, and if they didn't disappear under pressure, that meant I had meningitis. I promised him that in that case, I'd go immediately to Casualty.

Hari told me one last cheery tale, about a cousin who'd dropped dead only twenty-four hours after developing a sore throat, and then, thank goodness, went downstairs.

I soaked in the bath and afterwards felt much better. I went back downstairs and told them so.

'It's started to rain again,' Ganesh said. 'I really don't think it's a good idea for you to go out to Egham, if that's what you're planning. Not that you tell *me* what you're planning these days! Besides making yourself worse, you'd infect all those sick people out there and they've got enough symptoms to be going on with.'

I conceded the point. He let me ring the hospice to check on my mother and explain why I wouldn't be coming that day. Sister Helen said that Mum was tired and it was just as well I wasn't planning a visit. She wasn't up to visitors really. If I came, I could only sit by the bed, not talk to her. She hoped I felt better soon.

Just to make sure I didn't slip out, Ganesh offered me a morning's work behind the counter on the grounds that Hari had to go to the bank plus a couple of other calls. We were fairly busy despite the weather. The shop doorbell jangled regularly and we dispensed papers, magazines, ciggies, sweets and oddities like stamps and lottery tickets in a steady stream.

You'd think Gan would be pleased at all this trade, but all he did was stare morosely at the cold drinks cabinet and say that Hari ought to install a tea and coffee machine. 'Who's going to buy a cold drink on a day like this?'

Hari returned from his errands, announcing gloomily, 'Brass monkeys, isn't it?' as he came in. He studied me for signs of cholera, Black Death or Ebola, or failing that, simple old flu, and seemed disappointed that I was not only still on my feet but improved. Hari, though, isn't one to give up easily.

'All this wouldn't have happened if you were eating properly. And frankly, my dear, I have a bad conscience about you. Sleeping in that garage, it has made you ill.'

I tried to convince him that sleeping in the garage wasn't the problem. I'd stayed out in the rain too long the previous evening, that was all. At this, Gan gave me a reproachful look.

Hari went upstairs.

'I am trying to find somewhere to live,' I said. 'I can always move into Norman's place if nothing else.'

'Why were you out so long in the rain?' Ganesh demanded.

'I missed the bus. Oh, all right, I was watching for someone.

I can't tell you, Gan, honestly. But I will just as soon as it's all settled.'

'You're looking for Duke's killer,' he snapped. 'And you've got a suspect, haven't you? At least tell me who it is, then if you go missing, I'll have a name to give Inspector Morgan, somewhere she can start looking for you.'

Oddly, this made sense. I was nervous at the idea of meeting Jerry Wilde again. On the other hand, I didn't want Gan haring off to the police if I was just gone a few hours, nor to give him a name which could lead to Nicola. He might inadvertently let it slip. I compromised by writing the Wildes' name and address on a scrap of paper and sealing it in an envelope.

'You're not to open this unless I've been gone twenty-four hours without any contact, right?'

He grumbled a bit about this being the sort of thing characters in corny old films did, but agreed. I watched him tuck the envelope inside his blouson jacket and felt quite reassured. Not having Ganesh at my side in all this had been an extra difficulty. Having to continually put him off was placing a strain on our friendship.

'If ever I can tell you,' I said, 'you'll understand, I swear it, Gan. If it's any consolation, I really wish I could. I'm truly sorry.'

We exchanged sheepish smiles.

Jerry Wilde rang at twelve thirty, just as Hari had ordered me to go upstairs and have some lunch. His voice vibrated with ill-concealed fury. 'I'll meet you, but there had better be a good reason for this! I don't want you coming anywhere near Kew. Nicola tells me there was a beggar cadging loose change in the street last night. We never have beggars in this street. Was that you?'

'I don't beg!' I prevaricated. 'I'm an actor, and in between I work where I can.'

He made a disbelieving noise. 'Pull the other one. Anyway, shouldn't that be actress?'

'We don't say that any more.'

Another snort. 'Tomorrow's Sunday and I can't get away without Flora suspecting something. It'll have to be Monday, and well away from Kew.'

We argued a bit about where to meet, and settled for five o'clock on Monday afternoon at Oxford Circus Tube station, by the ticket dispenser. It would be rush hour and like a madhouse. It was unlikely anyone would notice us.

'Oxford Circus Tube?' Ganesh said suspiciously, as I put down the phone.

'The best place to hide is in a crowd,' I retorted.

That afternoon I went back to Susie's. I couldn't help but be concerned about her, and anyway, I wanted to tell her I'd seen Allerton, though I wasn't sure if that would prove any help.

The block of flats didn't look any better by daylight. But Susie did look a lot better than the last time I'd seen her. She recognised me, which surprised me a bit, remembering her fuddled state.

'Hello,' she greeted me, pulling open the door. 'C'mon in.'

She teetered ahead of me on insecure-looking black slingback heels. First sight of the living room showed me she'd tidied up the place and turned down the heating. No bottles or glasses were on view, though the ashtray was still filled with stubs. She made me coffee and we sat down to drink it under the gaze of the pottery cat in the fireplace. Susie had combed her hair back and twisted it into a roll secured with a big tortoiseshell clip. As well as the heels, she wore a black sweater, skirt and tights. A thought occurred to me.

'It wasn't today, was it?' I asked cautiously. 'Rennie's – um – you know.'

'Funeral?' She shook her head. 'No. I'm all done up like a dog's dinner because I'm expecting my sister. I've got to look like I'm holding it together or she'll be on to me to go back with her to Margate. She's got a good heart,' Susie conceded, 'but she's bossy, you know what I mean? If I give her a hint I'm not managing, I'm finished. So, I'm managing, right?' She grinned at me wryly.

'You're doing great,' I said, and meant it. I liked her a lot. I didn't understand what she'd seen in Rennie, but, well, that was one of life's many mysteries.

She held up a packet of fags to me, and when I shook my head, she took out one for herself and lit it. 'I ought to give up, cut down at least. But right now, it's not the moment.'

'Have you had any more thoughts about keeping the business on?' I asked.

She waved a hand to dispel the smoke. 'I dunno. I've had some funny old news. Seems Rennie was holding out on me.'

I perked up at that and tried not to look more than mildly interested. What had she found? A secret ledger detailing illicit income? A list of blackmail victims? In a way it was something even more surprising.

'He was insured,' she said. 'I never knew it. I found the policy, all paid up and everything in order. It was in there.' She pointed at the pottery cat. 'What a place to hide it. And he should've told me, shouldn't he? Daft to say nothing. It was only by chance I found it. I was looking at the cat, thinking of Rennie, turned it over and, I don't know why, looked through the hole in the base and saw there was something stuck in there, rolled up with an elastic band round it. I rang 'em up. I'll get a nice little sum of money. Poor Rennie.' She gazed meditatively at the cat. 'He did like his secrets.'

'So you can pay for the funeral, then,' I said, 'and still have a bit over. Perhaps you ought to think about taking that holiday in Ibiza.'

Susie shook her head. 'Not without Rennie. Like sitting on the beach with a ghost. No, but I've got time to think. 'Course, what I'd really like is to get away from here . . .' She gestured at the window to indicate the estate. 'But I don't know if I'll have enough to do that.'

She leaned back on the sofa and crossed her legs. The skirt was very short and if she flashed her pins like that at the funeral it would brighten up the undertaker's day. 'Rennie sometimes went to some really nice places in the line of business, you know. I don't mean clients invited him into their homes. They don't do that. The last thing they want is the neighbours knowing. But when he was carrying out enquiries, stake-outs, checking out the lie of the land, he went all over the place. He'd come home and tell me about it. There are some really nice places to live, you know, if you've got the readies.'

I thought of Mrs Mackenzie out at Wimbledon, and Flora and Jerry in Kew. None of them had even set foot in a place remotely like this flat in its crumbling, vandalised block. 'Yes, there are,' I agreed.

'Nice places and nice people,' Susie said dreamily. 'It must be lovely . . . Round here it gets worse every day.'

I told her I'd seen Allerton. She was interested but not hopeful. 'Thanks for trying, anyway,' she said. Her eyes rested on me speculatively. 'Why're you interested in who killed Rennie?'

I prevaricated. 'On the off-chance it might have something to do with me. He was found outside my place. I want to know if someone's tracking me.'

'You find that Mrs Marks?' she asked suddenly. She hadn't been as fuddled as she'd appeared last time.

Reluctantly, I admitted that I had. 'But Rennie hadn't been to see her. He'd phoned her and asked if he could, but he didn't – couldn't. She didn't know what he wanted. He hadn't said.'

I don't know if she believed I was telling the whole truth, and doubted she did. But she made as if she accepted that that was it. 'We'll never know what it was, then,' she said.

I left her, feeling cheered because she was making out a lot better than had seemed possible on my first visit. I passed a woman on the staircase. She was hurrying upwards. She wore a red raincoat and carried a dripping umbrella. She had the same blonde hair and thin features as Susie, but wore a truculent I-don't-stand-any-nonsense look. The Margate sister, a battleaxe, but one who cared. Susie would be all right. She'd been an additional worry lurking at the back of my mind, but now I could forget about her and concentrate on my own problems. No lucky pottery cats in my life.

Chapter Fourteen

On Sunday Ganesh borrowed Dilip's car again and drove me to Egham. It was quite a nice day, cool, but the rain was holding off and the sun managing to cast a pale glow over everything.

Ganesh came in to say hello to my mother, and when he'd gone, she said again what a nice young man he was. She then gave me the sort of look I remembered getting from Grandma Varady every time some unattached male personage of roughly suitable age with prospects of a steady job hove into view.

This visit I had some really nice news for her. 'I've spoken to Nicola, Mum. Only very briefly. I met her outside her house. She was on her way home. She'd got her violin case with her.'

Mum's face lit up. 'What did she say?'

This was a tricky one, but instinct told me that to invent a cosy conversation would only get me in deeper. It'd be a green light to Mum to ask me to go back and chat Nicola up again.

'She didn't know who I was,' I explained awkwardly. 'She, um, thought I might be a beggar.'

'I hope you told her you weren't!' Mum said indignantly.

I mumbled some reply before going on, 'Look, Mum, I've done all I can. I've found her, seen her, spoken to her. I've seen inside the house. I know she's musical and studying the violin. I don't think anyone could've found out more for you.'

'No,' she agreed. 'But it does seem a pity . . .'

'No, Mum,' I said gently. I put my hand over hers. 'She's a bright kid and she'll smell a rat if I follow this up any more.'

'I suppose so,' she said reluctantly. 'Thank you for doing so much. I don't think even poor Rennie could've done better. You ought to be a professional, Fran.'

It was a compliment, I supposed. I didn't tell her it hadn't been my first effort at tracking someone down and I considered myself to be quasi-professional already. In a sort of way.

When I rejoined Gan outside he'd been reading the map in the car and discovered Windsor Great Park was just up the road. So we drove there and parked and walked amongst the trees and lawns. It was all so nice and peaceful. There were plenty of other people walking, respectable, solid citizens with little children and little dogs. I felt happier than I had since Duke had first popped up in my life. I'd done what Mum wanted. She was pleased. All I had to do now was tell Jerry Wilde the police were looking for my missing sister and, having successfully passed the buck to him, skedaddle. How Wilde took the news and what he did about it was his own business.

Happiness took a bit of a dent at this point. If Wilde had killed Duke I wouldn't be safe until he thought he and his family were safe. The information I had for him told him they weren't, not by a long chalk. The most prudent thing I could do was to stay away from the Wildes as Jerry had demanded. Instead, I'd arranged to meet him the following day. And why? Because my conscience wouldn't let me rest if I didn't give them a warning. Sooner or later, I guessed,

Mrs Marks would pass on to the police what she'd told me. From then on, to the Wildes, it was only a step.

I got to Oxford Circus Tube station at ten to five on Monday afternoon and took up position by the ticket machines. I wanted to see Jerry Wilde coming before he saw me. I reckoned he'd come up the escalator from the northbound Bakerloo Line, having changed from the District Line at Embankment. At Oxford Circus, the Central, Victoria and Bakerloo lines intersect. That and its central London location, with direct access to the shopping of Oxford and Regent Streets, make the station a hive of activity at most times. At this hour of the afternoon it was just a rugby scrum. Everyone was in a hurry to catch a train, to get home. They'd spent long hours in the area's offices or trailing from big store to big store and were tired and bad-tempered. It's difficult to keep your cool in those circumstances. I was already feeling hassled myself, having got there via the Northern and Central Lines, as a journey a general free-for-all.

At least down here in the Tube it was warm, gusts of hot, stale air billowing up from the depths. The homeless would come down here to thaw out, given the chance, but the police regularly chase them out. The buskers are better at eluding authority, and despite notices everywhere on the Underground system, few of the corridors are without music. Personally I think the travellers like it. One or two of the buskers are really good. Some, like a chap I once knew called Sam, aren't. He was really rotten; his guitar playing was crap and he couldn't sing to save his life. Day after day he assaulted people's eardrums with discordant yowlings, but he made more money than some of the better ones because people pitied him for his lack of talent and admired his sheer brass neck.

I sipped from a can of Coke and kept my eye on the automatic gates at the head of the escalators. I saw one kid slip through without a ticket. He was about twelve and skinny. He'd been hanging about, waiting for a suitable person to follow. He spotted one in an absent-minded matron laden with Selfridges carriers. She fed her ticket into the slot and at that precise moment, beautifully timed, the kid stepped right up close behind her. The gates flew open, and both went through before she became more than marginally aware from the slight pressure at her back that she'd acquired a shadow. The gates snapped shut but only skimmed the kid's backside.

An orange-jacketed London Transport employee had spotted the manoeuvre, however, even in the milling crowd. He yelled out, 'Oi!' but he was too late: the kid was off, diving down the escalators, pushing by other travellers. The LT man was joined by a colleague and they debated what to do, before abandoning the prospect of a hopeless chase. As for the elderly shopper, she just looked bewildered, still not quite understanding what had happened. One day soon, when the kid had grown a fraction bigger, it wouldn't work any more. The gates would slam shut against his diaphragm, winding him. Then he'd have to think of something else.

I leaned back against the wall. The palm of my hand, gripping the can, was sweaty. I was nervous, even with so many people around. I was wearing my puffa jacket and clean jeans (courtesy of Hari's washing machine), but any claim to respectability was let down by my right boot, still laced with Ben's garden twine. I tipped that foot sole-up against the wall to disguise it. Then I glanced about me and froze. A little way off, intently studying the Tube plan on the wall, stood a familiar figure, hands in the pockets of his heavy winter-wear leather jacket, long black hair falling over his face. My heart sank. Just what I didn't need but should have foreseen. Ganesh had appointed himself my minder.

I'd not had the slightest idea he'd followed me. I was surprised Hari had given him time off and wondered what excuse he'd given. There was nothing I could do about it now. I couldn't march over there and demand to know just what on earth he thought he was playing at and did he mind not screwing up my nicely made arrangements. Sod's law meant that Jerry Wilde would choose just that moment to appear. If he saw me with someone else, ten to one he'd turn round and go back down to the trains and home. So I turned my head, ignoring Ganesh. He was ignoring me too, but I knew he'd located me. I wondered how long he thought he could stand there studying the map before one of the undercover boys hanging around central London's Tube stations decided he was a likely drugs pusher and nabbed him. You can spot the undercover boys with practice; they're the scruffiest and least likely-looking ones. In addition, London Transport police had arrived in the shape of a couple of uniformed coppers, probably looking out for beggars. Jerry Wilde wouldn't like the sight of them, either. To my relief, they moved off to check out elsewhere.

Not a moment too soon. So distracted had I been with all these possible spanners in the works materialising around me that I failed to see Jerry Wilde until he appeared in front of me.

'Well?' he said, by way of greeting. He loomed over me in a way that was meant to be and was intimidating. Though not a burly bloke, he was quite tall and appeared fit, the lean and muscular type. He probably played tennis or squash.

I pushed myself off the wall and tried not to look disconcerted. I couldn't see Gan, who'd abandoned the wall map and was presumably lurking elsewhere in a manner meant to be inconspicuous.

'I've got some news for you,' I said to Wilde. 'You won't like it. The reason I'm telling you at all is because, despite what you think, I want to protect Nicola from learning the truth too.'

'You are so sure you know what the truth is,' he hissed at me.

One of the Transport coppers had returned. He was watching us suspiciously. He'd probably noticed me before, and now I'd been joined by this well-heeled gent was deciding I was on the game and this was my pitch. Damn it, we were going to have to move out of here.

'We've got to go somewhere else,' I said to Wilde.

'You arranged here,' he replied stubbornly. 'I'm not changing the agreement.'

'So tell our friend in blue over there about it.'

He glanced sideways and his thin features twitched. 'All right. We'll go and find a coffee shop. There must be one around.'

We set off up the litter-strewn stairs to street level. People poured past us coming down to the Tube from the pavements above. I guessed Ganesh was behind me somewhere, a little like the kid who'd followed the woman through the gates, though not quite so close. It's a curious sensation when you know someone's following you but you don't know exactly where they are. The urge to check is instinctive. You have to concentrate on not turning round. I knew how Orpheus must have felt when Eurydice was following him out of Hades and quite understood how he hadn't been able to resist looking back.

Luckily Wilde was too concerned with his own problems to worry about mine, and didn't appear to notice my nerves. We struggled along wet Oxford Street pavements past the window displays, the roast chestnut braziers and *Big Issue* sellers, and finished up in the basement cafeteria at D.H. Evans with a couple of cups of coffee on the table between us. Two or three women shoppers sat a little further off, resting their feet, but there was no sign of Ganesh. I'd checked in every plate-glass window we'd passed, pretending an interest in everything from fashion to cookware, without spotting my very own knight in shining biker's jacket. I didn't think we'd lost him. He might have been there, close behind, but it was twilight now and the brightly lit windows didn't reflect as they did in daytime. Whatever his shadowing skills, I hoped Ganesh had more sense than to come into this café. He'd look a bit obvious, all on his own, ears flapping in our direction.

'So, what's this news?' Wilde was keeping to the lofty tone he'd adopted from the first.

'Before I begin,' I said, 'let's establish that you're no longer pretending Nicola isn't my sister.'

'I shall never think of my daughter as your sister!' he said angrily. 'However, without admitting anything, I understand why, in her present circumstances, Eva is expressing interest in her. This is despite the fact that nearly thirteen years ago she abandoned any claims she may have thought she had. What I don't admit is that she has any justification in pursuing that interest through you in the way she has. This is hounding me and my family. We have done nothing to deserve it.'

'Will you come off that high horse?' I'd had enough of this. 'You're in the wrong and you know it. Am I the one with something to hide? If you weren't dead worried, you wouldn't be here with me now. Like it or not, you and your wife and I are all in this together. I asked you to meet me today so I could warn you that the police have found out my mother had a baby. They know the baby was called Miranda and left the hospital with my mother, alive and well. They're now curious to know what happened to her.'

That rocked him and knocked all the pomposity out of him. His face turned a ghastly greenish-grey. I thought he was going to throw up and got ready to dodge.

'Police?' he whispered.

I nodded. 'But don't worry. I haven't grassed and I won't. Nor will my mother tell them what she did if they get to ask her. She isn't afraid of the police, not with things being the way they are for her. They might not get to question her at all if the hospice has anything to do with it.'

'I don't believe this!' he burst out. 'It's some trick of yours to con money out of me.'

'Please yourself,' I told him. 'I don't want your money. It'd be like the thirty pieces of silver they paid Judas Iscariot, and that didn't do him any good. I'm warning you for Nicola's sake, that's all.'

He licked his lips. 'All this has happened because of you and your damn prying.'

'No, this particular thing has happened because someone croaked Clarence Duke and brought the cops in on it.'

I waited for his reaction to that. I don't know what I expected. That he'd start back with exaggerated gestures like an actor in a silent movie? Roll his eyes, look shifty and say he didn't know what I meant? If so, I was disappointed. He was either a lot better actor than that, or he really didn't know what I was talking about.

He looked puzzled, then faintly annoyed. 'Who the devil is Clarence – what?'

'Duke,' I said. 'He was a private detective. Now he's a dead private detective. His death is what brought the police into this business. Not me. Not my mother.'

'Private detective,' he muttered. 'Flora said you'd mentioned one to her. Said your mother had set one on to finding you, nothing about finding Nicola.' He raised his head, eyes filled with suspicion.

'He found me,' I said. 'Then someone found him.'

'I don't know.' He was shaking his head. He looked confused and, for a moment, quite ill. 'This is – is shattering. What am I going to tell my wife? She's of a very nervous disposition. But look, even if the police know your mother had a child, they can't track her down, not if your mother doesn't tell them where to look – or you don't.'

He didn't, fortunately, know about Mrs Marks and her daughter Linda, and I wasn't about to tell him. I didn't need to.

I scotched his hopes for him with, 'Don't bet on it. The police are professionals when it comes to tracking people down. They're quite capable of checking all the births in that hospital at the time. The inspector in charge, Janice Morgan, is really bright. Give her time and she'll think of it.'

He passed a hand over his brow in a gesture which struck me as slightly theatrical, but perhaps that was just my prejudice.

'I don't know what to think . . .' he mumbled.

'All right, get your head round this. Far too many people know about my mother's other daughter. It's only a matter of time before they track her down. So what are you – are *we* – going to do about it?'

He stared down at his cooling cup of coffee for a moment, then appeared to make a decision and, in doing so to get back his nerve. He raised his head and the familiar self-righteous aggressiveness was back in his face.

'We have kept scrupulously to any understanding with your mother. It is she who is breaking the terms of the agreement, not us. Perhaps we were wrong, as you put it, to reach any such understanding. Though I dispute your use of the word. It was only technically wrong. Morally, it was justified; more than that, it was right. Can you imagine how my wife and I felt when told our child had died? That Flora couldn't have another? No, of course you can't. Can you just try for a moment? We were devastated. Our world had fallen apart. Flora was almost out of her senses with grief. She couldn't believe it had happened. She didn't want to believe it. She talked of our baby as if she – as if she were still alive. At that point, our darkest hour, we walked into your mother. I believed then and still believe now it was meant. Whoever rules our lives, whether it's God or Fate or whatever you believe it to be, that power put your mother in our path at that moment.

'It was so – so simple. Your mother couldn't keep Nicola. We could offer her a loving, secure and comfortable home. It would save my wife's sanity as well. What's wrong with any of that? It wasn't done legally, by the letter of the law, I know. If we'd had time to think it over, had clearer heads at the time, we might have gone about it differently. But we didn't.

Once the dice have been rolled, you can't change them. Life doesn't give you a second throw. We took Nicola. We made her ours. She *is* ours.'

It was a pity, from his point of view, that he spoke the last words. He'd been doing well up to then, undermining my confidence. He'd about talked me round to his and Flora's viewpoint on the whole business. What did I know of how a parent who has lost a child might feel? What did I understand of the emotions of a woman who longed for children but had been told she'd be forever childless? A woman who, before Nicola arrived in her life, had had to content herself with fussing over lonely little boys like Ben? What allowance had I made for the desperate state the distraught Wildes had been in at the time they'd made the pact with my mother? It was I, not Jerry, who had been adopting a tone of moral superiority.

Or that was how I'd begun to think until he'd spoken the word 'ours'. Then I remembered that there was probably nothing, but nothing, he wouldn't do to protect the child he saw as 'his'. Something I suspected might even have already led him to murder.

Fired up, and as obstinate as he was, I retorted, 'People don't own other people, right? We don't have slavery in this country. They banned it a couple of centuries ago. Parents don't own their children. The only person to own Nicola's life is Nicola herself. It's up to her how she uses it. Perhaps she'll make a career in music, as you seem to think she should. Perhaps she'll chuck it all up and do something quite different. You know, be an air hostess or a nuclear physicist, or a singer in a sleazy bar in Soho.'

'We wouldn't stand in her way,' he said stiffly, 'unless, of course, she chose the last.'

'I bet,' I said sceptically. 'But what are we going to do now? That's the big question.'

An angry red suffused his face. He pushed away his untouched coffee. 'Whatever I decide – my wife and I decide – it's our business, ours alone. You are not required to do anything but stop hanging around my house. If anyone is going to lead the police to us, it's going to be you, by your behaviour. How do I know they're not watching you? How do I know we weren't tailed here this afternoon?'

He gave a hunted look round the area but saw only the lady shoppers gathering up their packages in preparation to leave.

It was a bit late for him to think of that. But just as well he hadn't thought of it earlier. He might have spotted Gan. Where *was* Gan?

'All I want from you,' Wilde was saying, 'is your assurance that you'll stay away from my house and my family.'

I had nothing further to gain from going back to his neck of the woods. 'I'll stay away,' I promised.

Wilde got to his feet, towering over me again as I sat at the table. 'I hope you remember that, Fran Varady. I really hope you remember.' His voice was quiet but scared the living daylights out of me.

I watched him go with relief. My coffee was cold now and undrinkable, which was a pity. I fancied a cup. I gave Wilde time to get clear and then left the café. Ganesh was in the luggage department in the basement, reading all the price tags. A sales assistant was bearing down on him, the light of enthusiasm in his eye, determined to make an unexpected sale this late in the day. He'd be lucky.

I could've hailed Ganesh and rescued him but I was entitled

to express my displeasure at his interference. I sailed past him and out of the shop. I only went as far as back to Oxford Circus, where I waited at the top of the steps down to the Tube, leaning on the balustrade.

After about ten minutes, he joined me.

'Couldn't find what you wanted?' I asked.

'At those prices? Are you joking?'

'Gan,' I said, 'believe me, I appreciate your concern. But it could have gone horribly wrong back there if my companion had spotted you in the Tube station.'

'It could have gone horribly wrong full stop,' argued Ganesh. 'That's why I was there.'

'Gan, I can look after myself. I am more than capable of dealing with one bloke in the middle of Oxford Street!'

'You know, Fran,' Ganesh looked at me seriously, 'sometimes you really act too big for your boots.'

That reminded me. 'Boots! I need new laces.' I looked back at the brightly lit stores.

Ganesh took me firmly by the elbow. 'We sell them back at the shop.'

We rocked back home on the dear old Northern Line tumbrel. At least Ganesh didn't pepper me with questions about who said what during my chat with Wilde. He asked just one, but it was a good 'un.

'This guy you were with, you think he did for Duke?'

'I don't know. He's the best suspect I've got.'

'Tell Morgan about him.'

'Can't. Involves other people.'

'Right,' said Ganesh, and lapsed into silence.

The person sitting next to me jumped up and leapt out at

Euston, in such a hurry to catch his train he forgot his *Evening Standard*. I snaffled it and buried my head in it during the remainder of the ride, just in case Ganesh thought of another question. The news on offer that evening was pretty routine. Politicians were up to their usual tricks. There was a good deal about the forthcoming selection of candidates for the London mayoral elections. Some media personality had a new girlfriend. I wasn't interested in the financial reports. I read the cartoons, considered doing the (easier) crossword on the back page, abandoned the idea as I didn't have enough time before we got off, and was about to chuck the paper back on the seat for the next person when my eye caught a small paragraph tucked away at the bottom of a page with the heading:

MOTHER APPEALS
Police widen hunt for missing nurse.
Enquiries to date have failed to turn up . . .

'Come on,' said Gan, tapping my arm. 'We get off here.'

I tossed down the paper. We always feel we're the only person to have a particular problem. But the world is full of people struggling with a variation of the same thing that's bugging us. That other hunt for a missing daughter was still going on. The country was full of missing persons, that was the problem. People go missing for all sorts of reasons. They're scared of someone; they have abusive home lives; they're in debt; they just feel like dropping out; they suffer amnesia; a few are victims of crime. Families go on looking. They never give up that hope. You see the appeals in the *Big Issue*. Some of those people have been missing for years, just as my mother dropped out of our lives for years. But, like my mother, they can still turn up. I wondered for how many, when they did surface, more problems were created than solved.

But none of it, any longer, was my concern. I'd warned Jerry and Flora that the police were looking for a child who'd slipped out of the records thirteen years before. I couldn't do any more except keep out of the Wildes' way, which I was happy to do. I'd done as Mum had wanted and told her about it, and no one could ask anything more of me. There was still the question of who'd killed Rennie Duke. But the more I thought about it, the more my brain kicked in with reasons why Jerry Wilde wasn't the culprit. Duke was a private detective and a nosy one. His wife said so and she should know. He liked to pry. Who knows what he was up to besides checking on what Mum might have done all those years ago?

'You know, Gan,' I said as we walked from the Tube back to the shop, 'Rennie Duke was just the type to upset any number of people, some of them dangerous. Any one of them could have been tracking him or put out a contract on him. It just so happened that the killer found him outside the garage that night. His death doesn't have to have anything to do with me at all.'

Which meant that I wasn't in any danger, either. Duke's killer, whoever he was and whatever his motive, would have gone to ground and wouldn't surface in this part of London for a very long time. I felt like dancing.

'Inspector Morgan will be checking all Duke's cases,' said Ganesh.

I recalled the confidence in Morgan I'd expressed to Jerry Wilde. 'Yes, she will,' I agreed. 'Naturally she quizzed me to start with. She was bound to, wasn't she? You and I, we found him. We knew him. But if the cops are enquiring into Duke's background, by now they must have come up with a bumper file of suspects.'

Ganesh looked at me suspiciously. 'You're very chipper all of a sudden.'

'Of course I am. The heat's off me. Whoever killed Duke probably hadn't the slightest idea I was sleeping in Hari's garage or that there was anyone around at all. He doesn't know about me, Gan. I'm in the clear.' Euphoria made me generous. 'I'll take you out and buy you a veggie burger and a beer tonight.'

'I don't want to rain on your parade or anything,' said Ganesh, sounding a little embarrassed. 'I'm the last person who wants you setting up rendezvous with dodgy blokes in Tube stations. As far as I'm concerned, if all this means you're not doing any more detecting, that's great. You are sure about this, though? You're not going to wake up tomorrow with some new and wonderful idea for investigating Duke's death?'

'Sure I'm sure!' I promised. 'Rennie Duke's death had nothing to do with me or my mother. I'm leaving it all to Inspector Janice.'

Who would have been very pleased to hear me say it, had she been there. Failing that, I had to make do with Ganesh's approval, but having that was nice too. Also rare.

Chapter Fifteen

Though my mother was constantly on my mind, as far as other things went, I was still well in control on Tuesday morning. So much so that I was able to think about things which were *not* connected with the Wildes or the late Clarence Duke. I trotted round to Reekie Jimmie's to see how he was getting on with transforming his potato café into a trattoria and when I might expect to start work.

I had a bit of a shock when I saw the place. I had imagined that Jimmie intended to slap a little paint around, hang up a couple of Chianti bottles, install a plastic plant or two and be happy with that. But the first thing I saw as I approached was a signwriter just putting the finishing touches to the legend *Ristorante Pizzeria San Gennaro* above the door. Beyond him, the interior of the place had been gutted. Carpenters were hammering and sawing and a plasterer was relining the walls. Various other guys milled around gesticulating and arguing.

I sidled through the doorway. I could now hear that they were all talking to one another in Italian. This seemed to be carrying thoroughness in conversion of the café to unheard-of extremes. How genuine did Jimmie want to get? How much money was he spending? I avoided a hole in the floorboards and a crouching electrician, tried not to breathe in too much dust and sought out Jimmie in the back room. On my way, each workman I passed looked up, flashed teeth at me and managed to suggest by body language that he was the best chance I was likely to get all week.

Jimmie wasn't alone in the back room. With him was a small neat man in a black overcoat who appeared about to take his leave. He had gathered up a document case and a pair of black leather gloves. He gave me a razor-sharp stare which contrasted startlingly with his smiling mouth beneath a rather droopy moustache.

'Come on in, hen!' urged Jimmie as I hung back, unwilling to barge in unwanted. 'Just the person. Now then, Silvio, this young lady is going to be one of our waitresses. We're lucky to get her.' He gestured at me proudly, before qualifying his enthusiasm by adding, 'Don't worry about the boots, she's a nice Catholic girl from a good home.'

What? I live in a garage, Jimmie! I didn't say this, probably because I was too startled, but I certainly thought it.

Jimmie was beaming at me and urging me forward with a beckoning hand. I walked towards him obediently, feeling stupid. You know how when you're small, proud but misguided relatives want to show you off, as they put it, though they really mean show you up? They get you to sing or recite or play the piano or something else really grim. You do it knowing that it's awful; that you've forgotten the words of the poem or middle C on the piano has gone mute so that it only rattles when you strike it. I had that feeling again, just as when I was five.

Silvio studied me carefully from head to foot and apparently decided I passed muster. He asked me my name. His accent was only faint and his hands didn't look as if they ever did any rough work. His nails were manicured and he wore a broad wedding ring and what I fancied was a genuine Rolex, not the sort bought from a chap with a suitcase full of them. Otherwise he was a middle-aged, well-dressed balding version of the blokes out front. When I told him I was called Fran, short for Francesca, he flashed his gold teeth at me and informed me that I had an Italian name, as if I rather than my parents could claim some personal credit for this. I didn't point out that my family was Hungarian in origin and the choice of name had just been because my dad liked it.

Anyway, to my relief, Silvio had lost interest in me. I had the feeling I'd been let off lightly. He walked out briskly, drawing on his black leather gloves as he went. I heard him issuing what sounded remarkably like orders to the men outside. I swear one of them replied, '*Si, Don Silvio.*'

Jimmie shut the door and gave me a somewhat sheepish look. 'Cup of coffee, hen?'

'Jimmie,' I said, 'who on earth is that? And what do you mean by giving him that spiel about me? I am not and never have been what he probably calls respectable.'

He avoided my eye. 'Silvio? He's my new partner. He's a very nice feller, a gentleman. Guys like him, they're sort of traditional, do you know what I mean? That's why I said what I did about you. Every word of it true, mind you!'

Jimmie wagged a nicotine-stained finger at me. I wasn't to be diverted.

'Partner, Jimmie? I didn't know you did business with a partner.'

Jimmie looked defensive. 'It costs money to turn this place from what I had into an upmarket eatery. We're going to apply for a drinks licence. Where my old counter was, that's going to be the bar. The whole area's going to be tiled with genuine Italian glazed tiles from a factory owned by Silvio's cousin in Naples. Between you and me,' Jimmie added, looking furtive and lowering his voice, 'Silvio's putting up most of the cash, but I'm going to be the front man, I mean, manager. I wouldn't want a lot of people knowing about that. But I know I can trust you.'

He could trust me, but I wondered how far he could trust Silvio and his crew. 'They all seem sort of the same,' I said, indicating the workmen in the front of the premises.

'They're all Italian,' said Jimmie. 'Hadn't you noticed?'

'I couldn't fail to notice,' I retorted. 'That's not what I mean. It's something else.'

'It'll be the family resemblance,' said Jimmie. 'They're all sons and nephews and so on of Silvio. He believes in keeping things in the family.'

Why did the word 'family' have a slightly ominous ring in my ears? As tactfully as possible I asked how this partnership had come about.

'A bit of luck,' Jimmie told me. 'Silvio was planning to go into the restaurant business. He heard about my idea for turning the old spud place into a pizza speciality and came round to take a look. He explained that if I went into partnership with him, we'd be looking at a chain of places, all in the same style, you know, so the punters can recognise them. He had the money. He just wanted a premises to start up, and this is a prime location. I mean, I couldn't turn down a chance like that, now could I?'

All I needed to hear. As far as I could see, Jimmie had had an offer he couldn't refuse, and hadn't refused it, even without realising that there wasn't an alternative.

'Jimmie,' I began, but changed my mind. This was definitely a moment to turn a blind eye. 'When do you think you'll be ready to open?'

'Shouldn't be too long,' said Jimmie confidently. 'We've had none of the usual problems with the suppliers, and Silvio's boys are ace workers.'

'Cheers, Jimmie.'

I picked my way back through the ogling craftsmen in the front of the shop and went back to the newsagent's.

'How's Jimmie getting along then?' asked Ganesh.

'Fine. On his way to being a partner in a nationwide chain of money-spinners. There's a little matter of being taken over by the Mafia, probably to launder dirty money, but hey! Jimmie's happy, so who am I to quibble?' I explained the reasoning which had led me to this conclusion. 'Maybe at least one of those stories you always hear about Jimmie is true. Perhaps he did rule an underworld gang from behind that baked spud bar.'

'Don't be daft,' said Ganesh. 'You've seen *The Godfather* too many times.'

'You're probably right,' I admitted. After all, I'd had second thoughts about Jerry Wilde being a murderer. My problem was, I concluded, I had too much imagination. It came from being a frustrated creative artist.

My gung-ho attitude to the Wildes lasted only until lunchtime, when I received a telephone call at the shop.

'For you,' said Ganesh, handing over the receiver.

I left the cigarettes I'd been stacking and mouthed, 'Who?'

'Girl.'

Girl? I took the receiver gingerly and put it to my ear as if it would explode and perforate my eardrum. It didn't do that, but it gave me a shock, even so.

'I want to speak to Fran Varady,' said a firm young female voice.

'Speaking . . .' I replied cautiously.

'This is Nicola Wilde.'

I didn't say anything. I couldn't.

'Hello? Hello?' she was shouting into the phone at her end. 'Are you still there?'

'Where did you get this number?' I croaked.

'I haven't got time to go into that now,' was the impatient retort. 'I'm phoning in my lunch hour. I'm at school. I've had to shut myself in the sports equipment cupboard.'

'They've got a phone in there?' This was some private school.

'No!' Irritable. 'I'm on my mobile.'

Of course. Silly me.

'I want to talk to you.' She was on the offensive again.

'Not a good idea,' I managed, rallying.

'Why not? You were hanging around outside our house the other evening, weren't you? I bet it was you. You asked me for change. You knew my name. Well, I'm fed up with being left out of everything. I want to know what's going on. I want to meet you.'

'No,' I said.

'Why not?'

'I promised your father.'

'He needn't know. Listen, I've told my mother I'm going over to a friend's house tonight after school to do some homework. I've done that before, so she's quite happy. I'll meet you at Earls Court Tube station, at the foot of the stairs up from the platforms, Upminster line.'

A clammy sense of déjà vu swept over me. Fixing up rendezvous at Tube stations seemed to be a Wilde speciality. The only thing lacking was for Flora to ring me and suggest a meeting at Notting Hill Gate.

'About five,' ordered the voice in my ear. She was used to getting her own way. If she was feeling left out now over present events, it must be a first, and she didn't like it.

I found myself meekly agreeing. Perhaps, after all, a subconscious urge to take a closer look at her moved me.

'So?' asked Ganesh as I put down the receiver. 'You look pretty rattled.'

'I am rattled,' I said. 'I've got to go and hold a schoolgirl's hand.'

It took me longer than I'd allowed for to get out to Earls Court that evening, and she'd arrived before me. I saw her as I walked towards the meeting point. She was in a crowd, but for me it was as if no one was around her. I felt everyone would be looking, everyone would see us together. Any of these hurrying regulars on this line might know Jerry, recognise Nicola, pass on the word.

My sister did not look pleased. She was scanning faces, frowning, and chewing on her lower lip. When she saw me, she just looked grumpier.

'I thought you weren't going to come!' she greeted me truculently.

'Hey, it's rush hour, all right? Nor do I jump when you shout, okay? Just so we're clear on that. You're lucky I'm here at all.' Curiosity overcame me. 'What were you going to do if I didn't turn up?'

'Phone that number again and keep on phoning it until you did come.'

'I bet you scream and scream until you're sick, too,' I said.

She looked blank. She hadn't read the same childhood books I had.

'Just for starters,' I said, 'how *did* you get my number?'

'Oh, that.' She tossed her hair. No longer in the wet rat's tails as when I'd seen her under the lamplight, it was pale blonde and twisted in a mass of narrow curls. She had well-defined eyebrows and pale-blue eyes. Her nose was short and straight, cheekbones wide and pronounced, mouth generous even set, as it was now, in an angry line. She looked like my mother – our mother. Or as I remembered my mother all those years ago, before her illness. She looked more like her than I did, certainly. I'd taken after the Varady side. Grandma had repeatedly told me so. As for Nicola's father, Mum had given no clue as to who he had been, but it didn't matter. He hadn't got to pass on his looks. This girl was a Nagy.

'It was the evening you waited outside the house,' she was saying. 'Later on Ben Cornish came to have dinner with us. He was a bit late. Mummy was out in the kitchen cooking. I'd gone upstairs to sort my books for the next day. I heard Ben come and I went out on to the landing. I meant to lean over the banisters and call down to him. I like Ben. Do you like Ben?' She peered at me in a manner I can only call hostile. Ben was the subject of a crush, clearly. She wanted to know if I'd strayed on to what she saw as her territory.

'Never mind what I like,' I said. 'Go on.'

She looked miffed and chalked up a mental black mark again me, but she went on. 'Well, before I could call down, Dad and Ben had started talking. Ben looked sort of shifty.

They were whispering. So I listened. They didn't know I was there. Neither of them looked up. I heard the name "Fran Varady". Ben said he'd been talking to you. Dad swore.' She seemed vaguely entertained by this.

'Then Dad said that my mother mustn't know. Ben said, of course not. He took a bit of paper from his jacket pocket and showed Dad. Dad said he'd call you; I mean, he said, "I'll call her when I get the chance, but for God's sake, keep it from Flora." Then he took out his pocket diary and copied down a number from the paper Ben held out. Ben folded it up and put it back in his jacket pocket. Then he took off the jacket and hung it in the hall. They went into the kitchen to say hello to Mummy. I came down. I could hear them in the kitchen talking about some new wine or other Dad wanted to try, so I knew they weren't coming back at once. I looked in Ben's pocket, found the number and made my own copy. Easy.'

Now she definitely looked smug. Trains were coming in and out. People swirled around us. It was chilly and not very comfortable standing on the platform but it was still the best place. I didn't know of a café around here and I could hardly take her into a pub. I suggested we walk up and down. It's easier on the legs to keep moving, rather than just stand planted like a couple of posts.

'Look,' I said to her, 'the bit of business I had to discuss with your father, I'm not prepared to talk about it to you.'

She thrust her angry little face at me. 'Well, I'm fed up with being left out! Don't tell me it hasn't got anything to do with me, because I jolly well know it has! They've been talking about me for a while now. I've heard them whispering together. Then last night Dad came out with this crackpot idea that Mummy and I should go on a holiday abroad, right away, like now! I mean, it's term-time. I've got a violin exam coming up. I've been practising like mad. I kicked up a fuss and said I wouldn't go. They both looked so upset. Something's going on and I want to know what it is!'

'Have you asked them?'

'Of course I have!' she shouted. Then, more quietly and sullenly, 'But I didn't get anywhere. What can be so secret? It's stupid.' She stared at me. 'You know, if I hadn't seen you that evening, in the rain, I might have thought you were Dad's girlfriend. My friend Naomi's dad is always having different girlfriends. Her parents row over it. But my dad hasn't ever done anything like that. Anyway, I'd seen you, and obviously you couldn't be anyone's girlfriend, well, not someone like my dad.'

'I'm not your dad's girlfriend,' I said sniffily. 'He wouldn't be my type.' Cheeky little madam. It just so happens several blokes have told me I'm attractive, and not everyone is put off by muddy boots, one of them laced with string. I didn't think Ben was, for a start, and if I'd wanted revenge on her for the cutting remark, I could have taken it there and then. I remembered she was only just on thirteen and nobly kept silent. Only fight your own weight.

'So, are you going to tell me?' she insisted.

'No, I'm not, and you can phone the shop until you're blue in the face, but I'm not meeting you again. I'm wasting my time meeting you now. This conversation is going nowhere.'

I then made the mistake of adopting the superior adult approach. I ought to have known better. It had never worked with me when I was her age.

'Believe me, Nicola, it's nothing for you to worry about.

Just go home and put the whole thing out of your mind.'

Whoosh! Did she blow up then! She actually stamped her foot. 'How can I? Everyone treats me as if I were a kid, as if I were thick! I'm not a kid, I'm almost thirteen and I'm not thick! Something's wrong and it's been wrong for several weeks. So don't tell me not to worry or not to let my imagination run riot or any of the other crummy things people have been telling me!'

Something wasn't right here. I didn't know how long Mum had been in the hospice, but I had only started looking for Nicola just over a week ago. Yet here she was claiming something had been wrong for several weeks, well before my arrival on the scene. Her parents had been discussing her surreptitiously for 'a while'. The only other person I could think of who might have been stirring up muddy waters was the late Clarence Duke. All my old suspicion of Jerry Wilde came back. What if Duke had been on the track of Nicola before me? What if Jerry had found out and was panicked into drastic action?

'Nicola,' I began carefully, 'does the name Clarence or Rennie Duke mean anything to you?'

She shook her head. 'Who is he?'

'Just someone I met the other day. I thought he might have been to see your parents. He w – he's a little thin bloke, drives a jade-green car.'

'I don't know anything about him,' she muttered. She kicked at the ground. 'No one tells me anything. You could but you won't. But I know something's up and it all started when I told Mummy about Nurse Cooper.'

I whirled round so fast I nearly stumbled over the edge of the platform into the path of the approaching Barking train, putting paid to my investigations altogether. 'Who's Nurse Cooper?'

Nicola looked surprised. 'Oh, she came to talk to my class. We've had all kinds of people coming in, different professions, to talk to us. It's the headmistress's idea. Supposed to give us ideas about what we'd like to do when we leave school. Nurse Cooper came to talk to us about being a nurse, you know, and how long it takes to train and the different sorts of specialities. I wasn't really interested because I want to be a professional musician. But she said she'd trained at St Margaret's Hospital, and that interested me because I was born in St Margaret's. So afterwards, when we were all chatting to her, I told her that. I didn't have anything else I wanted to ask her but I felt I had to say something to her. She was interested. She asked how old I was and said I must have been born there when she was just starting her training . . . What's up?' She broke off and stared at me. 'You look funny,' she said.

'I'm cold,' I said. 'And pretty fed up with standing around here listening to you. Did you see this nurse person again, after she spoke to your school?'

She shook her head. 'No, but I went home and told Mummy about it all. I didn't think she'd be really interested, but she was. She kept asking me if I was sure it was St Margaret's. Later on that evening when Dad came home, she told him about it. It seemed sort of odd to me. Why would they care?' She shrugged. 'Anyway, it was after that that things started to go peculiar. There's been an atmosphere ever since. Really freaky.'

'It's been nice talking to you, Nicola,' I said briskly, 'but I really think you ought to go home now. You never know, your mother might ring your friend's house with a message for you or something. You don't want her to find out you lied, do you? Nor is it a good idea for either of your parents to know you've talked to me, right? I really mean that. As for whatever it is your parents have got worrying them, you have to respect their right not to tell you about it.'

She looked mutinous, lower lip thrust out.

'Nicola,' I urged, 'part of growing up is learning to respect other people's need for privacy. I'm sure you've got your secrets from your parents. If they have some problem they don't wish to discuss with you, I think it would be mature of you to accept that.'

She still didn't look happy, dragging her toe through the grime on the platform. 'I'm not agreeing to go on some stupid holiday when I've got my exams coming up.'

'Fair enough. Explain that to your parents. Then leave it at that, right?'

She mumbled something and we parted. I wasn't at all sure she was going to leave things alone. She was persistent and curious and, heck, a lot like me. I wouldn't have given up easily at her age. I'd just have got more devious. Nicola, a kid who listened in on other people's conversations and searched their pockets, would, I fancied, think of some other stratagem. But I had no time for that. I had other things to do.

Lights shone from almost every window at Newspaper Norman's place. It looked as if everyone was in for supper. I rang the bell and called through the letter-gap and eventually Norman came shuffling down the hall.

'Come in, dear,' he invited. 'I've been expecting you. Come about the room, I expect.' He had a grubby apron tied round his middle over his red jogging pants.

'Well, no, Norman, not exactly. I haven't quite made up my mind about that.'

He looked surprised and reproachful. 'I've been holding it for you. Several people have been to look and expressed lively interest.'

I suggested, as tactfully as I could, that perhaps it would be best if he let it to one of them.

'Norman, I've actually come round to see if you can help me over something else. It's about a newspaper story . . .'

Norman brightened. 'Let me go and switch off the cooker. I was just about to start on a few chips.'

He trotted off towards the kitchen. I made my way into the room on my left and gazed with misgiving at the stacks of newsprint lying around everywhere. I wished Norman hadn't mentioned making chips. Chip pans are a prime source of house fires.

'You know, Norman,' I said when he came back, 'you ought to get a smoke detector put in the hall. Just think, if anything happened to destroy your newspaper collection, what would you do?'

He looked horrified. 'Don't even speak of it, dear. It would be a disaster! Now I can take you back to nineteen seventy-three.' He pursed his lips. 'Those would be in the other room.'

There was another room like this? Norman was considering the smoke alarm idea. 'I'll give it some thought, dear. What can I do for you? Offer you a sherry, perhaps?'

I declined the sherry. 'Recently there's been a running story about a missing nurse.'

Norman clicked his fingers. 'I know the one. All of them have covered it. Do you prefer a broadsheet or a tabloid account?'

'The fullest one, please. Oh, and last night's *Evening Standard*.'

He sat me down in a sagging armchair and began ferreting away happily in his boxes and cupboards. 'I have an infallible filing system,' he told me.

'Great, Norm,' I said. Goodness only knows what it was.

Eventually he came back with an armful of papers, and after searching through them one at a time, he laid a selection before me. 'Sure you won't have a sherry while you're reading? It'll take a while.'

I'd already grabbed the first paper and was scanning it eagerly. Norman must have taken this as acceptance of his offer, and produced a bottle and glasses from a small wall cupboard which must have been the only one without newspapers in it.

I read on, then sat back, my head spinning. LeeAnne Cooper, the missing nurse whose mother had been appealing for news, was a thirty-one-year-old divorcee who shared a flat with a nursing colleague. Her former husband worked abroad, had been traced, and was out of the picture. She had no current boyfriend but was described as friendly, outgoing and capable. She had done a lot of work with young people and charity. No one could imagine what had happened. To disappear was not in her character.

Then, one line in one paper only, a tiny bombshell hidden among all the rest. Asked if LeeAnne had expressed any worries, the flatmate had mentioned that the missing woman had been concerned that she wasn't earning enough to buy a flat of her own. This was followed by some general observations by the paper on nursing pay.

I sat back. It was horribly, hideously clear to me. Fate had led LeeAnne Cooper to give a talk at Nicola's school. LeeAnne, one of the few people who would know that baby Nicola Wilde had died in St Margaret's Hospital thirteen years ago, without ever going home. And Nurse LeeAnne Cooper was feeling short of money.

'Drink your sherry, dear,' said Norman. 'You look a bit pale, in need of a restorative.'

'Yes,' I said. 'I think I am.'

Chapter Sixteen

I don't like breaking promises and generally do my very best not to, but this time it was being forced on me. I just couldn't handle this alone any more. I was going to have to tell Ganesh everything.

I hoped my mother would understand, even though it was going directly against her expressed wish. Hadn't she said to me that all anyone can do is make a decision and then live with it afterwards? What I couldn't live with was the thought of a killer. What I didn't know was what I was going to do about it. I didn't expect Gan to come up with the answers, but I needed to share the responsibility. He had, after all, been feeling left out. He was about to be brought in with a vengeance.

They were just shutting up the shop when I got there. I nipped in through the door as Gan was closing it. He flipped the card hanging in it round to *Closed* and slid the bolts. Hari was busy behind the counter. Gan and I looked at one another. I knew my face was a picture of misery.

'I see your good mood didn't last long,' said Gan. 'Am I to be told what's happened to knock you off your happy little cloud?'

I rallied with, 'Not if you're going to be sarcastic!' and

then surrendered with a pitiful. 'I'm in an awful fix, Gan.'

He glanced at Hari. 'Just give me half an hour to finish up here and we'll go somewhere quiet and you can tell me all.'

I told him I'd wait in the garage. I exchanged a brief 'Good evening!' with Hari, who asked me absent-mindedly how I was as he shovelled cash into little bags. I don't know what I replied. Whatever it was, he probably didn't hear me.

Bonnie jumped up happily when I appeared in the storeroom, but even she sensed my mood and her exuberance was dampened. She followed me out to the garage and sat down, head on one side and one ear cocked, wondering what was going on. I opened a tin of dog food and spooned out her supper. She might have been worried about me but she didn't let it come between her and her food. Like me, Bonnie is a survivor. You don't turn down a meal when you're not sure where the next one's coming from.

Gan appeared in twenty-five minutes holding two cans of Coke from the cold cabinet. He handed me one and hauled up a crate to sit on.

'Are you in trouble with the law?' he asked, popping his Coke can.

'Yes and no. I will be if Morgan finds out what I've been doing.'

I took a deep breath and, starting at the beginning, explained the whole deal to him. He sipped at his Coke but didn't say a word. When I'd finished, he shook the can to check it was empty, set it down on the floor and said: 'I know what I'd like to say to you.'

'I can guess.'

'Fine, so I won't say it. But I'm glad you've told me now, Fran.'

'I did feel mean leaving you out,' I confessed. 'But I'm not too happy now I've told you, either, because I've dragged you into it with me. I wanted to keep you out of it, out of the Nicola bit, anyway. I couldn't keep you out of the Rennie Duke bit.'

'About this nurse—' he began.

'Don't say it's a mix-up of some sort, because it isn't. How many Nurse Coopers are likely to pop up in one connection? I can see what happened. She obviously had a good memory. When Nicola started talking to her she remembered the Wildes. Who knows? She was new on the job at St Margaret's when all this happened. Perhaps it was the first time she'd had to deal with parents who'd lost a child. It made a big impression on her. Anyway, even though it was thirteen years ago, she knew that what Nicola was saying was all wrong. Nicola may have been born in St Margaret's but she wasn't Flora's kid.'

'She might have been adopted quite legally,' Ganesh interposed. 'Nurse Cooper wasn't to know.'

'Nurse Cooper smelled a rat,' I said obstinately. 'So she trotted off to see Flora Wilde and check it all out. If she was right, and Nicola wasn't legally adopted, there was money in it. Blackmail's a nasty thing but things hadn't been going well for LeeAnne. She was short of money. Her marriage had busted up. She'd turned thirty and life was going nowhere. Maybe she thought, hey, these people are living in a pretty expensive part of the world. They won't miss a couple of thou. I don't suppose she meant to blackmail them for *ever*.'

Ganesh took a deep breath. 'Even if you're right so far – and it's all supposition, remember – are you now saying that Nurse Cooper's disappearance is down to the Wildes?'

'It has to be, Gan!'

'No, it doesn't.'

'Oh, come off it!' I argued. 'I've met Flora and Jerry. Flora's an outright screwball. She's violent. She knocked me flat on the floor. She tried to beat my brains out with a tin of chickpeas. As for Jerry, he's more of a thinker and worrier than his wife but I haven't the slightest doubt there's absolutely nothing he wouldn't do to protect Flora and Nicola. In fact, I'm not so sure he didn't mean to run me down that day he just missed me at the hospice. If I hadn't thrown myself into the rhododendrons I'd be dead meat right now, and wouldn't that just suit the Wildes fine!'

'So,' asked Ganesh, 'are you going to the police?'

I sighed and shook my head. 'No. How can I? As you say, it's all supposition. I think that either Jerry or Flora killed LeeAnne Cooper. Then Rennie Duke came sniffing round and they killed him. I can't prove it. Look, I've had doubts myself! I'd almost persuaded myself Jerry hadn't killed Duke, but now . . . LeeAnne Cooper's got to be dead, Gan. She's been gone three months without a sign of her anywhere. She disappeared two days after giving that talk at Nicola's school. I've read it all up in Norman's newspapers. They even mentioned her visit to the school as an example of how she worked with young people. You should see how the press have written this up. They've made LeeAnne out to be some sort of saint. Her mother's been seen on telly pleading for information. Here am I saying she was a blackmailer. Am I going to be popular, I don't think!'

'I don't think you're very popular with Morgan as it is,' said Gan.

'So suppose I tell her all this and she goes to the Wildes

and they swear they've never set eyes on Nurse Cooper. Oh yes, she came and talked to the school, but that's it. Who can prove otherwise? What will come out is Nicola's real identity. I can't let that happen, Gan.'

Ganesh said carefully, 'I don't see how you can prevent it happening, Fran. Inspector Morgan is on the trail of your mother's other child and she's got as far as Mrs Marks. As I see it, Mrs Marks is where all this is eventually going to blow sky-high. Think about it from her point of view.'

Ganesh began to tick points off on his fingers. 'First, Duke contacts her to talk about Eva Varady but doesn't turn up. Second, the police contact her to talk about Duke. Third, you turn up and want to talk about your mother and Duke. The poor woman's practically got a queue of people outside that crèche of hers. It's been made pretty clear to her that she's sitting on some really explosive information. All right, she didn't want to get daughter Linda in shtuck so she's kept quiet till now. But I bet she's had a long talk with Linda by this time and the two of them are going to end up going to the cops. They're a law-abiding couple of citizens. They run nice little businesses. No one in business,' concluded Gan, 'can afford to upset the police.'

'So why not just keep quiet?' I argued. 'Wouldn't that suit them better?'

'Fran,' he said patiently, 'we're talking about people who live well inside the law, not wavering on the edge like a lot of people you and I know. I'm not including Hari in that, by the way. Hari's so law-abiding they wouldn't need coppers if everyone was like him. But that's just what I'm saying. Mrs Marks and Linda are like Hari. They're honest, hard-working and have consciences. You can bet your life they're worriers.

They are going to spill the beans, sooner or later, take my word for it. What's more, I reckon it'll be sooner rather than later.'

'So what can I do?' I wailed.

He shrugged. 'Sometimes it's just not possible to do anything. Sometimes it's even worse if you do something than if you don't. When in doubt, sit tight. It's the best policy. Face it, if it's action you want, you've got a straight choice. You can go to the police and blow Nicola's identity, or you can keep shtum, stay here and let Morgan sort it out. It'll come to the same thing in the end.' After a moment he added gently, 'You don't always have to do everything yourself, Fran. You're not the world's fixer.'

'I'm not trying to save the world. I'm trying to protect my sister. You're always telling me how much family matters.'

'Yes, it does. But I've never said families never make problems. You've done your best, Fran.'

I sometimes think those words 'you've done your best' are the bleakest in the language. There's surrender in them and I'm not a person who gives up. Call me stubborn or what you like, *I* don't like being beaten by circumstances. I said as much to Ganesh.

'You don't think,' he asked, 'that's a bit arrogant? Thinking you're the one who can always beat the system?'

'No,' I said. 'I just don't like being beaten by it.' There was a silence, during which I brooded and Ganesh waited. 'Poor kid,' I said eventually. 'It's going to be a heck of a shock to her. What will they do? I mean, the police, social services, all the rest of them. Will they take her away from the Wildes and put her in care? She'd hate it. She's never had to rough it. The other kids in a care home would eat her alive.'

'They won't put her in care,' Gan comforted me. 'She's been with the Wildes thirteen years and don't tell me they can't afford good lawyers.'

'They'll need them if they're both on a double murder charge. Who's going to look after her if they're both in gaol?' I threw up my hands in despair. 'That's it, then. I can't do anything. I have to sit tight and let matters take their course. I wish I didn't feel that this is all my fault.'

'It's not your fault. Duke was out there looking too. It was Duke who led the police to Mrs Marks, not you.'

'All the same,' I told him, 'I swear this is the last time I'll ever investigate *anything*.'

'If only . . .' said Gan. He smiled sadly.

It seems hard to understand now, and I can only put my decision down to depression, but it was at that point that I made up my mind I had to accept Norman's offer of a room – even if only for a short time. I'd already caused Hari so much hassle. If the storm broke over Nicola, it would only get worse. I had to get out of the garage. I trotted round to find Norman.

'Well,' he said coyly, 'I was just about to offer it to someone else, but seeing as it's you, dear, the room is yours.'

'I don't want you to break any arrangements or anything,' I said hastily, back-pedalling.

'No, no.' He held up a hand blackened with newsprint. 'I always said that room was yours if you needed it. I'm a man of my word.'

'Norm,' I ventured, 'have you done anything about a smoke alarm yet?'

He looked shifty and said he was thinking about it. Right, I thought, if I move in here, my first good deed is going to be fixing a smoke alarm in my room. Norman asked if I wanted to see the room again but I declined. If I took another look at that hole before agreeing, I'd chicken out.

I scraped together the first week's rent out of my slender funds and then trekked down to the council to report my change in circumstances and apply for housing benefit. I filled in the form and was advised that it would take some time to process and that, even if successful, I should realise I would only receive what was considered 'eligible' rent. I would have to meet any difference and they would take into consideration the suitability of my accommodation. I assured them the accommodation was neither too generous nor too lavish. Quite the reverse. They still pursed their lips over the amount Norman was charging me and looked doubtful. 'We'll let you know.'

I asked how I was supposed to pay the rent meantime. I didn't think Norman would be charitable indefinitely if I ceased to come across with the rent money. 'There's been a lot of fraud,' they told me. 'We check everyone carefully now.' I asked if there was any chance my rent allowance would be back-dated, if and when it was approved. They smiled pityingly. 'Only in exceptional circumstances. Generally not.' I guessed I wasn't exceptional. I was definitely a generally not. Well, I'd have to carry on paying Norman myself for the next few weeks. Perhaps I could give up eating.

So I toiled back to the shop and told them what I'd done.

'I'll clear out tonight,' I promised.

'What did you do that for?' asked Ganesh angrily. 'You can't live in that place. It's lethal.'

I assured him I only meant it as a short-term stopgap arrangement. He wasn't convinced. Neither was I. I had to agree to let him come and inspect the room, though I told him it wouldn't make any difference, my mind was made up. Ganesh, after one look, insisted on going back to the shop and returning with a bottle of Jif, Hari's vacuum cleaner and a puffer-tube of Nippon insect-killer. Between us we cleaned the room up. I'd like to say it didn't look too bad when we'd finished, but I'd be lying. It looked just as awful but a bit shinier and without the fluff under the bed. I suppose it was some consolation that the woodlice would be zapped by the Nippon. Gan fixed the washbasin so it didn't sag off the wall so badly, then went into the bathroom and had a go at fixing the stuck window there, without much joy.

'Apparently,' I told him, 'there's a bloke called Sid living up in the attic who's good at fixing things. I'll get him on to it.'

'A nutter in the attic. This place is like a bloomin' Hammer House of Horror set,' Ganesh said gloomily. 'Bet if you go up to the attic you'll find this Sid dangling from a beam by his toes, waiting for nightfall.'

'Shut up, Gan,' I said wearily. Nothing about this was funny. It was as well he hadn't met Zog.

'Take you out for a meal,' he offered. 'Take you to the Greek place, OK?'

Anything to get out of this hellhole for an evening. I agreed. We carted the vacuum cleaner and the other cleaning materials back to the shop. Hari looked up as we came in and said: 'There is a message for you, my dear.'

He hunted among various scraps of paper behind the till and produced a piece on which was written what appeared to be a mobile phone number.

'Did you get a name, Hari?' The number meant nothing to

me. I just hoped it wasn't Nicola again.

But Hari hadn't taken down a name, only remembering that the caller had been a man. He had been trying to keep an eye on a suspicious-looking customer at the time.

'Ten minutes by the magazine rack, looking at everything, buying nothing. I asked him, what you think I am, public library? Then he bought one little pack of cough sweets and went. More customers like him,' added Hari, 'and I'm ruined.'

'Phone from the flat,' said Gan. 'I'll just help Hari finish up down here and I'll come up and fetch you.'

I toiled up the stairs to their flat, feeling about ninety years old. Ringing a number when you don't know who's at the other end is always awkward, and I nearly didn't do it. There were too many people I didn't want to talk to. But it had occurred to me it might be Mickey Allerton with some vital piece of information. Not that I wanted it now. Things had slipped out of my hands.

It wasn't Allerton, it was Ben Cornish.

'Hi,' he said. 'How are things?'

'Could be worse,' I told him, though I didn't at the moment see how.

'I thought,' he said, 'you might like to come over to Kew Gardens and let me show you round, show you what I'm doing here. If you're free, of course.'

'I don't think I ever want to go near Kew again,' I said.

'You won't see anything of the Wildes. Come on. Anyway,' he added, 'to be honest, I thought we might put our heads together and see if we can't sort something out.'

'Like what?' I asked suspiciously, alarm setting my spine a-tingle.

'Flora's confided in me,' he said. 'I know.'

One more person in the know. They'd be broadcasting my sister's identity on the Ten O'Clock news next. My heart sank but I wasn't surprised. I'd confided in Ganesh, Flora in Ben. There comes a moment when we all need the support of a friend.

'There's nothing you or I can do,' I said. 'You've just come into this and you think we can find a way to fix things. I've been in it longer and I know there isn't.'

'Hey, come on!' Ben urged. 'We certainly won't find a way if you keep that attitude up! Perhaps you just need a fresh point of view, and I can provide that. Come and see what I'm doing at the Gardens, anyway. I'd like to show you.'

I was tempted. I liked Ben, and an afternoon away from it all amongst the lawns and hothouses of Kew would be nice, provided I could make Ben see that we couldn't prevent the police getting to Nicola eventually. I dithered and made a token effort to refuse again.

'Well, thanks,' I said, 'but I'm going to see my mother tomorrow afternoon.'

'So come in the morning. We can have lunch in the coffee shop and I'll drive you down to Egham to see your mother afterwards. I'll meet you in the Palm House, in the middle, by the spiral stair.'

My first night under Norm's roof was wretched. I couldn't sleep. Someone, presumably Norman, was snoring somewhere below me. Boards creaked overhead. Probably Sid, getting ready to go out for a night's burgling. Zog I knew was out doing his cleaning job. The room was bitterly cold. There was a coin-operated gas fire but I couldn't afford to keep it burning all night, so I huddled in my sleeping bag on the sagging bed, with Bonnie pressed up tight against my back, and dozed fitfully. In the early hours Zog came home, clumping up the stairs and mumbling to himself. I finally fell asleep about six, which meant I woke up just before nine with a head which felt as if it had been hit with a sock full of sand.

I splashed my face at the washbasin, not surprised to find the hot-water tap was dry. Then Bonnie and I went out shopping for breakfast. I brought back some milk, a packet of cornflakes and a box of teabags. I boiled my little electric kettle to make the tea and we both breakfasted off cornflakes. By this time I was regretting my promise to trail out to Kew Gardens to meet Ben. It would be just my luck to run into Jerry at the Tube station or Nicola with a bunch of her chums. But as I said before, to me a promise is a promise.

I took Bonnie round to the shop and left her in the storeroom again. Poor dog, she must be beginning to think of it as home. Ganesh wasn't there, he'd gone to see some suppliers, and Hari was busy. I was glad, because I wasn't in the mood to answer any questions about my first night in my new abode. I waved at Hari and slipped out of the door into the street.

It had been drizzling as I walked to the shop, and now it had started to rain in earnest. Just the day for a stroll round a botanical garden. By the time I got to Kew, the rain had lifted but the sky still lowered greyly, suggesting more rain wasn't far away.

I entered the Gardens at the Victoria Gate. Not surprisingly, this wasn't a good day for visitors. The café and shops looked deserted. One or two diehards wandered round in macs or anoraks. A cold breeze blew damply into my face as I set off towards the ornate glass structure of the Palm House. The only happy-looking creatures were the ducks on the pond.

Even the line of heraldic beasts rearing up before the Palm House looked cheesed off. I pushed open the door and went inside.

I was met by a cloud of steam and a wall of sweltering heat. From a drizzling London I'd been transported into some tropical jungle. Rampant greenery burst out everywhere and reached up to the glass roof, pressing against the panes as if it would escape and, like Jack's beanstalk, go on growing up into the clouds and out of sight. With a hissing noise a fine spray of water issued from hidden nozzles amongst the leaves and settled in droplets of moisture in the suffocating air. I made my way down the paths between the beds and found myself by the white-painted spiral staircase. I couldn't see anyone else around. A pair of slat-seated benches set at right angles to one another formed a cosy conversation corner – if anyone could bear to sit and talk, or even just sit and look for long in these sauna-like conditions. I sat down. After a minute I had to take my puffa jacket off. I'd suffer some form of heatstroke if I didn't.

I'd just done this when Ben appeared, strolling towards me in a sweater and body-warmer, looking as cool as a cucumber.

'How do you stick it?' I asked him.

'Got used to it. I shan't be working here much longer anyway. This is my last week. I've done all the research I wanted. Now I've got to go away and write it up.' He sat down on the other seat and leaned his forearms on his knees. 'You look a bit stressed out,' he said. 'It's not that bad.'

'I had a rotten night. I've just moved into a new place.' Sweat trickled down my forehead, behind my ears, down my neck.

'Thanks for coming, anyway,' he said.

'If you know about Nicola,' I said, 'you'll know there's nothing we can do. The police will find her eventually.'

He was shaking his head. 'No, not necessarily. You've got too much faith in the law, Fran. They're not that damn efficient.'

I opened my mouth and closed it again. What he didn't know – and neither did Jerry and Flora – was that Mrs Marks and her daughter Linda could put the finger right on the Wildes. Somehow this wasn't the moment to tell him.

'Then there's Nicola,' I said. 'She's a bright kid and she knows something's up. She might just work it out for herself.'

'Don't be daft,' he said comfortably. 'Even if she starts to suspect she's adopted, she isn't going to think the adoption isn't legal, is she?'

He seemed so certain, and I was so hot and sticky and wanting to get out of there, I was almost ready to agree. Why *not* agree if it made him happier? I said cautiously, 'It's possible there's a way out of this, I suppose.'

He leaned forward, moving nearer to me. 'Of course it's possible, Fran. We can make it possible.'

'We can? How?'

'Your mother isn't going to tell anyone, is she?' When I shook my head, he went on, 'So it's only you and me who know, apart from Jerry and Flora. If we don't talk, that's it. No one finds out.'

What with the heat and steam and the bad night my head was furring up like an old kettle. I still didn't want to tell him about Mrs Marks; some instinct prevented me. Instead I said, 'It can't be that simple. We don't know if there's anyone else out there who knows. Anyway, the Wildes got themselves into this situation.' I was tired now and wanted to put a stop to all this. 'Let them get themselves out of it.'

Ben's face twitched. 'I won't let anyone destroy Flora's whole world.' His voice was suddenly low, hoarse and filled with a terrifying passion.

'What?' I snapped out of my fogged state. His eyes had a wild shine to them. His whole face seemed to be trembling. Either from heat or emotion, sweat now trickled in rivulets down his cheeks. The old casual, cool, in-control Ben had totally disappeared and the reason was all too clear.

'You're stuck on Flora Wilde!' I gasped. With this explanation, a host of other facts crowded into my mind, swirling about and parting, forming a pattern, a pattern of violence and death. 'She knows it and she's using it. She wants someone to pick the chestnuts out of the fire for her. You must be able to see that.'

'I'm not stuck on her, as you so crudely put it!' A tide of dull red crept from his throat up his face, and his lips were drawn back, bared animal-like. 'I worship her, and you – you scruffy piece of street rubbish – don't you dare say a word against the way I feel or against her! What would you know about someone like her? What would you understand about the way I feel? I've loved her since I was a kid. As far as I'm concerned, Flora's perfect. She's beautiful, loving and kind. She's a wonderful mother. She's devoted to Nicola. She'd never dump her like my people dumped me! She even had a place in her heart for me when I was a kid. She's – she's just wonderful!'

'She's bonkers,' I retorted unwisely. But I was angry now and didn't care. 'What's more, I don't stand for being called rubbish. You say I know nothing about you and Flora, but you know nothing about me, you patronising git. I was dumped

275

too as a kid, but I learned to get on with life. You, you've never stood on your own feet. You've always found someone to latch on to, someone to look after you. You know what? There are takers and givers, and you're a taker. By the way, does Jerry have any inkling how you feel about his wife? I bet he doesn't. He dotes on her. He'd sling you out on your ear and Flora wouldn't raise a squeak of protest. All she cares about is Jerry, Nicola and her nice home. She's using you, you dope! Can't you see it? She's fighting to preserve what she has and she doesn't care what it costs. You're just a handy footsoldier, running round to do her bidding. When it comes down to it, you're expendable, cannon fodder. So get those stars out of your eyes. She doesn't give a damn about you and she never will.'

'I knew,' he said softly, 'I knew we couldn't trust you. I told Flora we'd have to shut you up!'

That was when I noticed the knife in his hand. He saw the discovery register on my face and smiled. 'Gardeners,' he said, 'carry everything in their pockets.'

'Yes,' I said, bracing myself, ready to leap aside if he struck out. 'They carry bits of string to act as bootlaces or to wrap round Rennie Duke's neck!'

The smile twisted into a sneer. 'That pathetic little private eye? He was so damn obvious, and getting rid of him was so easy.'

'Easy but stupid,' I said. 'It brought the cops into it.' My leg muscles were tense now as I got ready to jump.

'Will you shut up about the bloody cops?' he snarled at me.

At that moment, voices echoed through the vegetation. At least two people had entered the Palm House through the door at the south end and were coming towards us. Ben flung up his head. I seized my chance and leapt up and away from Ben, dashing into the far aisle, twisting right and making for the door at the north end. Behind me an American voice was saying, 'Oh, do you work here? Can you tell us—'

I blessed the unknown tourists, but Ben wouldn't be caught up with them for long and would soon be behind me.

Outside the wet air hit me with the force of a cold shower. I began to run along the front of the Palm House, past the heraldic creatures, their paws raised as if in dismay. Then Ben burst out of the main doors, forcing me to double back. The pond now lay between me and the exit and I had to work my way round it. I ran like the clappers down the paths, circling the water, towards the Victoria Gate exit. I could see it – and escape – ahead of me. But then I saw something else, a diminutive figure in a red showerproof jacket with the hood pulled up, standing between me and the way out. Flora, looking like Little Red Riding Hood and preparing to act like the wolf.

I glanced back. Ben was striding my way. He broke into a run. I was sandwiched between them. I could have taken a chance and barged straight at Flora, bowling her over, but in the first place, I didn't know if she was armed in any way – I suspected she probably was – and in the second place, I didn't know if Jerry Wilde was stationed somewhere, about to arrive on the scene. I couldn't take on the three of them united.

I wheeled left and found myself running down the path which leads past the grassy mound on top of which stands the Temple of Aeolus. The grass on the mound had been left to grow wild, and even at this time of the year stood in tall, blackened wet ranks. I leapt up the mound and threw myself full length amongst it. I'd left my puffa jacket in the Palm House, which was a good thing, because its bulk and its bright colour would've betrayed me. I was panting and sweat-drenched. The cold, wet ground came as a shock, water permeating my clothing, the wet grass dripping on to my head. I heard running feet passing by. After a moment I raised my head cautiously and peered between the grass stalks. I couldn't see anyone below. Beyond the Temple of Aeolus, the path split, one fork turning to the right, into the Order Beds, the other leading straight on towards the Princess of Wales Conservatory. I guessed Ben and Flora had taken one direction each. But they'd soon realise I hadn't gone either way and would double back.

I skidded down the mound and made for the pond and the Victoria Gate. But I'd calculated wrongly. Flora stood at the top of the path, outside the museum. I whirled and doubled back, and as I did so, she began to run forward. I wheeled right down a path at the end of which I had an idea there was a smaller gate. It was there, but disused and locked. I was trapped in a dead end.

I plunged into the bushes by the path, crashed my way past the rear of the gents' loo, and ran across the grass towards the museum block. Flora had realised her mistake in quitting her post by the museum, where she could have cut me off. She had doubled back too, and was close behind me. I could hear the thud of her feet and a hissing noise she was making. Then Ben appeared on the right and slightly ahead of me. They had me in a pincer movement. I had nowhere to go but up the high, unscalable wall.

And then Heaven took pity on me. Out of the gents' loo came the dignified uniformed figure of a park constable. I shot between Ben and Flora towards him.

'Help!' I yelled.

He stopped, startled. 'Whazzamatter?'

If I told him that Ben – whom he probably knew – and dinky little Flora were a pair of murderers hellbent on adding me to their list of victims, he wouldn't believe it. So I said the only other thing I could.

'I've been mugged!' I wailed. I'm an actor. I sounded good.

'What?' he exclaimed. 'Where? When? Who by?'

I pointed dramatically at Flora. 'Her!'

He peered doubtfully past me at the tiny red-clad figure. That was when Flora blew it. She should have stayed put and told him I was a druggie, out of my skull. Instead, frightened by the uniform, she turned and ran. To any kind of policeman a running figure means only one thing: Guilt.

Ben too realised she'd done the wrong thing. I heard him call out to her, '*No!*' But the constable was pounding after her, and with a final glare of hatred at me, Ben took to his heels, disappearing through the Victoria Gate. He might think Flora wonderful, but saving his own skin came first. Left alone, I sank down on the ground and rested my head on my knees. It had been altogether too close for comfort.

'Let's get this straight,' said Janice Morgan. 'You weren't mugged.'

'No, of course I wasn't!' I snapped. Honestly, the police mind is beyond me. Even Morgan, who I'd always thought of as bright, had turned into PC Plod. What makes them so pernickety? They must read the rule book morning, noon and night.

'You made a false report of a crime.' She looked just like

my old headmistress, beady-eyed, disapproving, rigid with moral outrage. Carpeted again, Francesca Varady. 'That's a serious offence.'

'It's not as serious as attempted murder!' I howled.

'Certainly not as serious as that, which is why it seems very odd to me that you told the officer only that you were mugged. Which, it turns out, wasn't true. I can't understand why, if you believed an attempt had been made on your life, you didn't say so at the time. Why didn't you tell the park constable the truth, if that's what it is?'

If that's what it is. They didn't believe me. They just didn't believe me. Was this possible? Oh yes, most definitely. People like me can't be believed, but people like Ben and Flora – nice people, who live in nice places – everyone accepts their word.

'I didn't tell him then because –' I gazed at her in bafflement '– if I'd told him they were trying to kill me, he'd just think I was a lunatic.'

'If he thought you were a lunatic, he'd escort you out of the park. Isn't that what you wanted?'

I tried hard to keep my cool. 'Listen, perhaps you keep your head when all around are losing theirs. I just panic like an ordinary person. If I'm being chased by a pair of nutters with knives—'

She interrupted me. 'Mrs Wilde was not armed.'

'Wasn't she heck! She managed to throw it away in the bushes or the pond.'

'Did you actually see her with a knife?'

I had to admit, I hadn't. 'But she was in with him, why else was she there? Why else was she trying to cut me off from the gate? Why did she run when I called up the park police?'

Janice Morgan sighed. 'Fran, Mrs Wilde lives in Kew, a stone's throw from the Gardens. She walks there nearly every day, rain or shine. It's her way of keeping fit. The regular staff there know her well. As soon as the constable reached her and saw who it was, he realised there must have been a mistake. Flora didn't even know you were meeting Ben Cornish there. When she saw you running towards her like a wild creature, of course she ran away.'

'You can't believe this?' I gasped.

'The trouble with you, Fran,' said Morgan, 'is that you see everything from your own perspective.'

I clenched both fists and thumped the desk. 'I know what I see – saw. I saw Ben Cornish threatening me with a knife, and that's a fact, right? I didn't imagine it. Look, he phoned and invited me to go out there and look around. Does he deny that?'

'No, he says he asked you to come there, offered to buy you lunch and then drive you to Egham to see your mother. It sounds very nice of him.'

'Yes, he did all that!' I wailed in growing despair. 'But the reason he wanted me there was to talk about the Wildes. Then he threatened me. If he's innocent, why did he run when the copper went after Flora? Have you picked him up? If you'd searched him at the time, you'd have found a knife on him!'

'Mr Cornish left the Gardens to run and tell Mr Wilde, who happened to be at home that day, what had happened – that is, that you'd accused his wife of mugging you. We've talked to him and he denies your account completely. He admits he did have a pruning knife on him, quite a small knife. That's understandable. He's a gardener, engaged at the time on gardening work.'

'He's also a murderer. He killed Rennie Duke. He throttled him with garden twine.'

'Proof?' she asked sweetly.

'Well, was garden twine used?' I challenged.

She didn't bite. 'I ask the questions, Fran.'

I thought for a moment, then stooped and hastily unlaced my boot. 'Here, Ben gave me this for a bootlace. Is it the same string as you found round Duke's neck? Send it over to forensics.' I offered up a quick prayer of thanks that I'd not bought a replacement pair of laces from Hari, largely because I'd been so cross with Ganesh for trailing me to Oxford Circus Tube.

She took the string. 'I will. But what I want to know is what else you think you have against Cornish.'

I sighed. 'One or both of them also killed LeeAnne Cooper, the missing nurse.'

'Fran . . .' she began warningly. 'This is getting totally out of hand, as if it wasn't already bad enough. You seem just to be flinging accusations of all kinds, anything that comes into your head. I admit we're looking for LeeAnne Cooper, but nothing so far has suggested either that she's dead or that she has the slightest connection with Ben Cornish or Flora Wilde.'

'There's a connection,' I said. She waited. I couldn't go on. In the end I said dully, 'I can't be the one to tell you. Perhaps you should have another talk with Mrs Marks. Tell her you've talked to me and I said you should ask her.'

Morgan was quiet for a few moments. Then she said, 'What gives you the idea she's dead?'

'She has to be.'

'No, she doesn't. She's missing. No more than that. People sometimes go missing for years and turn up safe and sound.'

'You don't have to tell me,' I said. 'My mother was missing for fourteen years. But I know—'

'How do you *know*?' she asked gently, but there was steel inside that low-pitched calm voice.

I forced myself to match her self-control but it wasn't easy. What I was going to say would stir up a hornet's nest. Yet it had to be said even though, as a result, yet another person's life would tumble in ruins.

'I think,' I said, 'I know where her body is.'

Morgan expelled her breath in a long sigh. 'Where? And how long have you known it?'

'Not long. Not consciously. Maybe it's been bothering me a while, but I only just put it all together when Ben pulled the knife on me in the Palm House.' I met her gaze as firmly as I could. 'If you go out to Wimbledon,' I said, 'you will find LeeAnne Cooper's body in a raised flower bed Ben Cornish built for his great-aunt, Mrs Dorothy Mackenzie, while she was away visiting her sister. I haven't got any money, but if I had, I'd wager every last red cent on it.'

Morgan had paled. 'You wouldn't mess me around on this, Fran? You know what you're saying?'

I nodded. 'I'm sticking with it.'

Morgan rose to her feet. 'I'll have to request a warrant. Fran, if you're wrong, you are in more trouble than you've ever been in in your life!'

Chapter Seventeen

'Do you have any idea how many times I've bent the rules for you, Fran?' Inspector Morgan asked.

It was over a week since our previous conversation. I had expected Morgan might have stopped off at the shop, as she'd been so keen to do before, and let me know what was happening. But not a word.

'You can't,' Ganesh had said, 'expect the police to take you into their confidence.'

'Why not? They expected me to take them into mine. They must have found something in that garden. If they hadn't, they'd have been round here like a shot, accusing me of dishing out false information and wasting police time.'

'That's if they followed up your idea and looked in that flower bed.' Ganesh had been in a negative mood. He and Hari had had a long argument over installing a hot drinks machine. He'd half got Hari talked round to it, but it had been an exhausting process.

'You would think,' Gan had continued, his mind clearly running on his own problems to the complete disregard of mine, 'he'd want to make that shop pay.'

'Doesn't it?' I asked, forced to follow the conversation down the path he wanted to lead it.

'Yes, but not much, not as well as it could. And why not? Because he's so damn cautious! The hot drinks idea is a really good one. He sells cold drinks so why not, in the winter, sell hot ones? Look, what's the difference?'

I played devil's advocate and pointed out that whereas customers expected to find a cold drinks cabinet in a newsagent's, a hot drinks dispenser would be a novelty. It might not catch on.

'Go on, take his side,' grumbled Ganesh.

'I'm not taking his side. It's just that he's probably worried about your ideas after the business with the washroom.'

'There's nothing wrong with that washroom!' Ganesh was indignant.

'No, but the whole business wasn't incident-free, was it? Gan, can we get back to talking about whether the police have found anything in Mrs Mackenzie's flower bed?'

'They've probably dug up nothing but a load of bulbs,' said Gan, getting his own back for my lack of support over the hot drinks idea.

But they hadn't, or if they had, they'd dug up something else as well. That same evening, at long last, in the *Evening Standard*, we saw a report that human remains had been found in the garden of a house in Wimbledon. Just that. No mention of any names, but as I pointed out to Gan, unless there'd been a massacre recently in SE19, it had to be poor Nurse Cooper.

A few days later I received a message that Inspector Morgan would like to see me. I was round to the nick in record time.

I couldn't help noticing, as soon as she walked into the room, that she'd got rid of the Miss Marple gear and the change was pretty startling. She was wearing a charcoal-grey pin-stripe business suit, black tights and low-heeled courts. Clearly finding a body wasn't the only thing going on. The new look gave her a super-efficient air. She was certainly in bossy mood.

'Nice whistle,' I observed of the suit.

'I'm giving a press conference later,' she said, a bit starchy but not quite able to hide a smirk.

Now that smug look riled me because, after all, without me they wouldn't have found out what happened to LeeAnne Cooper, let alone Clarence Duke. But does anyone invite me to come along to a press conference? Does any journalist hotfoot it to my dingy room at Norm's asking for my personal account? Do I get any much-needed publicity? What do you think?

'You found her, then, or so I read in the *Standard*.' I couldn't help but sound sarcastic. Morgan ought to be cringingly grateful, not sitting there dolled up for the cameras. 'I wasn't flinging accusations, as you said, and I wasn't wrong about the flower bed.'

'Yes, we found her.' Morgan sighed and tapped her teeth with her biro in a very un-Superwoman manner. 'And despite the fact that an attempt seems to have been made to hasten the destruction of the body by the addition to the soil of some lime-based garden product, the remains have been identified and there are sufficient details of her injuries in the pathologist's report to point to her being the victim of a knife attack.'

'Nasty,' I said queasily. I stopped feeling sorry for myself. It was a horrid business. I said something more to that effect.

Morgan nodded and picked absently at a bit of cotton on her sleeve. 'A very unpleasant business altogether.'

'And you've charged Ben Cornish?'

'We've charged Cornish with the disposal of the body of LeeAnne Cooper. That's all for the moment, but it's enough to hold him on. The elderly owner of the property was very upset when we arrived to dig up her garden. She was on the phone to her solicitor straight away, trying to stop us. She couldn't believe we had anything against her great-nephew. Kept telling us what a lovely, kind boy he was. Then, when we found the remains, she collapsed and had to be taken to hospital. We end up carrying the can when that sort of thing happens to a member of the public,' added Morgan grimly. 'Accusations of insensitivity when dealing with an old lady and all the rest of it. Anyone would think *we* had buried the body along with the daffodil bulbs.'

'I feel sort of responsible too,' I said. 'But I had to tell you.'

'There are a number of things you should have told us, Fran, right from the beginning. We now know why LeeAnne Cooper and Clarence Duke were so interested in the Wildes. Mrs Marks eventually put us on to it. But you knew too, didn't you, Fran? About your sister? You knew all along.'

'I didn't know she existed until my mother told me. It came out of the blue to me,' I said bitterly. 'And how could I tell you? Mum was counting on me.'

'Withholding evidence is a serious matter. It could be said you tried to impede our enquiries. That's an offence.'

'I didn't impede your enquiries into Rennie Duke's death. I only tried to protect my mother and sister,' I protested.

'You could have told us straight away,' she insisted, deaf to my argument. 'Especially when you knew we were seeking the whereabouts of your mother's other child. You could have saved us several wasted man-hours which could have been given to the Duke murder investigation. The superintendent was not pleased.'

I told her I realised that and was sorry. 'But what could I do? Now you know it all, you ought to understand why I didn't speak up. I couldn't grass up my own mother!'

'I know, and that's why I put up a strong case in your defence. No charges will be made against you, Fran, but you're very lucky. You've got away with it by the skin of your teeth, and not for the first time!'

Sergeant Cole, who was sitting in on this interview, complete with fresh set of spots, gave me a jaundiced look. Left to him, he'd have thrown the book at me.

'Thanks,' I told her. 'But it seems to me the police are being a tad ungrateful. You wouldn't have found LeeAnne and you wouldn't have got Cornish but for me.'

'Cornish nearly got you,' she pointed out mildly.

I didn't need to be reminded. I was totting up far too many close shaves in my life to date. Next time – I'd make sure there wasn't a next time.

'What happens now about Rennie Duke's murder?' I asked impatiently. 'When are you going to charge one of them with that?'

'Charges against Cornish in regard to the death of Mr Duke are being prepared.' She was being evasive.

I smelled a rat. 'What about the Wildes?' It seemed I had to force them into the conversation. Morgan was being altogether too damn careful not to mention them.

'That's a separate matter. Clearly there's a lot to sort out before any steps are taken. Because it involves the future of the child, however, it's likely it will be treated as a civil matter rather than a criminal one, left to social services to sort out.'

'You can't leave it to them. They'll take her away and bung her in some crappy kids' home,' I objected.

'Not necessarily. They're letting her stay with the Wildes until it's decided what steps to take. It was wrong of your mother to hand over her baby as she did, whatever her motives or circumstances. Of course, it's not illegal to ask someone to look after your child for you as a temporary measure. But this was a definite attempt to circumvent official adoption procedures and use a genuine birth certificate to establish a false identity, plus all the later misrepresentations which follow from that. I can't say for sure that there will be no charges. All I can say is that the welfare of the child will be put first.'

Morgan smiled thinly. 'Mr Wilde has his legal team working on it. He's a wealthy man. He can pay for the best. Naturally, even if she stays with the Wildes, her situation will have to be regularised. Legally, she's Miranda Varady. It's astonishing that they got away with it for so long. It's all there in the records: registration of both births, issuing of a death certificate, record of the cremation of the infant Nicola Wilde . . . The Wildes must have spent thirteen years terrified someone would check.'

And someone had eventually checked, I thought. Rennie Duke, a methodical little guy with a knowledge of where to look and a nose for a secret. Not to mention poor foolish Nurse Cooper, who'd thought her boat had come in but had instead paved the way to her own violent death.

Very carefully, I asked, 'So neither of the Wildes is being charged in connection with murder?'

Morgan shrugged her tailored shoulders. 'Why should they

be? Cornish has made a statement taking full responsibility for both deaths, but confessions have to be supported by evidence these days and that's why he's only being held over the disposal of a body until we get everything right. He'll be charged eventually, I'm sure. But there is no evidence involving either of the Wildes in the deaths. Admittedly, both victims represented a threat to them. But there's nothing to suggest they themselves turned to murder. Well, it's not likely, is it?'

I wanted to shout out that hey! even the middle classes kill! But I didn't bother. What Morgan was saying was that china-doll Flora, living in her own little doll's house, and respectable professional Jerry were what Susie would call nice people living in a nice place. People with clean hands, clean records, good lawyers and good contacts. Murder? Perish the thought.

The dissatisfaction must have showed in my face, because she went on, 'They admit LeeAnne Cooper came to see them with the aim of getting money from them. Wilde told her to clear off and reminded her that blackmail was a serious offence. He called her bluff, in other words. Jerry Wilde himself was satisfied they'd seen the last of her after that. Unfortunately, Flora had been very distressed by the episode and, unknown to her husband, confided in Ben Cornish, an old friend. He took it upon himself to remove the threat permanently from the scene. Neither of the Wildes was aware of that.

'Later, Rennie Duke showed interest. This time, both Wildes confided in Cornish and asked him to meet Duke, acting as their go-between, and see if some sort of pay-off couldn't be arranged. LeeAnne Cooper had been a rather nervous amateur. Duke had a seedy reputation. They didn't think he could be frightened away so easily and they were prepared to pay.

'But there's nothing to show that they were prepared to resort to violence. They've admitted they had discussed skipping out, going abroad, if that was the only way they could protect their daughter, as they saw it. But Wilde says it was only a contingency plan. He really didn't think it would come to that. He was content LeeAnne had already been scared off and he really thought he could do a deal with Duke. Their foolishness was in taking someone like Cornish, a real loose cannon, into their confidence. They'd no way of knowing he was a killer. He was to be their middle-man, not their executioner.'

'Wilde acted really cool when I mentioned Duke to him,' I said sullenly. 'He's one very good actor. Perhaps you ought to remember that when he starts spinning you his tales.'

'He was one very frightened man,' said Morgan, 'because, by then, he knew Duke was dead. To go back to the beginning, first LeeAnne had appeared, then Duke. The Wildes were very, very jittery. Then a bombshell. Mrs Mackenzie told them about you and your mother, Eva Varady, and that you'd asked for their address. Jerry Wilde went at once to the hospice to see your mother, to discover if she were the source of Duke's information, and to beg her not to tell anyone else the truth. But before he could see her, he received a call on his mobile phone from Cornish, telling him that Duke had been found dead and the police were involved. Cornish urged that it was imperative all three of them, himself and the Wildes, close ranks and deny they'd ever heard Duke's name. Neither of the Wildes suspected Cornish had killed Duke any more than they suspected he'd killed LeeAnne Cooper. It was all Cornish's doing from start to finish.'

'I see,' I said. I did, but what I saw was a different picture to the one Morgan had painted. I'd had personal experience of Flora's instability and tendency to violent reaction. I felt sure, though I couldn't prove it, that LeeAnne had sought her out alone. To tackle the Wildes together wouldn't have made sense. Why let yourself be outnumbered? Anyway, LeeAnne might have reckoned the mother would be the more vulnerable of the two. When she saw that tiny blue-eyed doll she must have thought it was going to be a doddle. Instead, Flora had flown into a rage, perhaps in that very same cosy farmhouse kitchen where she'd attacked me, grabbed a knife and killed LeeAnne in a frenzied attack. Then she'd phoned her devoted slave, Ben Cornish, and asked him to help her get rid of the body. 'No problem,' says Ben, and buries LeeAnne in the raised flower bed he's constructing in Mrs Mackenzie's garden. It was at least possible, at that point, that Jerry had not even known of LeeAnne's existence. Whether he'd found out later was another matter, and one we'd never get to know the truth of. But one aspect of his behaviour really bothered me.

Both Sister Helen and I had witnessed his panic at the hospice, after according to Sister Helen, he'd made his call by mobile. But she'd made a mistake. Wilde hadn't made a call, he'd received one. This bit of Janice Morgan's account I believed. Sister Helen had thought he'd walked outside to use his mobile to make a call. Instead, he'd walked outside because he was so jittery he couldn't just sit in the foyer, waiting. However, it was after speaking to Ben that he'd leapt into his car and driven out of the grounds like a bat out of hell, nearly running me down. Was that just because he'd heard Duke was dead and the police were investigating, as Morgan apparently accepted? Or because he knew how unstable his wife was; had maybe even learned by then that she'd killed once?

It was a funny thing, I thought, but Jerry Wilde, whom I'd suspected from the first, had turned out to be the only one in that trio without blood on his hands. I'd been right to judge him a thinker. With Ben arrested, he'd rapidly stitched up a pretty neat version of events to protect his wife and get himself off the hook. It'd been easy with Ben playing along, taking all the blame. What better for Wilde? It left Flora and him in the clear and got Ben out of their lives. Two's company, three's a crowd. Jerry must have sussed out by now how Ben felt about his wife.

So Ben and Flora were killers in my book, partners in crime. But they weren't, it seemed, in Morgan's. Did I argue with her? No. Cornish would never implicate his beloved Flora. Even given the unlikelihood that he did, it wouldn't be backed by evidence. Enough people's lives had been messed up. The important thing now was to try and salvage something for Nicola from all of this wretched tangle. She was having to come to terms with the information that her 'parents' were not her parents. To learn that one of them was a killer would be to lose them twice.

'If you're not going to charge me with anything,' I said, 'can I go? I want to visit my mother.'

They let me go, Cole reluctantly. Morgan walked with me out of the building.

'A lot of people are very unhappy with your role in all this, Fran,' she said. 'I managed to swing it in your favour but don't let me down. It's on file. You know what that means. Keep out of trouble from now on, please!'

I promised to do my best. 'I appreciate what you've done for me,' I told her. 'Though I still don't think the cops appreciate what I've done for them.' I eyed the charcoal suit. 'You might mention a public-spirited, currently resting actor at the press conference.'

'Don't push your luck,' she said. 'The less mention made of your name the better at the moment.'

With that she trotted off for her fifteen minutes of fame. I went to Waterloo to catch the train out to Egham.

The afternoon was wearing on and the commuters starting to make for home, so Waterloo was quite crowded. My journey was squashed and uncomfortable. Apprehension about what I'd find when I got to the hospice made things worse.

My mother had clearly been going downhill during the last couple of visits. I'd agonised over whether or not to tell her that her secret was out. But since it was quite likely that the police or social workers would turn up, I'd had to forewarn her.

She'd taken it quite well, all things considered. 'I suppose it had to come out eventually,' she said pettishly. 'It's a real nuisance. It was such a *good* arrangement. Why do people have to interfere? But they won't take Miranda away from the Wildes, will they? Not after all this time?'

I told her I thought it unlikely, not because I believed it, but because it was what she wanted to hear. I didn't point out that the person doing quite a lot of the interfering had been me, on her instructions. She still didn't seem to think that either she or the Wildes had given rise to the basic situation.

Instead she fixed blame on Rennie Duke.

'Rennie could never leave well alone,' she grumbled. 'I didn't tell him anything, really I didn't, Fran. I don't know how he pieced it together. But that was Rennie for you.'

I'd had an idea or two, but I'd kept them to myself along with everything else. To begin with there was my mother's letter to me, which, as I told you earlier, I suspected he'd managed to read. But perhaps things had gone wrong even before that. They'd started going wrong when she'd called Rennie in to find me, so that in turn I could find Miranda-Nicola.

Of course, she hadn't mentioned Miranda to Rennie. But on the other hand, she was very ill when she spoke to him, and on medication. Little wonder if she'd been confused at times, especially when discussing such a stressful subject. Was it possible that, in talking to Rennie about me, she had sometimes slipped into calling me Miranda – 'Find Francesca for me' alternated with 'Find Miranda' – and that Rennie had sussed pretty quickly she was talking about two different daughters? Like a lot of other theories I'd had about this business, though, it would remain in the realm of 'perhaps'.

It had been one of those clear, cool days following rainy weather when the light seems to make everything look crisp and distinct. Although by the time I turned into the hospice grounds evening shadows were gathering, the light still seemed to hold a special quality. The surrounding vegetation had a curious luminosity. The big, irregularly shaped rhododendron bushes were like slumbering beasts. Their shiny dark-green leaves looked softer and more tactile. Everything looked about to move, to reach out and touch me. This Surrey garden was as exotic as the rampantly tropical Palm House.

A light breeze blew across my face. For a second, I felt as if I were someone else, that I stood in the dusk and watched me walk up the path. The house ahead of me looked unreal. As I approached the front door, I saw a movement. Sister Helen had appeared on the other side. She pulled the door open and stood waiting for me.

I knew what had happened, what she was going to say, and anticipated her. 'Mum's died, hasn't she?'

'I am so sorry, Fran,' she said. 'It was only about an hour ago. I've been trying to find you. I telephoned the shop and they said you'd gone to the police station, so I called there but you'd left. I guessed you were on your way.'

She stood aside and let me into the foyer. Delicately, she asked, 'Would you like to see her?'

I nodded.

'Have you seen a dead person before?'

'Yes,' I said. I'd seen my dad and my grandmother, both nicely laid out. I'd seen a girl I shared a squat with hanging from a ceiling fixture. I'd seen Rennie Duke collapsed in his car. I was notching up more than my fair share of scenes of death.

'You have to remember,' she said, 'the undertaker hasn't been yet. We're waiting for him. We phoned our regular funeral parlour. Do you have an alternative wish?'

'No,' I said. 'I'm sure the usual man will be fine.' I thought of Susie Duke and wondered if I was going to be expected to pay for the funeral. I hadn't those kinds of funds and it was too much to hope that Mum had been insured. Hideously embarrassed, I began, 'I can't – I'm unemployed . . .'

She put a hand on my shoulder. 'It's all right. We're a registered charity, and one of the things we take care of, in specified circumstances, is the funeral costs. Don't worry.'

I followed her down the corridor. It seemed wrong to have been discussing money like this, but I didn't know what I was supposed to say or do.

Mum was lying nicely in her bed by the window. Through it I could see the birdbath and a pair of starlings jostling one another in it. I wondered if she'd been watching them when she died. She looked surprised, as if despite living with the knowledge of her own mortality, Death had still seemed an odd sort of visitor to have turned up in her room. Her lips were parted as if to ask what he was doing there. I wanted to cry but there weren't any tears. I felt, if anything, numb.

I heard my voice asking, 'Was she alone?'

'Yes, but she'd just had visitors,' said Sister Helen's voice in reply.

That permeated the fog surrounding me. 'Who?' I asked.

'A young girl and a social worker.' I must have looked shocked. She asked, 'Are you all right, dear? Do you want to sit down?'

I sat down on the chair she pushed forward. She stretched out her hand to Mum's water jug, but I waved it aside.

'Was the girl Nicola Wilde?' I asked hoarsely.

'Yes.' Sister Helen put her head on one side, much like one of the birds out there in the garden. 'You knew about her?'

'Yes, I knew.' This was awkward. 'Do you – did anyone explain?' I asked.

'I had a chat with the social worker while Nicola went in to see Eva. I gather the girl was adopted and Eva was her birth mother. I had a feeling, you know, that Eva was waiting for something. I can tell you now that she hung on far longer than we were expecting when she arrived here.'

Waiting for me to bring Miranda back. Sister Helen had spoken of love making sacrifices. Perhaps my mother had been self-centred in some ways, but in one she hadn't. She'd left me with Dad and Grandma, so she reckoned I was all right. But Miranda had faced the kind of life facing the wailing baby in the squat I'd visited with Marty. And then Jerry and Flora had walked out of the hospital, deep in their grief, and into her path. She'd given away the baby she truly loved because she wanted a better life for her daughter.

'I'm glad she came,' I said.

'I think it made Eva happy,' Sister Helen replied. Happy, and ready to let go.

I travelled home in that curiously numb state. Of course, Nicola had been told by now that she wasn't the Wildes' own child. Perhaps she'd demanded to know about her real mother and brow-beaten the social worker into taking her to the hospice. I could imagine my sister doing that. I wondered how she was coping, poor kid.

In my head, I addressed my mother: 'I managed it, then. I got Miranda back for you.' I felt I had her approval, and that she'd found her peace.

It was dark when I got back to Camden. Given the way I was feeling, even the idea of going back straight away to that dingy room of Norman's was unbearable. I wanted company, and to talk to someone. I started to walk towards the shop. Before I got there, however, a fire engine raced past me, followed by another.

When I got to the shop, Hari was there alone. As soon as I appeared in the doorway, he threw up both hands, darted out from behind the counter and swooped on me.

'My dear, my dear! You are safe! We have been so worried!'

'Yes, of course I'm safe!' I said. I looked round. 'Where's Gan?'

In the storeroom, Bonnie, hearing my voice, began to bark.

'At the fire, of course,' said Hari. 'Because he was afraid, you see, that you would come back from visiting your mother at the hospice and have gone there, to that room you rented.'

'Oh my God,' I exclaimed. 'Norman's place is on fire!'

Chapter Eighteen

As I approached the scene of the fire, I saw that the winter evening sky above the area was glowing an angry orange. The air was filled with smoke and tiny specks of burning debris. Breathing was difficult and painful. My nasal passages and throat were beginning to feel sore. There was a terrible stench of blistering varnish and paint, charred wood, smouldering carpets and furnishings.

Fire engines blocked the street. A crowd had gathered at the end of the road and was being ordered back by a couple of coppers. The watchers still hung on obstinately, fascinated by fire, by destruction and the sheer terrible power of the scene. At my old school, one of our teachers had attributed civilisation to man's mastery of fire, allowing him to heat and light his cave and cook his bison steaks. Fire is something so important the ancients reckoned someone stole it from the gods. The gods must have had a few good laughs since then. Fire isn't so easily mastered. It's like trying to domesticate a caged wild beast. It's waiting, just waiting, for you to turn your back.

Here, in this street, the beast was free and destroying all about it. Despite the gallons of water pouring down on it, the fire hid, waited and pounced. As I watched, a giant spray of water from a hose soared into the air. The burning roof hissed and crackled. The flames subsided for an instant before breaking out again. From what I could see of the house it was a blackened, windowless shell. The houses to either side hadn't escaped unscathed, blackened with smoke, windows shattered from the heat, paintwork blistered.

A man standing next to me said, to no one in particular, 'There's gotta have been somefing stored in that house, somefing what burns up fast. I never seen a place go up so quick.'

More water arched into the air. The flame subsided again and this time didn't reappear. I shook the man's arm. 'Did they get the people out?'

He looked at me in surprise. 'I dunno.'

I pushed my way between onlookers until I was stopped by a copper. 'Here,' he said, 'what d'you think you're doing?'

'I live there,' I shouted above the surrounding clamour.

'What, in that house? Hang on!' He attracted the attention of a nearby firefighter. 'This girl says she lived in the house!'

The fireman lumbered towards me in his heavy protective kit. 'What's your name?' he asked. I told him. 'Right, Fran,' he said, 'you can tell us how many people might have been in there. A neighbour says the old chap took in lodgers.'

'I don't know how many lived in the basement,' I told him, 'but four of us lived in the rest of the place, including the owner. Do you mean you haven't got anyone out?'

'We got two out,' he said. 'The old boy who owns the place is one of 'em. He's not making any sense. Keeps going on about his collection. What did he collect?'

'Newspapers,' I said unhappily.

'News—' His jaw dropped. 'Bloody hell.'

'What about the others?' I persisted.

'One other. But he run off, jumped out the ambulance and legged it down the street.'

Poor Zog, still running. Would he ever stop?

'So that makes three, with you accounted for,' said the fireman. 'You say one more lived in the main part of the house?'

'Yes,' I said. 'In the attic.'

As I spoke there was a great rending crack and crash and the roof of the house caved in.

Shrieks and cries rose from the watchers. We all surged back. I cannoned into someone and hands gripped my shoulders. Someone was yelling my name in my ear. I turned and saw Ganesh.

'Oh my God, Fran,' he gasped. 'I thought you were in there.' His face was running with sweat, which had streaked long rivulets through grime. His long black hair was plastered down. He must have been standing as close to the fire as he could get.

'I just came back from the hospice,' I said. 'I went to the shop.'

'Come on,' he said, 'let's get you out of here.'

'Hang on,' said the fireman, reappearing. 'Where can we find her? She'll be needed for the enquiry.'

Ganesh told him to contact me at the newsagent's, then put his arm round my shoulder and steered me clear of the crowd and away from the horrid scene.

At the shop, Hari had been fretting. When he saw us, he seized us both, dragging us inside with a frantic, 'Come, come, come!'

'I'm closing up early,' said Ganesh in a voice which brooked no argument, and Hari didn't utter a word of objection.

We all went upstairs to the flat and Hari made us herbal tea. Ganesh and I reeked of smoke. Gan had pulled off his sweater and put on a fresh one. He brought one for me, too. I realised I had nothing but what I stood up in. Even when I'd been flooded out of the flat, I'd managed to rescue a few personal bits. Not this time. This time my loss was doubled. In one day I'd lost both my mother and my home. I thanked God for Bonnie, safe downstairs in Hari's storeroom when fire broke out, and now, by special dispensation, allowed up here in the flat.

I sat on the sofa, sipping at my tea, while the others watched me, two pairs of dark eyes filled with concern. I wanted to thank them for caring, but it would have embarrassed them. Bonnie had jumped up on the sofa and lay with her head resting on my knee as if to make sure I didn't slip out again without her knowledge. Her bright little boot-button eyes were rolled up in their sockets to fix on my face, and the fur above them was puckered in a worried canine frown. I touched her head reassuringly and her tail moved uncertainly.

'What will you do now, my dear?' asked Hari. 'There is still my garage—'

'She can stay here,' Ganesh interrupted him. 'She can sleep on the sofa. Tomorrow I'll go with her to the council. They must find her somewhere.' He hesitated. 'While you were gone, that Sister Helen person from the hospice rang, wanting to talk to you. I told her you were down at the copshop, adding to a statement. I wondered—'

'My mother died today,' I said. 'About an hour before I got there.'

They were kind, commiserating and comforting. I sat there letting their condolences and kindness wash over me. I still felt numb, not knowing how I was supposed to reply. After a while, Hari went into the kitchen to start chopping up vegetables for the evening meal, which they assumed I'd eat with them. I wasn't hungry, but I couldn't refuse.

When he'd left us, Ganesh asked, 'You want to talk about her?'

'I want to talk,' I said. 'But I don't know what to say. Nicola had been to see her with some social worker in tow. So I guess she died happy. It was what she wanted. Maybe she just let go after she'd seen Nicola. I don't know. I wish – I can't help wishing she'd waited for me to come.'

'Dying isn't a time we have the picking and choosing of,' said Ganesh.

'No. I think she was glad to have seen me again. What she really wanted was for me to find Nicola, but I've got my head round that now. I still think she was pleased to find me, for my own sake.'

'Of course she was!' said Ganesh firmly.

I met his gaze. 'What I do know,' I said, 'is that I'm glad I saw her again. When Rennie Duke first came to see me and told me she was alive and looking for me, I thought meeting her again would be the last thing I wanted. But I did want it, really. It's as if a bit of me was amputated long ago and now it's been sewn back. Perhaps she felt that way too.'

Ganesh reached out and took my hand. 'She is at peace, Fran. She got her children back. Whatever Morgan says to you, you did all the right things.'

I pulled a face. 'Morgan's not pleased with me!'

'Let her stick to catching crooks and murderers,' said Ganesh. 'Some things are none of her business.'

* * *

In the end, the basement tenants were accounted for, both out at the time of the fire. Zog had vanished. They found two charred bodies in the burned-out wreckage; one was identified as Sid, the attic tenant. They never identified the other.

Ganesh came with me to my mother's funeral. Nicola wasn't there to say goodbye, which I was sorry about. Perhaps the social worker had jibbed at going, or there'd been some fuss over Nicola visiting the hospice. Morgan was there. She was nice to me, but Ganesh glowered at her, all the same.

Social Security made me an emergency cash payment for some clothes. The council found me a temporary room in a hostel. I hated it there. An air of hopelessness permeated the place. There was one girl who sat on the stairs all day long with her head in her hands. She was always there. You had to step round her. For all I knew, she stayed there all night. The people who ran the place were mostly volunteers. They meant well but they had that kind of waterproof cheerfulness that drives me nuts. I thought that if I didn't get out of there soon, I'd go as mad as that poor creature on the stairs.

Then, out of the blue, I got a visitor: Sister Helen.

'How are you, Fran?' she asked, looking round the tiny bare room with its hard bed on which the bright-red duvet only served to draw attention to the dearth of other furnishings and the pitted walls.

'Surviving,' I told her.

She smiled. 'You'd like to move out of here, of course you would. I've come with a suggestion. I have a friend who's involved in a charity which buys houses, renovates them, divides them into flats and lets them out at controlled rents to suitable homeless young people. Of course they only work on a small scale and can only offer places to very few, but it so happens that one flat is available, and when I explained your circumstances to them, they thought you would be very suitable. Would you like to go and see it?'

Would I!

I took Ganesh along when I went to view the flat. There was no leaving him behind, actually. After my near-disaster with Norman's place, Gan didn't trust me to make a decision about my living accommodation. The house was late Victorian, double-fronted and divided into five flats. The one offered to me was on the ground floor. It was basically one large room formed from knocking two smaller ones into a single unit. There was a kitchen corner with a breakfast bar, and a shower room and loo built on. It had basic furnishings, a bed, a table and four chairs, but plenty of built-in cupboard space. Even Ganesh approved.

He went back to the shop and I went to the office of the charity to arrange details. As soon as I signed up, the man in charge shook my hand and welcomed me to 'our number'. This was a bit spooky. He then passed me on to a capable-looking woman in the Sister Helen mould who led me to a stock cupboard of donated blankets, pots and pans and assorted dishes and cutlery. Between us we decided what I needed to start out and she promised someone would deliver it all to the new flat.

I came out of there unable to believe my luck. It really had seemed that there was nothing else left to go wrong, so perhaps, at long last, things were on the up.

I set off with quite a bounce in my step to tell Ganesh and Hari about it. But there was another, rather less welcome surprise in store for me. A few hundred yards away from the shop, a large sleek car purred up beside me and stopped. The rear-seat passenger leaned across and pushed open the door.

'Get in,' he invited.

Did I need this? Just when, for once, the sun was trying to shine on my little world? I stooped, stuck my head in and was about to tell this kerb-crawling Johnnie to get lost when I recognised the man in the car as Mickey Allerton. I managed to bite back the choice observation I'd prepared and got into the car instead. I had a feeling argument would be wasted. I made sure to leave the door open so that if the chauffeur tried to drive off, I could roll out.

Allerton looked as prosperous and well fed and watered as he'd done before. Clearly his life held none of the discomforts which dogged mine. His fish-silver eyes studied me with the same mix of amusement and disapproval they'd held on the previous occasion we'd met. 'I hear,' he said, 'that someone's been charged over Rennie Duke's death. A little bird also tells me that you led the coppers to him.'

I wondered just which little bird in CID he was supplying with millet. 'Something like that,' I admitted.

'You done well,' he said with heavy approval. I was startled. I hadn't expected praise, certainly not from Allerton. He reached into the inner breast pocket of his expensive bit of bespoke tailoring and took out a fat envelope. 'There you go, darling.'

It had to be cash. 'Whaffor?' I asked suspiciously.

'Just take it, darling.' His mouth formed a smile shape. 'No strings. Don't be offended, but I can't say I fancy you. I like women with a bit of shape to them. Let's say Rennie played it straight by me and I like things tidied up.' He ran an eye over my general appearance and heaved a sigh. 'Buy yourself some decent schmutter, for Gawd's sake.'

When in need, don't quibble. I took the envelope, thanked him and scrambled out of the car. It drove off at once. I wondered if I'd seen the last of him, and felt uncomfortably that I hadn't. Having his approval was more worrying than having him criticise me. Worst of all, he seemed to think I'd been efficient in finding Rennie's killer. This private-eye lark was more complicated than I'd ever imagined. I peeked in the envelope. Two hundred quid. Why did it feel more like a retainer than a reward? There again, who was I to look a gift horse in the mouth? And while we're on proverbs, cross your bridges when you come to them.

Two more people walked back unexpectedly and briefly into my life. One was Susie Duke. She called on me on my second day in the new flat, while I was still fixing it up.

'Nice,' she said, sitting down on one of my chairs.

'I'm looking out for a second-hand sofa,' I said.

She was delving into a large plastic carrier. 'Here,' she said, producing a wrapped object. 'I brought a house-warming present.'

I thanked her, hoping it wasn't a pottery cat. It seemed too heavy. It was a fruit-juicer, and I guessed quite an expensive one.

'Don't say I shouldn't have,' said Susie before I could speak. 'I owe you over Rennie. Without you, they wouldn't have got that Ben Cornish feller. Besides, I told you, with Rennie's insurance paying up, I'm in the money, for a while anyway.'

'What about the business?' I asked. 'Will you keep it going?'

She pursed her scarlet lips. 'Thinking about it. Actually, I wanted to talk to you about it. See, I couldn't manage it on my own. I wondered if you'd be interested in coming in with me, partners. You've obviously got the knack of it.'

I thanked her for the compliment but told her I wasn't sure about committing myself to any kind of permanent arrangement. I stumbled through a list of reasons: I'd promised Jimmie I'd work for him at the new pizzeria; Ganesh would make a heck of a fuss, and while I obviously didn't take orders from him, I didn't like doing things in the face of his opposition because I'd so often had to call on his support. He was still feeling sore about being left out of recent events. Chiefly, I was used to being on my own, deciding what I'd do and what I wouldn't.

Susie listened to all of this and nodded. 'Fair enough. But keep in touch, right? Perhaps if I find I need someone, I could ask you if you'd be willing? You could always turn me down. You'd be a sort of freelance.'

That sounded all right and I said so. It wasn't until she'd left that I wondered just what I might be letting myself in for. I decided not to mention it to Ganesh, not yet anyway.

The other person I saw again was Nicola. (I still called her that, since it was the only name she'd known, and she seemed still to be using it.) She rang the shop asking me to get in touch and leaving the number of her mobile.

I met up with her in a health-food café in Kew. She looked pale and tense, with dark shadows under her eyes, but she was still stroppy. She was my sister, after all. Our relationship was the point she raised at once.

'You should have told me!' she accused me. 'You could have told me that evening you were waiting in the street outside our house.'

'No I couldn't,' I retorted. 'You wouldn't have believed me, anyway. Nor was anyone supposed to know the truth, that wasn't the idea. No one would have known if it hadn't been for Ben.' I didn't mention Flora.

Her stroppy air faded, replaced by despair. She looked as if she was going to cry. 'I can't believe Ben did those things. He's too nice.'

'Yeah, well, nice people do nasty things,' I said unkindly. It was something she was going to have to face. It was just a pity that, on top of everything else, she'd had to find out her idol had feet of clay. When first love comes crashing down, it destroys your belief in the fairness of the world, in love itself, in any relationship, in what people are like and our own ability to judge them, everything, really, for a time. I remember. I'll tell you about it some day.

'Well, someone should have told me!' she said passionately, her pale little face flushed. 'I've been living a lie!'

It was true, she had. But it still seemed a corny way to describe it. 'You didn't lie,' I countered. 'You accepted what you were told about who you were. That's natural. Why shouldn't you?'

'But that was a lie!' she persisted. 'I've been walking around all my life thinking I'm one person, when actually I'm someone else!'

'No you're not, Nicola,' I argued. 'You're you. You're the same person. You like the same food, the same music. You just – just got a different name very early on, before you knew anything about it.'

'Doesn't a name matter? I'm this other person, this Miranda Varady, and I know nothing about her. It's no use telling me she's me and I'm her and I'm the same as I ever was, because

311

I'm not! I haven't got the same parents, for a start, and the ones I have got have lied to me all these years. How could they do that?'

'They love you,' I said simply.

'Then why didn't they trust me enough to tell me the truth?'

'You know why, because the deal they did with my – with our mother was unofficial. They've been afraid of losing you.'

This explanation didn't seem to wash with her. She was completely convinced that somehow, she'd ceased to exist. It was hard for her, and I was sorry. I hoped she'd get through it eventually, and in the meantime, I distracted her by asking if any decision had yet been taken about her situation. Obviously she was still living with Jerry and Flora.

'It's complicated,' she said moodily, twisting her finger in a lock of crimped blonde hair. 'I'm thirteen next week and Social Services can't just pick me up and dump me anywhere, like a three-year-old. I've made that absolutely clear to them. They've got to listen to what I say. All the same, I'm technically in their care now. Mummy and –' she broke off and amended '– the Wildes are fostering me until it's sorted out.'

'When's the violin exam?'

'Oh, that . . .' She shrugged. 'I've pulled out of that. I can't concentrate on music at the moment.'

'Don't let it go,' I urged. 'Don't ever let any dream go just because the going's got tough. I've not given up wanting to be an actor.'

She stared at me meditatively. 'It's funny knowing that my real mother was out there all the time and I didn't know her.'

'I didn't know her either,' I said. 'Even though I had a memory of sorts.' I hesitated. 'Whose idea was it that you go and see her?'

'Mine, of course!' she snapped. 'When they told me who I really was, I just couldn't take it in. I said, "Right, where are my real parents, then?" They hummed and ha-ed and said that my father – my real father – was dead and my real mother was dying. So I told them I wanted to see her. I wanted to see her with my own eyes. I felt, you know, I wouldn't believe it until I saw her. So I told that drippy social worker they've attached to me to get on and fix it.'

'And are you glad you saw her?' I asked. 'Did it help?'

'I think so,' she said. 'I think it will help, when I've got used to the idea. Anyway, my – our mother seemed pleased that I'd come. She kept calling me Miranda, which was a bit difficult. She knew I played the violin. Did you tell her? She knew about *me* but I didn't know about *her*. You should have told me, Fran, you really should.'

She seemed close to tears again, so I didn't argue, just gestured wearily.

'It wasn't nice seeing her so ill,' Nicola said after a moment. She paused. 'I thought I might feel cross with her, you know, for giving me away like that. But when I saw her, I just felt very sorry. Not just for her, but for all the things that had happened. The way it had turned out.'

She was messed up but basically a bright kid, and honest. She had guts, the most important thing. I wouldn't have wanted to be her social worker! I wished her all the best for her upcoming birthday and gave her my new address so that we shouldn't lose touch. I hoped she had enough nous to keep it hidden from Flora.

So I'm working at the San Gennaro. The place is doing pretty well. The barman is Italian and the accordionist, the one

Jimmie hired, has turned out to be called Pietro, so I guess that's where Don Silvio got to hear of Jimmie's plans. The other waitress is Polish. Jimmie is manager. That means he hangs about in the back room, now called his office, and makes phone calls to his mates. Mixing in new company has rubbed off on him, and he's taken to wearing a blue suede jacket, cream chinos and shades whether there's any sun about or not. He still smokes like a chimney. I gather Don Silvio has an accountant keeping an eye on the books. Silvio himself has popped in a couple of times, just checking. The barman and Pietro are both very polite to him. I've told Ganesh that if I ever see either one of them kiss his hand, just once, I'm off.

Marty has delivered a practically illegible typescript of his adaptation of *The Hound of the Baskervilles*. Or, as he's typed it, *The Hond of the Biskervils*. I suspect he's dyslexic, and if so, we must keep him away from the posters advertising the show. We're reading it through next week. Whether Irish Davey is bringing his dog along, I don't know. I rather hope not.

I sent Nicola a birthday card, though I don't know whether Flora intercepted it. I've seen Janice Morgan a couple of times. It seems that forensics did, after all, find traces of some special tropical plant potting compost in Rennie's car. So Susie was wrong to be sceptical about that. I haven't heard from Susie again, nor has Mickey Allerton reappeared – yet. Watch this space.